TIGER PIECES

WE Coble

MediaGenerationsPublishing

Omaha, Nebraska

MediaGenerationsPublishing
3000 Farnam Street, Unit 6H
Omaha, NE 68131
www.mediagenerationspublishing.com

Publisher's Note: This is a work of fiction. Names, characters, places, and incidents are a product of the author's imagination. Locales and public names are sometimes used for atmospheric purposes. Any resemblance to actual people, living or dead, or to businesses, companies, events, institutions, or locales is completely coincidental.

Book Layout ©2013 BookDesignTemplates.com
Book Edited by Peter Gaskin (gaskinpeter@hotmail.com)
Book Jacket Design by Rafido Francavilla
(http://www.wix.com/raphaelfrancavilla/rafido-digitalart)

Ordering Information:
Quantity sales. Special discounts are available on quantity purchases by corporations, associations, and others. For details, contact the "Special Sales Department" at the address above.

Tiger Pieces/ WE Coble. -- 1st ed.
ISBN-13: 978-0-9906646-0-4

To my family for their love and support

To my initial readers who encouraged me to finish the novel: Matthew Cotter, Nancy Pentak, Wayne Shearon, Tim Simonetti, Waiter at The Diner, Tanya Wells

To The Diner, the restaurant that allowed me to monopolize a seat for three months in the summer of 2010

To Scott L. whose invitation to the mountains set this all into motion

Part One

Tigers swimming alone through time

1974

I hang back and watch Big Mike survey the dusty village. He and the Sarge are swaggering around the village, yelling out orders, swinging their dicks around like they own the place. They up and pissed off the lieutenant from the South Vietnamese Lowland regiment, causing that bastard to hightail it out of here with all his men. Now, we're left to fend for ourselves, somewhat clueless as to where the hell we are.

"I wouldn't have fuckin' believed it," Big Mike says. "Lieutenant Minh and his men... poof. Just like them spooks. One minute here, then gone the next."

"When I get back to command, I'm going to tear that lieutenant a new asshole. Slant-eyed monkey freak doesn't get to hang us out to dry. Not Charlie Can Company," the Sarge growls. "Gordon, round up the fuckin' grunts! We're heading out for a walk in the park."

"You think that's smart, Sarge?" I ask. "Map isn't real clear. Shouldn't we just radio for backup?"

"You candy-ass, back mountain sister fucker! Get your ass in gear and jerk the fuckin' men!" Sarge screams. "I don't have the fuckin' time to babysit you, ya mama's boy." The glint in Sarge's eyes tears into me like a two-by-four punched through a tree during a tornado.

"Go on, sissy," Big Mike laughs. "Get up there so we can follow your cute ass out of here." The Company jeers and hoots after me as they fall into formation.

I take point and plunge into the jungle's gaping jaws. The trail is heavily canopied and light furtively breaks through at every other yard.

"Just ignore those assholes," Brady says as he comes up alongside me. "They're just as chicken shit scared as the rest of us." He smiles as a tiny sliver of sun glances off his sandy brown hair. He's the closest buddy I have in the Company. Some of the other guys jeer us with cat calls of being asshole buddies—guys who provide friends-with-benefits services.

Brady hails from a farm in New Hampshire. He's never experienced black widow green plants that can choke you to death, or breathed air filled with enough water to give you a drink, or felt his skin peel away from the sun's incessant clawing. The heat mauls him like a jungle cat on the prowl, and he's easy prey. Hell, I guess I could say the same for myself. I hail from the mountains of North Carolina, where two days above 75 degrees is considered a heat wave.

Brady takes a few weeks just to move without looking drunk. Doctors tell him he'll die of the heat if he doesn't get a handle on it. Die of heat? In this Godforsaken wasteland, where steel traps are looking to clamp you down at every turn? I think heat is the least of this boy's worries.

"Yep. I just wish we had backup," I respond. "Or at least someone who's better at understanding this singsong talk."

"There's something melodic about it," Brady says. "Love me some girls who speak broken English. It's like they're singing to me. I could listen to it all day." A devilish grin spreads across Brady's face. "Good eatin' here." He looks like a sinister carnival clown.

Hell. If we aren't killin' them, we're fuckin' them, I think silently. Brady's got that devil-may-care attitude keeping him warm at night.

About a few hours into the walk, we notice a clearing up ahead. We had come down perpendicular to it yesterday while marching towards the village. Hell. I think it was no more than 15 hours ago. That was our mistake. The Việt cộng let us through without so much of an exhale, so we never thought to survey the land with a fine tooth comb. They must have let the lieutenant through because the real prizes are us, the Ghosts. Our white asses can be seen in the deepest canopy and our smell can carry downwind for miles. Sometimes even I can catch the whiff of sour milk if the wind blows right.

A buzzing sound whizzes by me and I cock an eyebrow. What the hell—?

Shit.

I hear a second bullet whistle through the underbrush until it meets its target with a sickening *thud.* A scream hurls upward, pleads for salvation, and then a gurgle chokes off the horrific echo. The grunt drops to the jungle dust, his green fatigues now mired in red. A quiet before the storm expands time until a burst of whistling death elicits another deafening scream.

"Dammit Gordon, hit the fuckin' dirt! Ambush!" the Sarge screams at me.

Time crawls on all fours as I desperately struggle to my knees. Then, the swarm of whistling bullets cuts right through us. The first stinger hits my upper left shoulder, twisting me around, while another pricks my right thigh. I open my mouth, but nothing comes out. Two more stingers hit me, this time in the chest. The flak jacket cradles the impact but they still suck the air right out of my lungs. My head rings as another stinger opens the right side of my helmet. My back slams into the jungle floor, and my eyes are hooded in darkness. I hear trickling water; I see stars. I smell flesh.

"Sarge! We gotta get the fuck outta here!" Big Mike yells. He's always the can-do guy who'd stab you in the back while flashing his pearly whites. He comes from a big ol' southern family with four brothers and three sisters. They're about to lose another God-fearing son to this hell hole, 20,000 klicks from Sunday School.

Big Mike's southern drawl shoots into the dense canopy of twisting vines and crackling trees. Silence surveys the scene for a split-second, and then an explosion rocks the air. Using his voice as a siren call, the mortar shell kisses the ground just between Mike's feet and the Sarge. Body parts and fluids mix with the dirt and rain down upon the clearing. We are caught with our fuckin' pants down. Now the damn spooks are using our bodies as fertilizer. Company Charlie Can is being scrubbed out.

I crawl towards the river. I hear salvation whispering over the fast moving currents. "You don't want to survive and be a captive," I tell myself. The commie bastards parade soldiers around like monkeys to smile for the camera, do tricks for food, spit on your country. Dammit, no! I've got to get the fuck away. I won't lose control.

I crawl through the dirt with my blood leading the way. I feel light-headed. My whole body shudders when I hear the sing-song up ahead. Dammit. They are scrubbing us. Now, they're swarming out of their holes to pick the Company clean, like vultures dive-bombing fresh carcasses.

I've got to get to the water. Can't feel much, though. My arms are useless; my legs aren't much better; and I can barely see inches ahead. The pain in my left side makes me want to vomit up my insides. I plop into the water and smash into a piece of driftwood. My world bubbles out of view.

2

Down the river

"Vy! Where are you?" The sheer volume of the question underscores the concern creeping along the edge of her voice. "Vy! Vy! Answer me!"

"What, Mother?" I groan. I'd say anything to stop that mournful wail.

I stand at the river's edge and watch the current swiftly carry leaves and rocks past me. I wonder where they go and what they see.

"You scared me to death," she says. "I expect to find you with empty eyes. Why do you come here? Where the currents drag everything out to sea. It's not safe here. No telling who or what watches, waits, or wanders." Mother's black eyes study me. I wonder if this is how predators stalk their prey.

Mother worries all the time now. Ever since Father shimmered away like steam off the forest floor, she thinks her children will follow. One day he told us that he had found work with the Americans, the Ghosts. He said they needed roads to help save our people, and that they had big machines that required big roads. When he showed me the work he had completed, all I saw were track marks on the jungle floor, exposing the forest's insides. But his work fed us well. We grew fat. Complacent. Then, suddenly, our fortunes evaporated. The world blinked; the sun grew dark; the rain dried up.

Our father was no longer among us. We learned that a tree that his men cut had fallen where it should not have fallen. It crushed his chi and sent him into the cycle of rebirth. The family received the news from Sài Gòn as it traveled with the mưa[1]. It washed us in grief. Dry season gave way to rainy and we swam against the sadness. Mother claimed she already knew that Father crossed back into the stream of life and death. In her dreams, the Moon Goddess showed her two white birds fighting. White equals death in our culture. She wailed and wailed and wailed for days and days. During this time, she cut her hair nearly all off as penance for her karmic crimes. What unhealthy desires bound her to this life and stopped her progression

---

[1] Rains

towards enlightenment? This question echoed through her wail as a counterpoint to the pain of loss. Thankfully, it eventually ended, and life breathed through her again. Now she worries that her three children will shimmer away, leaving her behind.

Ngoc always plays close to the house. She is about three years younger than me and still looks up to her older brothers as teachers. She is entering adolescence with her innocence intact. She pounces on everything.

Minh is just 13 months younger than me, and shorter—like everyone else. We sometimes play twins and pretend to swap faces. We cut up all day. Minh is knee deep in the *lúa²*, harvesting rice to bring to the village. When the wind blows across the rice stalks, it enchants us as our inland ocean, our *sóng lúa³*. Just like the wind, it blows hot or cold, softly or harshly, or too little or too much.

"Mother, I like it here," I say. "No one bothers me. I can think. I can be at peace." Village life hasn't changed for hundreds of years. It is said that my family can stretch its hands back 500 years. We migrated from the *Đồng Bằng Sông Hồng⁴* region to the *Đồng Bằng Sông Cửu Long⁵* region.

"Oyez. You'll be the death of me. By the time someone bothers you, you'll be empty eyes." Mother

---

² Rice paddy
³ Rice waves
⁴ Red River Delta near Hà Nội
⁵ Nine Dragon River Delta or the Mekong south of Sài Gòn

shakes her head in annoyance. "Why do you need to be alone to think?" We Vietnamese are all about community and family. Individuals exist as part of something not separate from something.

"I'm searching for a path. I can go to the city and look for work or join the Army to fight the Việt cộng," I state. I sense that I am different from those around me but I can't find the words to express how I feel. When I see myself in the mirror, even my body betrays me. I am unusually tall for Vietnamese. I am lost among the villagers, even though I can see above their heads. It is as if the market closes before I can sell my goods.

"Vy, you are too young to think so much. You must first finish school before you do anything," Mother explains. "No Army. It's the fastest way to empty eyes. This war corrupts us. It's not the Buddhist's way to inflict death, for we may be ending the rebirth of an ancestor." Mother's faith has grown since she got older. She seeks solace during the wailing period, like a child seeks her mother for comfort and security when she is first born. Now she has a hedge against transgressions from her past, present, and future lives. Buddhists are condemned to rebirth until we learn our lessons.

"I seek an inner guidance," I reaffirm. "I try to quiet the thoughts to hear the whispering of the path. I do not know for what. I am restless like the trees caught in a big storm, rooted in place but bending in all directions."

Mother senses that I may be right. "This could be *chưng diên*[6] that grips you. Let's leave this foolishness behind," she says in a low voice.

As Mother approaches to lead me back to the village, she stops short. Her eyes narrow and then explode wide. In one movement, she hooks her arm around my shoulder and pushes me behind her in a quick half twirl.

"Ow! Why did you do that?" I yell.

"Shhh," she whispers, studying the surface of the river. I instantly fall silent and my breath catches on the steam trails, now rising skyward. I follow her line of sight and see a man's head bobbing in the current. At first, I see no body, like a crocodile protruding from the surface. Coming towards the river's edge is a Ghost.

The red holes on the body mimic the draping of multiple Japanese flags. I'd never seen so much white—the color of death—with red—the color of prosperity—mixed together. I'm not sure if it's alive. It could be another body with empty eyes, a *thây*[7], which seems so common these days. This is the first one I've come across in the water instead of crossing one along the paths of our daily lives.

"Go get the *Thich*[8] Hanh. Go!" Mother shoos me away as if I'm a fly buzzing around her food. I stomp

---

[6] Madness
[7] Corpse
[8] Buddhist Honorific Title

off in search of the Great *Thầy*[9]. As I peek over my right shoulder, I can see her cautiously approach the Ghost. At first it does not move, and then suddenly a moan skims the surface of the current, heading towards us as if it's one last shockwave of life. Mother drags it ashore and checks for a pulse.

---

[9] Teacher, Master

3

As I run up the path, I can't get the floating head out of my mind's eye. I watch it bob up and down like a lure on a fishing line, ready to clutch its unsuspecting prey. The matted, black hair and the coconut white flesh seem otherworldly. A Ghost it is, indeed.

I cross the center of the village and head east toward the tall, ancient trees. It is said that the founders of the village carried the saplings from *Đồng Bằng Sông Hồng*. Over a thousand miles to the north, the journey took many days. According to legend, a driving rain pushed them into this place where rivers crisscross and water sits. Where food is plentiful. To this day, fishing and farming rule our daily lives.

"Vy, why are you in such a hurry?" I glance down at my little sister. She beams two full moons up at me, rich with curiosity.

"Not now. Go back and play," I snap. I do to my little sister what Mother does to me. I shoo her away and quicken my pace. Still I can hear her pitter-patter desperately chugging along behind. Determined, I force my way through the *tam quan*[10] between the walls of the *chùa*[11]. I take the center path, leaving the other two entrances closed. The wind faintly rustles the overhead bell, heralding my approach. I feel the hair along my nape stand on end. I think of the many paths one can take. I shudder.

Forward I march, towards the *chính điện*[12], and carefully remove my shoes before I enter. As I approach the *Tam thể*[13] , time seems to blossom like a lotus in which past, present, and future become One. The coolness of the limestone floor freezes me in place.

"Great Thầy. Forgive the interruption." My voice is rich with reverence. I bow my head and keep my eyes on the Great Thầy, waiting for acknowledgement. The presence of time fills the hall as I listen to the monk's soft chanting. The smell of incense skips across the stillness of the air. By now, my little sister is standing

---

[10] Gate with three entrances
[11] Pagoda
[12] Main temple
[13] Trinity – representing the Three Bodies of Buddha

next to me with those full moon eyes, darting between my face and the Great Thầy's.

"My child, what brings you here?" Great Thầy asks, once his consciousness drifts back into the present. His meditation focuses his perceptions inwardly and he sits so still it's like watching a stone. At times, I swear he stops breathing.

"Mother sent me. A Ghost man bobs in the water down by the river's edge. He seems close to empty eyes." I barely register the flicker in the man's eyes when the other monks enter the room. They are all wearing the same mustard-colored robes, now flowing over the cool limestone. Their bare feet skate across the floor with hardly a touch. A dozen of them assemble in a crescent around us, with the Great Thầy at the apex. What was empty becomes filled.

"Come," he says gently. "Let's see if we can assist in keeping him in this life, or at least preparing him for his next." He speaks in such calming tones that my unsteady emotions are lulled into a state of stupor.

Great Thầy leads us all out of the temple, from the village, and into the open jungle. He moves without haste, yet covers the ground quickly. He skims across the surface while the jungle moves out of the way. The other monks effortlessly maintain his pace while I find myself hurrying to keep up.

Time slows its breathing. It holds it inside its lungs, keeping the past, present, and future awake in the same moment. I can feel the pressure building for an exhalation. Already, we can see Mother breathing for the Ghost. Her long, black hair drapes over their faces. There is no beginning or ending of the two. They've become One.

Upon hearing us, Mother stands and steps away from the Ghost. The sun's spotlight outlines her face as she pulls her hair back behind her ears. Her eyes catch mine and then little sister's. Her eyebrow twitches and I know I'm in trouble. I'll learn the crime I've committed behind closed doors, away from the villagers. Even my punishment will be a secret. A family's life is a secret life.

Great Thầy kneels beside the Ghost and places his ear against his naked chest. He then examines the body from head to toe. "Your efforts have saved this Ghost," he tells Mother. "His bleeding is staunched and he seems to be breathing on his own." Great Thầy is one of the oldest members of our village. Old enough to have played games with my father's father when they were both dust rats, scurrying amongst the feet of their elders.

Mother nods in silence. She seems satisfied, like a tiger that has finished cleaning its kill and is now amusing itself by surveying its game fields. Mother is trained in some of the Great Thầy's healing arts and is the school teacher. She helps out when people get sick.

Great Thầy tilts his head. The 12 monks lift the Ghost and in a solemn procession carry him back to the Pagoda compound. The whole village comes out to

see what all the commotion is about. If not for my up-
coming punishment, I would revel in this drama that
plays like a return of war heroes. Little sister and I
snake along the compound's wall until we get to the
monks' living quarters.

The monks swarm around an empty bed like the
great winds of the fall. When the air stills, the Ghost
now lies in the bed, stark naked. His people must be
barbaric. They have sliced his penis. I notice that
Mother and little sister do not follow us. They should
not see this. All in this space are me, Great Thầy, and
the Ghost. Time begins to breathe once more.

4

Present

"Hey, Vy! Snap out of it! Stop with all the S&M crap!" Jerry shouts.

Another sardonic Friday night in the same retread of a bar. The music has reached a piercing level, its distorted pitch banging into my brain like a sledge-hammer against concrete. I'm turning 40 in another two days and I am as single as the day I fell out of the womb on Mother's birthday. I never thought I'd still be pushing up a wall, looking for love, surrounded by men on the hunt, preening for the next thrill.

Jerry waves his finger between my eyes, clearing my vision. Jerry can be so impatient when I Stand & Model.

"Hey!" I flick his finger away. "Don't get my neck going." I laugh as I try my best possession-of-a-black-woman imitation.

"Oh no she didnun't!" Jerry bats his eyes. He transforms into an Eastern Carolina Black Woman who has been done wrong by her man. Jerry stands six feet with broad shoulders and thick black hair, making his impression even more comical.

"You got me," I say as I throw my hands up, mimicking an arrest.

"So... where were you this time?" Jerry asks. Concern hovers around his question. Jerry's been my best friend for about four years. I listen to his truth regardless of how spot on it can be, especially about men and my lack of procuring one on a regular retainer. Thankfully, I'm no lawyer, or this ho would need to find another way to eat.

"I was lamenting about being single as I hurl towards the BIG 4-0," I said.

"Oh! Stop the pity train, girrrlFRIEND! It's Friday night and these girls..." Jerry cups his palms under his chest, "...need some attention. Finish your drink and we'll head over to Cobalt to continue our S&M."

Gotta love Jerry. He's doing his best to help me celebrate my birthday weekend. This dive bar was our first stop—mainly because it was only a few blocks away from my home in Dupont Circle East.

"Guys!" Jack exclaims as he saunters up and lashes his brown eyes at us. His blond hair has been thinning since college. As long as he keeps it cut short, it looks full. "Round of drinks." He motions to the bartender. "We're going to crawl tonight. Where to next?"

I look over at Jerry who is rolling his eyes. He mouths, "Kill me now." Jerry wouldn't mind if Jack got lost in every sense of the word. As for me, Jack is a go-out friend, a bar companion, and a cruise director all mashed into one. We met while attending Georgetown University at the *Exorcist* steps, a flight of stairs made famous in the movie, *The Exorcist*, which connects Prospect Street with M Street. To ascend their steps is a rite of passage for most students. Funny how that seems so appropriate considering all the vices that Jack has brought into my life. Anyhow, one must have friends who fit this occupational role. They are the ultimate wingmen. They attract attention, deflect cattiness, and are easy to poach from. My last two 'drop trou' one-nighters came from this setup.

"Guess what?" Jack asks. He is on the edge of a full-on *In Living Color* skit. "Guess. Just Guess."

"No clue," I say as I look past Jack for an escape route. Exits are never easy to find when one really needs to go, like a police officer is never around when you need one.

"Don't know; don't care," Jerry chimes in. His level of irritation is beginning to peak along his brow. Jerry's kill fantasy is taking flight.

"I'll tell you anyhow," Jack says. "I've been invited to a Sunday pool party and want you guys to come along. It could be lots of fun." There is a hint of pleading in Jack's voice, just this side of begging. We often wonder why Jack wants us around. He seems to have his own clique.

I glance at Jerry, whose eyes are reflecting a direct, unvarnished message of "Oh-hell-no," but I go ahead with: "Sure. Jerry and I will be there. I don't plan on taking any clothes off, though."

"Darling, in your day you always told me that more—and I do mean MORE—was the name of the game." Jack says.

Jerry turns to me, surprised.

"There is no need to spill that much tea in such a short, and I do mean SHORT, time you've been standing here," I growl. I could have taken Jack's tight, blue t-shirt and used it to twist the asshole's head right off.

"You never told me about your gangbang years," Jerry says with a mixture of surprise, delight, and "why-didn't-you-tell-me" stare of death. We are best friends and yet I still need time to share my past secrets.

"Wasn't important," I reply. "AND, it happened during my twenties. In those days, more was the merrier."

Jack rolls his eyes. "Vy, you are running from your past again. Oh Darling. It makes you...so you."

"Let's move on, shall we?" I say with my best icy voice. "Weren't we going to Cobalt?"

"Oh goodie!" Jack smiles. He chugs his drink and dashes for the door. One would think his invitation would be rescinded and his name added to a blacklist if he didn't get there first.

"Later, you are going to dish about those gangbang years that Jack is so fond of telling," Jerry says. "Also, why the hell did you say YES?" Jerry's fingers dig into my shoulder, causing me to wince. His green eyes are locked onto mine.

"Ouch! Get off me," I demand. "This is my birthday weekend. Sunday I'm turning 40 and a pool party might put a smile on my face. And, as my best friend, you've got to be there," I cajole.

"There is no telling where in the hell it's going to be. It could be in the 'burbs. Ugh! Let's hope it's a nice neighborhood at least. We could end up being bridge people, commuters who come into the city BUT in reverse. How ugly would that be?"

"I think you are overreacting."

"You know Jack," Jerry says. "He does this CRAP all the time. He leaves out the most important details and then says, 'Oh, I meant to tell you...' Just wait."

We head up 17th and then cross over R Street toward Cobalt. Jack is standing just inside the entrance with drinks ready as his peace offering. Jerry enters, grabs one, and chugs it. Then he swings back and takes the other one and chugs it. He knows I no longer drink.

As if on cue, Jack rolls his eyes and delivers the news. "Oh. I meant to tell you, the pool party is at…" I can see Jerry's eyes grow large and accusatory, "…Michael's in Falls Church." With that bombshell, Jack disappears and heads for the bathroom.

"I just knew it!" Jerry explodes. "The pool party is at Michael's. Of all people. We are going to hell in a cheap hand basket and faux painted faces." He falls into overdrive brooding mode.

I'm not Jerry's fave right at the moment. Jack would never let us back out now. Jerry was clearly right about Jack—that jerk knew if he had led his invite with that piece of information—that it would be at Michael's place—a "NO" would have hit him upside his head, or maybe even some "Hell No's" would have stomped into him for good measure. Of course, Jack bolted, nowhere to be found, so we stew in our anger. He knew that Jerry and I had a falling out with Michael. What evil is Jack stirring up? He loves the DRAMA too much. We may not even see Jack for the rest of the evening, now that he dropped that A-bomb.

5

As I stand in Cobalt with a swarm of men buzzing around me, I can't help but think back four years to when I bumped into Jack on 17th street. It was a sunny Saturday in January and the temperature was hovering in the high 60s. I just didn't know that a dark cloud was trailing him like a bloodhound stalking an escaped convict. Jack was a harbinger of change, sometimes good and sometimes not so good. At least, he introduced me to Jerry, who would become my "bestiest" friend.

1996

"Hey you," a disembodied voice hisses in my ear. I turn to see who it is and I'm surprised to find an old, familiar face. "Well what do you know, it's Jack!"

"Ha Ha. It's been a while since we last hung out," he beams. "We had great times and I miss them. You know...between the touchy Fathers and the repressed, hot catholic boys. Mmm. Them's were good eatin' days."

I feel like I've been slimed and yet mildly aroused. Some of those adventures had been totally insane. My mind races through a litany of highlights, from suck-offs in bathrooms across campus, to the blow job in the walk-in closet of the Indian Ambassador's residence, and the Father who squeezed my knee and told me how beautiful I looked that day.

"Jack, we were in college," I say. "Young, stupid..."

"And full of cum!" Jack interjects.

"Yeah, that too. But that's not the point—I'm not interested in re-living leftovers." After college, Jack and I had drifted apart. He still wanted to drop trou' at every opportune (and inopportune) time. Our last adventure had nearly ended with a trip to the police station for public lewdness.

We had been cruising the "P Street beach", a wooded park area along the edge of Rock Creek Parkway, just under the P street bridge on the Dupont Circle side. It didn't take long for some hot guy to get on his knees and start sucking us off. When we heard a commotion down the path, we hightailed it out of there, just missing the police raid by a few moments. I swore never to do something THAT stupid ever again.

"Fine. Let's call a truce," Jack says, standing with the sun behind him. "Come on over tonight. I'm having a party with a few people from work, and from around the neighborhood. It would be nice if you showed up. At least for old time's sake. Around 7:00."

"Sure," I give in. I was as guilty as Jack for our adventures. I could have always said no.

"You still know where I live?" Jack asks.

"Unless you've moved, you're over on Corcoran, between 17th and 18th, Unit 1?"

"Right. I see you haven't forgotten everything. Ciao." Jack flashes a devilish smile and takes off. Classic Jack: tall, dark, handsome; a walking, talking, smooth operator. More boys than the US Navy have tried to board that ship. He knows how to have a good time. It's sewed into his genes.

I sigh as I rummage through my clothes. Nothing to wear. You would think a couple of stuffed closets would have plenty of outfits screaming for a night out. It looks like an all-black attire evening is in my future. It's time to put on a mime face, pull out my best cocktail conversation, and sashay on down the yellow brick road.

"Hey Jack," I coo as I step over the threshold. I squeeze my 5'10" frame through a cluster of men hovering around the foyer. I twist and turn through the men to avoid bumping into anyone. Even a slight touch can cause a pounce.

"Welcome...Vyah!" Jack oozes. "So good to see you, darling. Smashing in black. You always had an eye for fashion. Never could understand how you paid for the stuff."

"Jack...you know a girl never tells her secrets. Besides, a girl in trouble is always a temporary thing. Anyhow, thank you for the invite." I scan the room and see two guys laughing it up. They catch my eye and we mouth hello. One is shorter, about 5'8", thinning hair, pale as a Ghost, and the other is a little taller than me with dark hair and big chest. I find them both cute.

"Name is Vy," I say in a casual tone as I approach the couple. Whenever I am interested in someone, I have to force myself to remain calm or I'll start blabbing like a village idiot.

"I'm Michael and this is Jerry," the shorter one says. "How do you know Jack?"

"Jack and I went to college together." I grin right back.

"Really? Where?"

"Georgetown. We met while living on East Campus. It's right across from the 1789 restaurant." I pause to let the location sink in. I don't see any recognition flash across their faces, so I continue. "How do you guys know Jack?"

"Michael knows him. I'm along for the ride," Jerry announces.

I turn my attention like a sniper to Michael and wait to pull the trigger. Most guys who know Jack know him in the biblical sense. After what seems like hours, I prompt Michael. "Well?"

"We met at a club downtown," Michael mumbles.

I sense that there is more to this story but I drop it and take our conversation down another path. "So how do you guys know each other?"

"We work together, auditing pharmaceutical manufacturing plants. Pharma companies hire us to be third-party auditors," Jerry explains.

"And you?" Michael asks. He's batting his eyes and slurping down a rum and coke. He seems relieved that we are off the topic of Jack.

"I'm an instructional designer," I explain. "I build training programs. Nothing exciting." I lock eyes with Michael. He's so adorable at that moment, and seems to be available. "Tell me. Are you single?" I ask.

"Yes."

Immediately, I notice Jerry glaring at Michael. Michael notices, too, and decides to correct himself. He clears his throat and says, "Well. No. I just started seeing this guy. Nothing serious." Michael must have seen that my interest was starting to waiver because he quickly adds, "But we can still have dinner."

Damn. Why do I always pick men who are unavailable? I must have looked flummoxed.

"It's not serious," Michael reiterates. "You look like you could be lots of fun."

"Seriously?" I say. "You're quoting a *Dead or Alive* song?"

"Well?...What about it?"

I figure he's right. What harm could a dinner do?

As we exchange cards, a guy bumps right into Michael. "Excuse me," he says kindly. When the man looks up, a hint of recognition crosses his face. "Oh. Hey, Michael." He then quickly leaves, and disappears into the kitchen.

"Who was that?" both Jerry and I ask in unison.

"That's Gordon." We wait for Michael to offer more information, but he remains quiet. So Jerry and I both give him the dreaded "that-isn't-enough-information" look.

"I dated his roommate, Bob. He's probably lurking around here."

"When was that?" Jerry demands.

"Year ago, I think."

"Weren't you with John then?" Jerry's eyes are now drawn together.

"Yes. Bob was a third that we brought into our relationship to spice things up. I don't want everyone to know. It ended badly and I don't want to talk about it."

"So, then what is Gordon's story?" I ask.

"I think he was in the military. He now lives across the bridge in Falls Church. He might've been one of the last Americans to get out of Vietnam." Michael looks uncomfortable talking about Gordon, so I decide not to prod.

Once our conversation winds down, Michael says, "Call me and we'll have dinner."

"Sure, Michael," I reply, grasping his hand affectionately before we part.

I search the party for Jack and find Gordon talking to him. As I approach the two, I take the time to admire Gordon's physique. He is just shorter than me, and well-built with broad shoulders. He also sports silver streaks along the sides of his hair and chiseled lines marking his distinguished face. He certainly has the Daddy look down. What I like about him is that he keeps himself in fighting shape—no beer gut around his waist, and no sagging chest. From the looks of his exposed forearms, he's a hairy guy. I'm mesmerized.

"Hey, come over and meet Gordon," Jack says, catching me staring.

"Sure." I stride over to the inquisition and extend my hand. "I'm Vy and...not a friend of Jack's," I laugh. Jack rolls his eyes.

"Gordon," the man says, with a hint of bemusement in his words.

"I hear that you live over in Falls Church."

"Yes, I'm currently over there. You're pretty tall for an Asian guy." Gordon's rich voice blankets me with goose bumps.

"Well, do you like what you see?" I smile.

"Yes," Gordon replies.

"So, what brings you to D.C.?"

"Grad school—"

Commotion from the other room interrupts Gordon. Suddenly, a man bursts into the kitchen, half-crazed. When he finds Gordon, he rushes over and grabs his arm.

"We've got to go! An ugly reminder of a past three-way is standing in the living room." the mystery man exclaims. He then whisks Gordon away, and just like that, Jack and I are alone in silence.

I slowly turn to Jack, my mouth agape. "What the hell was that all about? Who was THAT?"

"That was Bob, Gordon's roommate," Jack says. "I don't know what's up." He shrugs his shoulders and calmly walks out of the kitchen.

I stare at the swinging door as it fans the empty space. Oh well. C'est la vie. Another one bites the dust, I tell myself. As I walk home, I can't get Gordon out of my mind. I find myself dreaming about the man's steel-blue eyes while a rogue question stalked the edges of my wishful thinking:

What was Gordon's part in the Vietnam War?

6

1974

I ache all over. Where am I? I remember hitting the water and hearing men scream all around me. I think my eyes are open but I see nothing. I hear sing-song. They must have captured me. Oh God! Must be some form of torture. I gasp and hear my voice echo as someone touches me.

"Shhh. You hurt," a soothing, male voice whispers. "I remove cloth, you see," the disembodied voice gently says.

I can't believe it. One of them speaks broken English. The light hurts my eyes. No telling how long I've been out. Seems like forever before I open my eyes without the light jamming my eyelids shut and tears flooding the whites. The room is bare. There is just one chair next to this platform I'm lying on. The walls are washed-out limestone; there is dust everywhere; and there are holes for windows. I'm in Việt cộng clothes, pajama-like bottoms and a top in all black.

"Eat," an old guy in crimson and gold robes commands. He's rail thin, and short as hell. I could take him if I wasn't so weak. I could break him in half. I've got to have at least a good 35 pounds on him. Even if I crush him, I have no idea what's out there. There could be commies running all over this compound. I'll just play along for now. If they wanted me dead, I'd be dead.

There is a spoon next to my lips. Looks like rice with bits of green in it. There are some fleshy white chunks in the center. I slowly bring my mouth towards the spoon and slurp the contents through my lips. At first I'm not sure what to expect. Then an explosion of flavors dances across my tongue. Salty, sweet, spicy, vinegary, and other spices tease and torment me. I suck down the gruel and then realize that the flesh is a fish. Tasty. Hunger claws its way out and devours the offering.

"Slow. No eat for two days," the old guy admonishes.

Every inch of me aches. Sometimes it is hard to breathe and I get dizzy trying to sit up.

Days roll by and I still have no idea where I am. I sometimes see shadows moving about, depending on the time of day. I have no idea how long I've been here. I think there is a small boy helping the old man. I decide to focus on the boy—maybe by starting a simple conversation, I will get my bearings.

"What is your name?" I ask. When he doesn't answer, I repeat it, but with a shout. "What is your name?!"

Damn. The boy runs off. I must have scared him to death. He doesn't look to be more than 10 years old.

"Loud. You words strong today," a voice says from my left. I snap my head around to see the speaker. "Not good, move sharp like. You might hurt something." The old man's face appears concerned, thoughtful. Over his left shoulder, I notice more monks have gathered outside, watching me and giggling. "Name?" the old man politely asks.

"Sergeant Maybray, serial number..." then the old man raises his hand with his right palm at me. I abruptly stop.

"No prisoner. You hurt. Found by water. Us help. Name..." he points to his face and says, "Thanh." Then he points to me. "Name?" he asks gently.

"Steve." I give him my middle name, just in case. Everyone here seems so thin and small, almost childlike. All around me I hear sing-song, further reinforcing my childlike misconception.

"Steve. You good. Soon go." A smile crosses Thanh's face, and the corners of his eyes crinkle. He is a good man.

I start to hear the sing-song, and I watch as the boy approaches the old man.

"Vy, come here." I stop sweeping the floor and approach the Great Thầy. "Go and bring the soup to feed our guest. If he can, let him feed himself. He needs to start taking care of himself."

"Great Thầy. He is so strange. Why is he a Ghost?" I ask.

Great Thầy laughs. "Not everyone looks like us. He reminds me of the French with his pale skin. I do believe he is what one calls an American, who hails from a great country across the water. Some say they are here to protect us from something called communism; others say they are here to steal from us like the French."

"He is a man like you, then?"

"Very much so, little one," Thanh smiles.

"But," I stop, confused. "He's maimed down there."

Again Thanh laughs. "Some cultures cut the extra skin away from it. We don't and that leaves us covered. Now go get the food."

"Yes, Great Thầy," I say and leave the room.

"Hey. Why was the small boy pointing at my crotch?" I had no idea what the two were yammering on about, and when the kid pointed toward my crotch, I got scared.

I see Thanh smile.

"He thinks you maimed," Thanh replies.

What is this guy talking about? "I...Is it..." Why haven't I noticed this before? I can't complete the thought out loud.

Thanh shakes his head and laughs again. "We," he points to himself, "extra skin... You no."

Relief washes over me in waves. "Oh." I gasp. I'm circumcised and they aren't. For a moment there, I thought a bullet had taken my manhood away. Of all the things that could happen, I'm not sure if I could go home half a man.

Soon, the small boy returns, carrying a bamboo tray with a bowl of soup, spoon, sliced mango, and a slice of bread. He motions for me to sit up and I comply. He places the tray on my chest and I wince. That startles the small boy, who quickly returns to Thanh's side. I turn my attention to the soup. It is filled with white noodles, beef slices, cilantro, bean sprouts, mint, and sliced hot peppers. It smells incredible. I taste it and practically wolf it down.

I look up and see the small boy studying me as I eat. It's like he's watching my every move like a cat of prey. His big black eyes act like spotlights, exposing everything I do. I must be some sight to him. Yet, I'm fascinated by this small boy's attention and can't figure out why.

I also notice the old man looking at the small boy and me. He seems deep in thought. I swear the old man has reached some sort of conclusion.

The old guy mentions something in sing-song to the boy before turning back to me. He's clearly happy that I finished my meal.

"Good. Appetite returns. You feed self. Strength back. Soon you go."

"Great Thầy. What are you saying?" I ask. It is exciting and scary to have a Ghost here in our village.

"I am speaking English to him. I was taught by a missionary, who wanted me to convert to his faith. I told them I was content being Buddhist, but that I would humbly accept the lessons," he replies.

"Why would you want a different worship?" I whisper.

"There are many paths one can take in life towards things we desire. It can be love; it can be success; it can be faith. One must remember that all this..." he waves his hand in a half circle, "is an illusion. It is desire that creates suffering for that which is temporary. One day you will understand." With that, he leaves the room.

I watch the small boy and he watches me. I motion him over and he takes my tray away. He must think that is why I motioned him over. Just as he turns to leave, I reach out and grab his arm. I wanted to touch him. I feel skin as smooth as silk and as soft as a lamb's fur. He shoots back a puzzled look. I see fear mixed with fascination in his eyes.

"Ok," I acknowledge and let go. He rights himself and continues to stare at me with innocent eyes. After he leaves, I realize that these people mean me no harm.

7

"He is ill," Great Thầy tells my mother. "We thought he was getting better. There must be infections inside the wounds. There may even be bullet scraps. Unfortunately, there is nothing we can do. Fever is taking hold and it will only get worse. He must go now, if there is any hope to save him."

"He cannot travel. Look at him," she replies. "The heat will cook him as surely as the fever. How can we begin to get the Americans here?"

"Take the cart and the water buffalo and head down the road towards the sea. It is rumored that Americans are pulling back in that direction. Some say the war is coming to an end."

"Are you filled with madness, Great Thầy?" Mother exclaims. "If the Americans do not shoot on sight, our brothers will make my children and me pay for harboring this foreigner."

"Việt cộng are moving towards Sài Gòn. There is a small window of opportunity to slip by. Take him and go. Leave your family here for safe keeping. Once you get him to the Americans, come back." Great Thầy's eyes implore her to go immediately.

"Great Thầy," Mother solemnly says. "I will not leave my children behind. There is no way of knowing what the consequences will be. We do this as a family and will face the future together."

Great Thầy sees the fire burning in her eyes and understanding fills the space between them. "Time for discussion is over," he says. "Time is now, before the sun rises. Grab what you can carry. I will see that the other monks prepare the cart. Your children, Vy, Minh, and Ngoc will ride next to the American while you walk. Go," he gently insists.

"Vy, come here," Great Thầy calls.

"Yes, Great Thầy?"

"Before you leave, I give you a sign to take with you on your journey. Have a seat."

I obey the Great Thầy.

"Ayyyiieee!" I scream as the Great Thầy pulls up my right sleeve and pokes me with sharp needles.

"Shhhhh, little one. It will be okay."

Other monks immediately appear as if materializing out of the wall.

"Great Thầy? We heard a cry."

"It's all right," Great Thầy says. "I will be finished soon. I'm giving a sign to Vy that I hope will one day lead to his enlightenment." He smiles as he meets my gaze.

"Go. Your family and your path await you," Great Thầy says in a gentle voice.

As I leave, I notice a single tear stream down Great Thầy's cheek.

"Come, Vy. Walk with me," Mother commands once I am outside.

"Yes, Mother." I hang my head low and march in step behind her. My siblings and the Ghost are already in the wagon. I notice that the moon has already begun its decent. I see Minh placing a cold towel on the Ghost's perspiring forehead. Little sister just watches and cradles a doll tightly to her chest.

The dusty roads never seem to change. How many generations have followed this road all the way to the sea? As we travel down, we notice how disheveled it has become. Scrub grass grows along its banks; the sounds of the dense jungle are just within earshot. And, we are all alone—not a soul passes us.

A moan escapes the cart, prompting Mother to turn around, startled. Her long, flowing áo dài glows a fiery red down the long skirt, and is complemented well

with the black pantaloons underneath. The top is em-
broidered with a colorful peacock, with its head on one
side and its feathery body draped gracefully across the
back. Despite the dirt we kick up from the road, her
dress remains immaculate. Radiant.

"His fever still holds him," Mother says with resig-
nation. Silence again descends upon us. A mournful
lament comes out to meet the rising sun. What harbinger comes with this light? The dusty path ahead of
us stretches as far as the eye can see.

"We must approach calmly, regardless of what is
happening," she tells me. "Promise me, you will hold
your tongue. Americans may not understand our sing-
song and will do rash things that cannot be undone."
Her eyes lock onto mine. "You are not like your brother and sister. They speak only when spoken to. But
you express your inner spirit; I can sense an inner
madness trying to escape your lips. You spring from
the jungle like a cat demanding attention. Promise me
that no matter what happens, you will remain a sleeping cat. Do not let others influence the madness inside
you." She lowers her voice when she says this, expressing so much between the spaces of the sentences. I hear
her words and resolve to reflect upon their wisdom later. I do not immediately understand what she is imply-
ing, but I do know that what she is saying is
important.

As the sun climbs higher and its ugly twin, heat,
bakes us, the Ghost moans even more. We stop but it's

too dangerous to leave the road. The cart might get stuck and then we'd be frozen in place. Time would leave us. The dust would settle on us like mist.

Mother tries to feed the Ghost food and water but he only sips. He coughs the food up, so Mother mashes some bananas and feeds him like a baby. With the sun directly overhead, the heat is so stifling that the dust is too drained to swirl. We all walk beside Mother now, gradually making our way towards the sea with the relentless sun stalking our every move. No clouds offer us any shade. Dry season has a vice grip on the very air.

No souls have passed us, yet I feel eyes following our every movement. We huddle close together as we march, mute and fearful. Strangers here bring great misfortune. Every sound brings a promise of violence.

"You there!" a shout comes from the thick grass. "Why are you on the road!" The voice is demanding, insistent. It reeks of malice. It coils around its words with venom dripping across the space between the syllables.

"Honored one, we are a simple family heading to the sea to meet my husband." Mother's voice wisps into the air, but she keeps her eyes downward. "He returns from fishing the great waters. He sends word for his family to join him." When she finishes, she gently nudges us forward.

"STOP!" the disembodied voice howls. It rises from the ground like a corpse forced to march in the land of the living. Mother clutches us into her chest as if we were her own skin trying to escape. We can feel the tension in her beating heart.

A band of armed Vietnamese men burst out of the scrub brush carrying guns and machetes. Mother defiantly steps forward, pushes us behind her, and meets them as a wedge. The four men halt. The space between us solidifies like amber. We are insects caught in the middle of it.

"Get down, NOW!" a man yells. The others point their guns right at us. We cower to the ground.

"Please. We have nothing," Mother pleas. "All we own is here." Mother extends her arm to show a jade bracelet, and points at the buffalo. "Why else would we be traveling alone, on foot, with our lives in danger?"

A moan escapes the cart, igniting a flare. The gunman swats Mother across her cheek with the back of his hand. She crumbles to the ground and we cry out.

"Silence! Or you will never speak again," the gunman hisses.

"Who else is there?" Another gunman has joined the fray. He kicks Mother as she struggles to upright herself. Tears fill our eyes and we suppress our sobs.

"Husband's brother. Sick. Americans used something that fell from the sky. The plants died, our people got sick," Mother wails.

"Why do you bring him along?" the first gunman sneers.

"I do as my husband tells me. It is not my place to question him," Mother responds. She projects surprise that someone would question her blind obedience to her husband. She conveys humiliation for having a stranger draw that conclusion.

"Get the brother out of the cart," the second gunman says to a third, who begins to move to the back of the cart. We all freeze. A collective breath is being held against its will.

"No!" Mother shouts with hysteria in her voice. "Disease. Americans did something. Here!" Mother lifts her left arm up, pulls back her silk sleeve, and shoves her flesh into the second gunman's eyes. There are welts and red bumps. Some rashes even have pus running out of them.

Shock spreads across the man's face and he shouts, "Get away!"

The third gunman grabs Mother and throws her toward the back of the cart. "You pull him out of the cart," he commands.

Mother dusts off her áo dài before obeying. When she does this, the fourth gunman grabs Ngoc and pulls her towards him. When she hears her daughter's screams, Mother freezes and slowly turns towards the fourth gunman. "I'll make you feel like you are number one," Mother says with a forced smile.

"Shut up, concubine. Your daughter will pay for your disobedience and lies," the fourth gunman declares.

"Disobedience? I do what I'm told. What you do now is dishonorable," Mother says. There is no emotion in her voice. "Lies. Truth. Illusion. Life is what we make of it."

The third gunman comes up from behind and grabs Mother by the neck. He presses the sharp edge of his hunting knife against her throat. A red stain glistens as an offering to a hungry sun.

Laughter springs from one hyena to the next. The gunmen are having fun with their catch. The peacock on Mother's top shrieks as the gunman tears apart the cloth, opening her áo dài and exposing the top band of her black pants.

Minh launches at the gunman as he mounts Mother, but the first gunman butts Minh across his head and he goes down, face-first, into the dirt.

"Wait your turn, boy. You'll get what your Mother gets," he laughs.

Ngoc's shirt flutters in the air like a bird taking flight. Her chest is bare. The fourth gunman exposes himself and laughs. "Here is a lollipop for you. Make me feel real good and you get yum-yum."

The gunman holding me slams me face down into the ground before I can react. I feel my pants strangling my ankles as my ass salutes the sun's fireball. I twist and turn, trying to break his grip.

Crack!

A gunshot splits the air apart and the fourth gunman screams in agony. He falls backwards, kicking and screaming. Half his face is gone and his dick no longer salutes.

"You fuckin' cunt!" Gunman three screams as he backhands Mother's head. Mother had lifted the man's gun from his waistband as he was mounting her. She smooth talked him into mounting her doggy style so she could get at his pistol. Instead of saving herself, she saved Ngoc. The momentum allows her to roll partially under the wagon.

The first and second gunmen fly towards Mother. Gunman three grips Mother's left leg, pulling her out from under the cart. Gunman one kicks Mother in the side, and Gunman two stomps her face. Mother's right arm deflects some of the blow.

Gunman two raises his boot once more to smash her nose in when a second *Bang!* slices the air open. The man rolls his eyes upwards and falls to his knees. Minh had picked up the gun that Mother had dropped and shot a hole through the gunman's back. As the bullet exited his chest, it grazed Gunman three's left shoulder, causing him to let go of Mother's leg.

"You all die now!" screams the first gunman as he pulls out his own gun. Suddenly a swarm of stingers slices the air, heading towards Mother, Minh, Sister, and me. Time holds its breath.

Silence. A red hole opens up in Gunman one's face, right where the bridge formed a T with the nose line. Another red hole opens up on Gunman three's left temple, and he slumps to the ground. We pile together on top of Mother as if an invisible magnet is pulling the iron in our blood together. Shock gives way to exhaustion. We crumble to the ground and wait for what the wind brings.

8

Ghosts swarm around us, their bullets flying through the air like clouds of mosquitos. They pull out of the scrub and witness the carnage of their weapons. Gunman one and Gunman three are lying on the dirt road, their heads no longer recognizably human.

I clutch my siblings over Mother's body. Ghosts swarm around us and the cart, making grunting noises. I feel their hands pulling us off Mother and I search their faces for understanding. I remember Mother's advice: "Remain a sleeping cat," so I shut my eyes.

In a few brief moments the dirt road reluctantly releases its hold and the convoy pushes off. The four gunmen are left to rot under the glare of the sun. It's as good a representation of hell as there can be, especially for Christians. For a Buddhist family, Karma's wheels will ensure a rebirth into a lower life form until they learn their lesson.

Mother holds her tongue throughout the journey. We siblings sit on the ledge along the left side of the truck, watching intently for the slightest sounds of danger. Mother clamps her teeth down on a white cloth as one of the Ghosts uses a tong to pull something out of one of the red holes in her side. Mother screams into the cloth and clenches her teeth. Rivers of water pour from her forehead and her silky black hair becomes a tangle of swamp grass.

We start to cry and one of the Ghosts approaches us. He unwraps a cloth and produces round balls on paper sticks, each with a different color, and extends his hand out to each of us. We do not take one of these strange, colorful objects. The Ghost smiles at us. He takes one and places it in his mouth. His eyes express joy. He offers the other two.

Minh and I take one each and do the same. Our eyes light up with joy, so the Ghost produces one for Ngoc as well. We each get a different color.

The Ghost they call "Lieutenant" sits next to Mother and says a few words in sing-song. "Safe. Children ok. Do you understand?" he gently says.

Her eyes flutter and a "Yes" squeaks out. Mother hangs in the balance of life and death—each breath is stretched to the breaking point before being snatched back. Her life force is like a rubber band being stretched back and forth. Each exhale could be her last. I realize that if we lose her, we will have this emptiness for the rest of our lives. The loss of a mother's love can be the harbinger of great, enormous suffering.

As the truck rumbles down the dusty road, the dirt clouds our eyes and gags our nostrils. We are bewildered by the moving beast. For as big as it is, it seems to be tossed back and forth like the luminaries on *Hồ Tây*[14] from the old, faded photographs that Mother carries with her. I used to catch Mother gazing at the pictures and smiling. Occasionally, she would look to the northern horizon after remembering some faraway experience provoked by the still images.

A great storm roils the land. Unlike the natural wind that measures its life in days, this wind is the collective breath of men and women who exhale together. The candles of the old ways are extinguished. Empires have fallen and democracy is still-born.

A new social order arises and forces a great migration between North and South. Mother and Father seek the ideals of freedom and land in the South. The Festival of the Moon gives birth to the photographs that capture an innocence that now transports Mother to a happier place and time as she hangs in the balance. Her life flashes before her eyes.

---

[14] West Lake, a freshwater lake in the center of Hà Nội

9

1996

As I clean off the stack of business cards on the coffee table, I come across Michael's business card. Six weeks have passed since I accepted Jack's sidewalk party invitation. I stare at the card and tell myself that it's time to find out if Michael is someone to get to know. I'm still attracted to him and need to be careful that I don't lose my heart over this.

"Hey, Michael," I say with a touch of excitement as I open the green apartment door. The green draws out Michael's eyes, which intensifies his grin.

"Nice of you to call. I wasn't sure that you would after I said I was seeing someone," Michael says with a mischievous smile.

"Actually, you said 'no' first, then you were prompted to say 'yes' by your friend Jerry, if I recall correctly." I lead Michael into the living room and offer him a seat.

"I don't really know where my boyfriend, Jay, and I are going. We've been seeing each other for a few months. I'm coming out of a 10-year relationship and I'm not really sure if I want anything serious," Michael explains.

I study Michael as he reclines in the chair. He's wearing a tight, navy blue t-shirt that shows off his pecs. The navy blue is dark enough to contrast nicely with his skin tone. White as a ghost. I can still recall the flutter in my stomach when he says yes to going out for dinner. "That seems the way to go," I say, "especially if you are recently out of such a long-term relationship. I think you need time to figure out what you want before plunging back in." I say this with the hope that Michael might consider me as an option during this self-discovery period. "At the party, you said that you were from the mountains. Which ones?" I ask.

"It's a small town in Virginia—you've probably never heard of it," Michael deflects.

"Try me. I lived in Virginia."

"It's Rocky Gap. Nothing special."

I laugh.

"What's so funny?"

"I grew up in the town of Pulaski in the next county over," I reply. "I know exactly where Rocky Gap is."

Michael laughs. "Why, oh why, did you end up in Pulaski?"

"Dad thought it would be best for us to live there, close to his family, while he worked in D.C.," I reply. "In fact, Pulaski was our first American home after six months at a base in Guam. The Americans had us go through intensive English and culture classes before sending us off to the mainland to settle down. When we moved into our new home, I hated it. Nothing seemed right. The food, the people, the weather. All I wanted was for things to go back to normal, but deep down I knew that there was no turning back."

"Sounds like a tough transition," Michael says.

I nod. "Mother told me that I needed to learn the American way now that we were living here. Learn all I could and then take action. What Mother wanted had produced an unintended consequence: we lost much of our Vietnamese language skills but we spoke English flawlessly."

"Well, good," Michael says, laughing.

"What? Why?"

"Because we can understand each other over dinner."

I freeze-frame on Michael's wink.

At the restaurant, I learn that Michael is quite talkative and flirty when he drinks. He tells me all about his breakup that ended a 10-year relationship, and how he had met Jay at a bar in the midst of moving out of the shared home that his ex had bought him out of. Michael gained no experience as a single gay man, but he did gain a new condo and new boyfriend, even before his buyout became official.

As we walk the three blocks back from the restaurant, we causally brush against each other. Our laughter skims the pavement. The air crackles to life with the hint of something to happen. Once we arrive at the front of my building, I gather the nerve to ask Michael up.

"I'd better get going. I'll hail a cab," Michael says quickly.

"Oh." A wave crashes over me into the sandcastle of my resolve and deflates me like an errant beach ball. I must have shown my disappointment like a billboard flashing over an empty highway, demanding attention. I realize that I had focused too much on a statement that Michael made at dinner—that he thought his relationship with Jay wasn't serious.

"You know...Jerry is having an afternoon tea party at his place tomorrow," Michael says. "You should go. It'll be lots of fun."

"I don't know Jerry. I met him when I met you," I say with caution.

"That's not a problem. You can let him know that I invited you. He's over at the Chastleton, which is only two blocks away." Michael points down R Street. "You know where it is?"

"Yes." Of course I know where it is. I only walk by the building at least twice a day.

"Apartment C. Use ring code 4466 to ding the apartment."

"Thanks for the invite," I answer with no enthusiasm in my voice. I want to get inside as fast as possible. This date imploded in its final moment and is now heading into a pit of no return.

Michael must have sensed my pull back. "I'd love to see you again. It won't be a problem. Jerry said to invite anyone I wanted."

"Well...sure," I reply. I don't hide the deflation in my voice.

"Wonderful. I'll see you there, then."

Once I'm face down on my sectional, I wonder why the hell I said yes. I got this vibe that we could have been doing a lot more than saying goodbye in front of my building. Now, I'm left to jerk off and sleep solo in a double bed. Thank you, Barbara Mandrell.

The next day, I find myself outside of the Chastleton, staring at the keypad. I'm chasing after a man who's got a causal thing with another man. Mother would be proud.

"Hey. Would you mind if I used the keypad?" a voice asks behind me, snapping me out of my stupor.

I turn and am immediately blinded by the most intense blue eyes I've ever seen. "Sure." I step aside and look over this guy's right shoulder as he punches in the code – 4466.

"Are you going to Jerry's tea party?" I ask.

He locks his blues onto mine. Unfortunately, the door's buzz shatters our moment. He grabs the door and pulls it towards him.

"Yes," he says. With that he enters the building and I follow. In silence we enter the elevator. In that confined space, I can smell him, hear his breathing, and feel the air slightly nudge between us. There is something very familiar about him.

As the door opens, we both step through without a word between us. But we do brush against each other. A shutter runs down my spine, goose bumps exploding on my arm. Suddenly, I recognize the man. His hairy arm touching my skin percolates the memory to the forefront of my mind. "Didn't we meet at Jack's?" I half whisper, dreading the response.

"You know, you do look familiar," he says as we make our way to C door. I hit the buzzer and we wait in silence.

A man I don't recognize opens the door. "Hey Gordon. Come on in," he says, smiling. When he turns to me, his countenance grows stern. "And who are you?"

The damage was done—Gordon was already out of sight.

"Vy. I was invited by Michael," I respond. Dammit, I knew this was a bad idea.

"I'm Taylor. Welcome. I'm here to help Jerry out." He opens the door for me and lets me pass, all the while feigning a housewife in distress. What a drama queen! We walk down a long hallway that basically spills us into the living room, which already has a dozen or so guests mingling about. It is a cozy one-bedroom apartment with an attached kitchenette.

"Drinks and some nosh are on the bar. Help yourself," Taylor offers.

Instead of heading straight to the bar, I look around the room hoping to catch up with Gordon. I then notice that he is already being served a drink by a group of guys, laughing heartily. Well. I wasn't going to break into that group. I had suddenly become an island in the center of the living room, with party guests obliviously circling around me. Now I know how a carcass must feel when vultures are circling overhead.

"Hey you," a bright sunny voice rings out.

I turn and see Jerry. "Hi. Michael said it would be ok to come."

"Of course. He called to tell me that he invited you. Welcome. He should be here any second now."

I'm already on gay time. I showed up a half-hour late and Michael isn't even here. The one person I wanted to see. "Thanks," I respond warmly. "Nice place, by the way. I love the red in the kitchen."

"Thank you," Jerry replies. "I was trying to decide what color to do as an accent, since you can see the kitchen." We move towards the bar island separating the kitchenette from the living room and prepare some drinks. "Where do you live?" he asks.

"Just a couple of blocks down, at 14th and R. I've been there a few years now," I say.

"Do you work downtown?"

"I wish. I drive out to Reston. I work for a technology company, putting training classes together for employees," I say.

I like this guy. He comes across as having good sense and a deprecating manner. "Where are you from?" I ask. "As you know, no one is from D.C. When you do meet someone who is, it's like catching a creature of myth."

"I was born in Norfolk, Virginia, and found my way here for a job. Now I get my kids every other weekend from my ex who lives in Maryland."

"Oh. You were married?" I ask, perplexed.

"Why do people find that such a surprise? You know this..." Jerry rolls his hands down the front of his chest to his belly button "...is God given and man built."

"I'm sure that it's not the body..." I begin.

"You..." he winks at me, "...should not be casting aspersions to my body." He laughs and I join right in.

"You know, Michael has a daughter."

"Really!" My eyebrows reach for the heavens. "He never mentioned that." Why would Michael have left that out?

"Michael may not have mentioned it since you can never tell how gay men will react to that type of news," Jerry explains. "On the one hand, they like the idea of sleeping with a real daddy. It's like sleeping with a straight guy. On the other hand, they don't want to deal with children. I have been through it all, being a dad myself and a single gay man looking for love."

"Look what I dragged in!" Taylor announces over the party's noise.

We both turn to look and watch as Michael enters the room. "Hey guys!" he exclaims, with Taylor hanging off his arm. He casts his eyes toward us and his feet follow.

"Lookie here," Jerry says to the two approaching men. "Twiddle Dee Tipsy and Twiddle Dumb Tipsy, together again." Jerry arches his eyebrow and mimics being drunk.

"Awww. Lighten up. Here. Take a drink and a load off your feet," Taylor smiles.

Jerry takes the drink and puts his lips to the rim. "Not bad for a Cosmo."

Taylor puts his hands to his face and screams, "Not *bad*? You are a hurtful, hateful BITCH! I can NEVER do anything right. Mommy is going to lie down now.

She can't take all this negativity." With that, Taylor grabs Michael and they disappear among the rabble.

"Is he going to be all right?" I ask, confused.

'Don't let that drama queen fool you," Jerry says. "I'll let you in on the secret. We dated. I know all about his games and tricks. We're friends now, even though I think he wants to get back together. At social events, he puts on the airs of being Mrs. June Cleaver. If he had a pearl necklace, he would be clutching it." We both laugh.

A few minutes later, Michael re-appears. "Are you laughing at me?"

"Paranoid, are we?" Jerry beams. "Why would you assume we are laughing at anyone in particular?"

"Better not be laughing about me." Michael pouts his lips.

"So how is the boy toy handling the key?" Jerry asks, trying to change the subject.

With alarm in his eyes, Michael quickly says, "Jay is not that young and you know why he has a key."

"What are we talking about here?" I ask.

Michael looks at me with hesitation on the tip of his tongue. "Jay is 12 years younger than me and I gave him a key a few weeks back." He says this as if it isn't a big deal.

"What? You gave a guy you're not serious with a key to your place?" I ask, incredulous.

"He's a huge help—he gets my mail and cleans up the place. It's great, especially since I travel a lot and visit my daughter every other weekend."

I can't believe what I am hearing. "I thought you were still in dating mode. Damn, did I get that wrong? I thought maybe we might have a chance at it."

"Sorry. I'm looking for friends more than anything else. But we can still hang out, though. I really am just looking for friends. Just before my ex left, he joined a whole new group of guys. Not only did he take most of our friends with him, he got himself some new ones." It's clear that Michael has been wounded by the breakup.

Hmmm. What am I supposed to do? Here is a cute guy asking to be friends; maybe he was misguided, maybe he had no experience being single, and maybe it's okay. Damn. Why am I attracted to this guy, especially since his relationship with this Jay guy is more serious than he lets on?

"Sure. We can hang out," I respond. With that comment, I turn my attention away from the group and spy someone I would like to at least get to know, hopefully horizontally. Luckily, he is coming towards us, headed for the drink station. I calculate a slight shift would lure my catch closer.

I brush up against Gordon as he swings around the bar. "Sorry. I didn't see you there," I say casually. I decide to keep the momentum going, so I turn to him and ask, "How are you enjoying the party?"

"I'm having a fun time. And you?" Gordon responds.

I find his smile intoxicating. And inviting. "Great. I enjoy meeting people. Actually, I recognize some of them from the gayborhood. I assume the others live out in the 'burbs, or on Capitol Hill. Are you still out in Falls Church?" I ask.

"Wow. Great memory. That was temporary, actually, with my friend Bob. But then a place on P Street became available. I thought I would experience this thing called city living while I'm young."

I recognize a smirk spreading across Gordon's face. "Well, you look good, whatever age you're trying on." I grin and flash a flirty smile. I feel like I know him. Why is that?

"What do you do?" I continue.

"I'm studying German. I got back from living there last summer. Berlin is sweet. I thought I would get my Master's."

I find myself staring into Gordon's blue eyes and wondering if he finds me attractive. I notice that he has gotten a little closer since we began talking. Encouraged by that, I continue my interrogation. "Where do you want to study?"

"GU."

"That's amazing. That's my alma mater. I got my undergraduate degree in Economics. It's a small world after all."

"I'm enjoying grad school. I thought once I finished, I would stick around and see if I could actually use it," Gordon laughs.

"What's so funny?"

"I was laughing at the idea of using German to find a job in D.C. It seems a bit surreal."

"My step-dad is of German/Dutch descent. I've never really thought of visiting Germany, though," I reply.

"You've got to see Berlin. It's an exciting, cosmopolitan city. There are lots of things...and people, to do." I laugh at the double entendre. "You can also simply hang out with friends and drink great beer."

I realize that Gordon is staring intently into my eyes. A few seconds pass and then he asks, "You're German?"

"No. I'm Vietnamese. My step-dad is American with the German/Dutch background. At least I look to him as my dad. My biological father died in a construction accident back in Vietnam—my parents met during the last days of the war," I explain.

"I fought in the war," Gordon says. I watch his face contort as some unpleasant memory rises to the surface. "It was a long time ago, but some memories die harder than others." His eyes glaze over for a moment.

I'm about to throw him a lifeline and haul him back to shore when his friends appear and pull him away with all the ferocity of an undertow. The words, "Don't leave," enter my mind, but not my throat. Instead, I watch his friends drag him back out to sea, until he is just a speck blowing in the wind.

10

As my friends pull me away from that cute guy, Vy, I can't help but think of the day in 1975 when I got back to Boone, North Carolina, from the war, and learned about Daddy's plans for me.

"Dear, it's been six months since we've seen you," my mother implores. "Please come out and have dinner with the family." I can hear her leaning against my bedroom door, listening in. She was so ecstatic when she learned I was coming home. She cleaned the house, called family, and chatted with her girls. Her prayers were finally answered. She could breathe and even watch the nightly news again. That faraway place that had captured her son was now returning him to her bosom.

Tommy and Sissy helped in as many ways as they could. They went shopping for her, worked around the yard, and helped Daddy paint the room and move furniture. Tommy got excited about teasing his little brother again, and Sissy couldn't wait to have anyone but Tommy to look after her. We would all be better and stronger than before.

When I first arrived at the house, my parents told me about their race to D.C. when they heard I had been taken to Walter Reed Army Medical Center. What they saw in that patient room stopped them dead in their tracks. They weren't sure where the machines began or ended as the tubes snaked in and out of my body. They whispered a prayer, pleading to God to keep me alive.

"Ok, Mother. I'll do it. I'll come down for dinner. Just give me a couple of minutes," I yell through the door.

"Wonderful!" Mother exclaims. I hear her footsteps race down the hallway towards the stairs.

I slowly swing my legs off the bed and stare out the window. I can see over the ridge and the mountains in the distance. It's definitely a long way from the jungles of 'Nam. The people there seemed so delicate, especially the women in their áo dài. I fondly remember being in Sài Gòn after my first monsoon downpour; sheets of water blocked my view like curtains over windows. As suddenly as it started, it stopped. The pavement glistened with sheens of moisture as the sun greedily sucked the puddles back up and the women floated across them as if walking on water. The skirt hem of the áo dài sparkled with bright colors and rich embroidery that mimicked swaying fields of bright, exotic flowers. The explosion of color washed across the city and even the dusty back roads of the surrounding small villages.

I also remember the heat. I never could cool off. The nights were as stifling as the days, but with the added detriment of not being able to see where I was going. Sweat beaded all over my body, becoming drinking fountains for every bug. The mosquitoes bit so much, they felt like an ancient Chinese torture.

The doctors told me that my walking would improve over time but my legs may act like weather forecasters. I'd always have the scars where the stingers of hot metal sliced into my flesh. Five holes, now scabbed over. It still hurt to breathe deeply or to laugh too hard.

I slowly edge down the stairs. Bending my knees causes me to wince. I have to remember: no quick, low twists or a muscle spasm in my back would have me twitching on the floor like an upside-down cockroach trying to walk on air. What I would give to be able to run up and down the stairs. It would be fun to launch off the next to the last step and fly. I hate feeling dependent on someone. I'm not an invalid.

"Hey everybody, look whose joining us," Daddy announces. He springs up and meets me half-way to the dining room. Before another word is said, he flexes his left wrist and the heavy, oak chair slides away from the table as if on wheels.

"Daddy, it's okay. I can take it from here." After I carefully crash into my chair, I look around the table. Tommy and Mother are sitting to my right; Sissy and Daddy to my left. I am at the head of the table, I realize. Why? I didn't feel like a hero. I shouldn't be at the head of the table.

"Let's pray," Mother says before reciting our family prayer. By the time she ends, I no longer have the heart to complain. I should be glad I'm alive. Yet the way they look at me, I can't tell anymore if Mother and Daddy see me as I am now or when they first saw me lying in the hospital bed.

All I remember is the haze that stood between me and the rest of the tangible world. I still occasionally hear the whirl and beeps of machines, like a long-lost school chum who suddenly turns up to say hi. Mother says she gasped when she saw all the bandages, and then the tubes running into and out of my flesh connected to cold, hard plastics. She trembles when she tells me about the stillness. She couldn't tell if I was alive. She wondered how much of me was me and how much was the machine. She kept telling herself I must live.

"Are you feeling better, Gordy?" Sissy asks.

"Kiddo, I have my good days and I have my bad days."

"Do you want to hike down to the river and..." Sissy begins, but Tommy cuts her off.

"Sissy! He doesn't want to go see your little fishies," he hisses. I haven't heard that type of curt, explosive anger in anyone's voice for a long time, and certainly not from Tommy. He's a couple of years older than me and tried to enlist for 'Nam, but an inner ear imbalance kept him out.

"Hey, Tommy," I say calmly. When I get his attention, I let my eyes tell him to shut up. I then turn to Sissy and say, "When I get a little stronger, Sissy, I'll go. I want to see the river again. I always loved hearing it whistle around the rocks and snap at the sandy shoreline." I see her smile.

Dinner wraps up in a somber mood. Our small talk contains the most profound messages, however. The weather is good; the family businesses are healthy; the new school is almost constructed; and there is a new housing development planned. We are drained of the fullness of life like ghosts. We hover over the food, eat it, yet it brings no fulfillment. We silently float out of the dining room and to the kitchen, carrying our dishes in a procession that would quiet the dead. Soon, I am outside on the porch, overlooking the sweeping land

and the huge oak just off-center on the property. As kids, we created our own joy around that tree, swinging, climbing, and playing hide-n-seek well into the night.

Ouch. I put too much pressure on my foot and the pain shot through me in weird right angles. Sometimes I see faces that are barely an outline in my memory, and hear sing-song that wraps it all up in a neat package. I try hard to concentrate on a face or a sound, hoping that it would become clear. I find it hard to be at peace with these ghosts, these shards of the living, these half-formed entities.

"Concentrating mighty hard there, son." Daddy catches me by surprise and I nearly jump off the porch. "Sorry. I shouldn't have snuck up on you."

"Don't worry about it, Daddy. I just think my nerves are shot," I say softly. I was jittery in my first few months out of 'Nam. Sudden noises could flash me back into the heart of the ambush. I broke out in a sweat, felt the blood pumping through my veins, and spiraled into a very dark, isolated space. But I was adapting, day by day.

Daddy lets out a big sigh. "That's good. A joke." Then a broad smile appears on his face, easing his chiseled lines. A spark of life flashes behind his eyes and he is back in the land of the living. "I want to talk to you about somethin'. It's been six months since you made it home and we're heading into summer." Daddy pauses to check if I'm preparing to rocket away.

I'm rooted into the ground. I'm too depleted to dig myself out. "What is it, Daddy? You look like the weight of the world is resting on your back, instead of your shoulders as usual," I grin.

"I got you in at my alma mater..." Daddy says.

It came out a bit too curtly, not the way he wanted it to, but that didn't stop me. "What?" I hit him with an accusing glare.

"Son. Calm down," Daddy says. He shifts into a more soothing flow. "It's going to be all right. Let's take a deep breath."

I don't put up much of a fight. "All right," I shrug.

"Just try it out for the summer. You can take one class per summer session. Some sessions run five, six or eight weeks. You might like it and want to continue," Daddy explains.

"I don't recall applying." Maybe Daddy just wants me to take random classes to get me out of the house. Chapel Hill is about two and a half hours away. At 19, what else am I going to do?

"Well. I was a trustee for half a dozen years and the Dean of Students is a personal friend," Daddy says.

"I don't know. Maybe I should just stay here." When I see the disappointment in Daddy's eyes, I add, "Until I'm stronger." But the tide is still rising. I realize that Daddy is doing everything in his power not to show how much I am letting him down. It's too much to watch, so I blurt, "I'll try it for the summer. Maybe one of the five-week sessions." With those words, relief glistens off his brow like beads of sweat after a hard day's work in the fields.

11

1978

"Hey! It's my man, Gordy!" Terry exclaims. "How's it hanging, Big Dog?"

"Sweet. I think Maggie is about to let me take her to the chapel of love." I show Terry my pearly whites across the living room. We're lounging around the house that Terry, Luke, Mitch, and I share a few blocks off Franklin Street.

"See that?" Terry says. "If you didn't follow your old man's advice, you'd be hooking up with some hairy, throwback mountain woman with more hair than you. At least your gorilla children wouldn't need clothes to stay warm on those frigid mountain nights." Terry laughs as he pops open the fridge, searching for his prize. Once I hear the bottle cap pop off his brew-sky, I know that Terry is starting the weekend party now.

"Ha. Ha," I jest. "Who are you shacking up with? Plump Cindy from Biology, more woman for you to love?"

"You know it. She's why God made brown bags." Terry leans on the couch and asks, "So where are you two meeting up?"

"You got to be kidding!" I snap. "You think I'd let you know? You'd ruin everything."

"Oh. You cut me to the quick." Terry shakes his head. "Please? Pretty please?" He comes over and starts petting me. He rubs his free hand through my hair, squeezes the nape of my neck, and then sits right next to me as if we can share the same seat. He puts his arms around me and starts snuggling his head into my armpit.

Another voice shoots into the room. "Oh, how cute. Look, Mitch, we're living with a bunch of fags. Can we join in or is this a private party?" Luke laughs.

I jump right off the couch and practically stand at attention. That Army stint still stays with me. "Hey guys," I respond as casually as possible.

Terry just rolls his eyes. "Oh puleaze honey, we ain't done. Come on back, shuug. Mo' lovin' I gots for you."

"Fuck you," I snap.

"Touchy, are we?" Mitch smiles.

"Honey, no," Terry says. "We agreed that you'd be bottom. So boy, bend over and take it like a man."

"Yawl can go fuck yourselves," I yell into the room as I push my way past Luke. I head into the bathroom and slam the door shut. I can hear them laughing. Why am I so sensitive? I know they are just kidding...I think. NO. They can't really think THAT.

"Pretty boy in there has a date with Maggie tonight. Thinks he's getting some'un," Terry whispers.

"I hear they are going to the restaurant, Top of the Hill," Luke says.

"How do you know?" Terry asks.

"I overheard her roommate talkin' about it in class. Didn't know it was Gordy, though."

"Yeah, but why is he so sensitive about all this man luvin' stuff?" Mitch asks.

Terry shrugs.

"Never can tell where Gordy is coming from. That 'Nam thing fucked him over."

"What the fuck?" Luke and Mitch burst out.

"Oops. Wasn't supposed to share that." A sheepish Terry ducks his head and gets up.

"Hold it right there, buddy!" Mitch commands. Mitch and Luke close in on Terry like a pack of wild dogs on a kitten.

"Guys? I'm not supposed to say anything about it. Leave it alone."

I open the door and cross my arms. I pretty much overheard everything Terry said, but I decide to play the naïve card. "What are you guys talking about?" I shoot the question at Terry like stinging venom.

"Nothin'," Terry says. I feel the guys' eyes focus with sniper precision to the dot between my eyes. Terry and Luke have cool, blue eyes like me, while Mitch's are dark brown. We're all fairly the same size; Terry is the tallest, though, at close to six feet. We're all getting a little pudgy from the partying, but overall we're still in good shape.

The pregnant pause bursts when Terry announces, "So the Top of the Hill?" He raises his eyebrow and mocks me with his devilish grin.

I go blank.

"Sorry bro'. Let the cat out of the bag," Luke shrugs.

"How?"

"Chatty, chatty, chatty," Luke smiles. "What do you expect from girls?"

"I better not see a single one of you there," I threaten.

"Free country, my boy." Terry grins like a carnival clown.

All day I'm nervous about seeing Maggie. She's a sexy number, with long brown hair and creamy white skin. We've been flirting in German Lit all semester, talking endlessly about Berlin and the go-go '20s before communism split the city. We focus on the culture, the craziness, and the bohemian lifestyle that appealed to me after the sedation of North Carolina and the adrenaline rush of 'Nam.

Maggie is actually about an inch taller than me, which is a little weird. But I can gaze into her baby browns and let myself drift away. Hmm. Life can be sooo good. It's senior year and we're talking about spending some time in Europe after graduation. Why go right to work? Hell, maybe I'll go to grad school. I see no rush to be an adult.

I bounce between seeing Maggie and wondering what nasty surprises Terry might come up with over the course of the night. My nerves are on full alert. No telling what the hell he'd do.

"Hey you," Maggie teases from across the table. "You seem a bit preoccupied. Everything all right?"

"Roommates," I sigh. "That's all. I should be shot. I'm here with a gorgeous woman and I'm not giving her the attention she deserves."

"You say all the right things, Mr. Smoothie," Maggie says. She then adds, "I know what you mean. Gaby, my roommate, is telling everybody all over campus that I'm heading out for a date at the Top of the Hill. She's even offered to rescue me. I tried telling her that I KNEW the guy. We've only practically been together for the last two years."

"Yeah. We've had a number of classes in German, haven't we? The language, the literature, the lifestyle," I reply.

"So..." she starts. She throws me a look that I know means one of those profound questions is about to come rolling off the mountain in a landslide. "Why'd it take so long for you to ask me out?"

"Dunno," I answer. "I'm real comfortable around you. You're easy to talk to, and certainly easy on the eyes."

Maggie giggles. "Mr. Maybray, I do declare. If you weren't so cute and personable I'd have you thrown overboard." Maggie exaggerates her 'Bama upbringing. Her dad's a big-time lawyer in Birmingham and is torn up to see his little girl go off to college so far from home. At least it's still in the South. He would have gone crazy if she had gone to one of those Yankee schools.

The date is going well. Too well. That's when I hear from across the room, "Well. Well. Well. What do we have here?" The voice grates down the back of my neck like hot wax, which is then ripped right off. I knew he couldn't resist showing up. But I'm not prepared for what I see when I turn around to face the annoying gnat. There, dressed in Army fatigues, is Terry and some goons I don't recognize personally. But I do recognize them as ROTC.

"Hey, my man!" Terry stumbles over with the stink of alcohol disinfecting the air. "My new best buds want to meet a real Army man." Terry burps. I can see Maggie's puzzled look growing across her forehead.

"Not now," I hiss under my breath.

"Did you really fight in 'Nam?" an incredulous, blond-haired, blue-eyed Aryan asks. They're staring me down like I'm a throwback.

"Guys. You've had too much to drink. Can't you see I'm with some company?" I try to play off the disclosure and change the subject. I really don't want Maggie to know this about me right now. Dammit. Why don't they just go away?

"Man. You can't make me a liar. Not with my new buds," Terry says. He's having a hard time standing up. Suddenly, he pitches forward and the goons grab him just before his forehead smacks into the table.

Out of nowhere, the waiter and the hostess are standing above us, eying the situation suspiciously. They must be wondering if the college kids are about to tear up the place. The goons shift their weight to balance Terry between them with an outstretched arm over each shoulder. It's the classic crucifixion pose that drunks have employed since time immortal, when they've needed a little help, even from the kindness of strangers.

"Nothin' happening here, officer," Terry slurs to the hostess. "We're going." With that, the goons pivot and haul Terry away. Just before they're out of sight, the Aryan goon throws an incredulous look back at us. He probably thinks I don't have what it takes to be in the Army.

Maggie is cool throughout the ordeal. The temperature between us is a few degrees cooler, though. She's been paying very close attention. Her face lines up with mine and then she drops her voice. "Any truth to that?"

"Not sure what truth you are talking about?" I innocently slide the response across the table. I even add a polite laugh and hope it's enough to throw her off the scent. She instinctively looks down at her lap, clearly disappointed.

I shift in my seat, waiting for something... anything. Thankfully, her eyes dart upward and the overhead light flashes off her irises for a brief moment. Our eyes, her browns and my blues, connect, and an electrical current builds, bringing more and more gravitas to her monosyllabic response:

"'Nam."

I realize that I am now required to respond. Truthfully. Otherwise, this date is over. I will be buried and forgotten in the field of collegiate love.

I begin my response slowly, carefully choosing my next words like it's an oral exam. "Yes. It was less than a year. I had just turned 19 and wanted to serve my country. I thought I would go in for a few years and then head off to college. If you count basic training, it was less than eight months."

Maggie's eyebrows knit together. The silence between us solidifies before she cracks it. "What was it like? Why were you there for such a short time?" She's eager to learn more about this. I am not sure if I am eager to share.

12

"It was October of '73 when I landed in Sài Gòn. I don't think I'll ever forget the heat. It was like nothing I had ever experienced. Up in the mountains it never gets hot like that. There's very little humidity, and it's fairly cool all year long. If you want that sweltering heat you head to the beach. In 'Nam, it's a physical thing. I remember them opening the door of the plane and like some wild animal, the heat devoured the air conditioning. The first few gasps of air were like breathing water. For a split second I thought I was drowning." I look up at Maggie and she's scrunched her face up into a grimace.

"It makes me think of our family vacations to Florida," Maggie says.

"I think it's much worse. The first three or four weeks, we spent our time getting used to the heat and humidity. I don't think I ever cooled down while I was there. It didn't matter if the sun was up or down. The heat baked into everything and shot right back out. I remember always being careful not to touch anything metal, which made it tough to keep my finger on the trigger."

"How do the people there handle the heat? What were they like?" Maggie asks.

"I guess they just get used to it as they grow up. They're smaller, almost childlike in appearance. It was a great confidence booster, because I was always the tallest guy in the room."

Maggie laughs, prompting me to continue.

"But the one thing I really admired about them was how much they smiled. I thought that strange considering their country was at war."

"Well, I guess that was all they had left. They sound like good people."

I let out a quick chuckle.

"What's so funny?" Maggie beams.

"You said they *sound like* good people. That got me thinking about their sing-song language."

"Sing-song?"

"That's how I refer to their speech. It's based on five tones, which means if you don't hit the right tone in your speech, you say something completely different than what you thought. I remember trying to say chào cụ (co), which means, 'hello, friend,' but ending up saying chào cu (coo), which means 'hello, little boy's dick.' The entire room burst into laughter."

Maggie's eyes go wide. "Mercy me! You said that in a room full of strangers?" She mocks me with a scandalous gasp.

"Well, I didn't mean to insult anyone. I just wanted to say hello in their language."

I just know that Maggie is going to torment me with this story for the rest of the school year. I plead with her using my puppy-dog eyes, but she already has a mischievous grin on her face. Too late. Only time will tell how she uses this new knowledge.

"Now tell me, why did you serve for such a short time?" Maggie asks.

I study her soft features. I've never told anyone about this outside of the Army. The MPs pounded me with questions about what happened before, during, and after the engagement. I remember wondering why they were asking me the same questions over and over while I lay there in the hospital bed, wishing I were dead. I hurt all over in places that felt like hot pokers jabbing into me.

"Hello? Earth calling," Maggie interjects.

"Sorry. Where was I?" I stall to gather my thoughts. "We were on patrol in a village somewhere south of Sài Gòn, near the coastline. We were ambushed. Our platoon was dropping like flies. I remember seeing body parts all over the place. God, the smell was awful. Like open sewage. I remember crawling away and falling into water, a river." I pause to let the memories wash over me.

"What happened?" Maggie is now sitting on the edge of her seat, perched like a bird waiting for birdseed.

"It's very hazy afterwards. A girl fished me out. I also remember a monk and boy taking care of me. I couldn't tell their ages. The boy looked ten but he could have been much older. The monk was the only one who could speak English, broken but understandable. I think at some point I started running a fever. One moment I was getting better, the next I was puking my insides up. But I can remember the monk and, I think, the female who found me, arguing about something in sing-song." I smile. "Then I was in a cart. I heard more sing-song, then crying and wailing, and then English. Before I knew it, I was out of the mire." Recounting the sequence of events builds up uneasiness within my throat. I realize how many moments are missing from the tale.

"Oh, you poor dear." Maggie reaches out and grabs my hand. Her voice is soothing. She squeezes my hand to give me the resolve to continue.

"I woke up in the hospital, Walter Reed, in D.C. Tubes were coming out of me like a potato with sprouts. I was bandaged from head to toe—they told me I was there for five or six months. When my parents showed up, they were horrified. They thought I was going to die. Believe me. I wanted to. I was in so much pain." I catch myself getting misty-eyed.

I pause, more for me to catch my breath than to get a response from Maggie. I can feel my body responding to the memories. My mouth is dry; my forehead is wet with sweat; and my left shoulder is throbbing from where that crazy tattoo was etched into my flesh. Maggie instinctively squeezes my hand again. That brings me back.

"When I finally see my body, I find all these scars and this crazy tattoo on my left shoulder." I reach up and grab it as if to remind myself that it is still there. I trace over the scars from where the bullets had dug into me and where the doctors wrestled them out of me.

All of a sudden I'm weary. Just recalling these memories takes a lot out of me. It's been about four years but dammit if it doesn't feel like it happened yesterday. We finish dinner in silence, and I pay the bill. Once Maggie is safely home, I suddenly realize that I was going through the motions but wasn't really there after I finished my story. I think I've ruined the date.

Suddenly, Maggie turns from her front door and plants a warm, moist kiss onto my lips. It takes me a moment and then I'm up against her, pushing her back. The door stops our backward waltz. Pressing up on her, I spring forward with a hard-on jabbing into her inner thigh.

"No!" Maggie whispers. "My roommates are home. I don't want them to catch us." She breaks my grip, pivots, and pushes the door open. She steps across the threshold, gives me a sly smile and closes the door behind her. She does all of that and it feels instantaneous. It's like she disappeared into thin air.

I'm standing, looking at a door with a raging hard-on. I think I've just lubed my pants. Sure enough, as I look down there is a wet spot. I walk home with it. I'm excited about that smile. That means another date.

I see the lights are on in her living room. Damn. One of the roomies is home. Doesn't matter, I'm heading to bed.

"Hey, Mitch," I say as I enter through the front door. He's sprawled over the couch with empty Vodka bottles on the coffee table. "Having your own private party?" I remark.

"No, man. Bud left and I'm headed to bed soon."

"G'night, then," I say and make my way to bed. Terry and I share a room with twin beds just as Mitch and Luke do. Sometimes the house feels too small but tonight Terry is out. Who knows what trouble he is getting himself into with those goons. I'm gonna bust his chops for spilling the beans the next time I see him.

Lying in bed, I remember Maggie and her creamy white skin touching mine. Her lips still taste of the wine she was drinking right before we left. My right hand grabs my hard-on and pulls it skyward. I'm stroking my meat when the door flies open. I freeze. Shit. Is that Terry? The figure sways at the threshold.

"Yeow!" I exclaim.

"What are you doing in my room?" Mitch belches.

"Mitch! Your room is down the hallway. This is my room. Go to bed!" I yell. I'm exasperated. My right hand is squeezing my hard-on under the sheets. I'm about to explode. I've got the cum rag ready and now this drunk idiot is too smashed to find his own room.

"No. It's too far." Mitch stumbles into the room and falls right on top of me.

"What the fuck?" I yell and push Mitch off of me, exposing my hard-on as he falls off the bed and takes the sheet with him.

Before I can cover myself, Mitch is already eye level to the mattress. He sees it. I freeze. Great. Now I'm going to hear jerkoff jokes for the rest of my life. I close my eyes and hope that Mitch just gets up and goes to his room or falls back to the floor and passes out. I wait. I don't want to make any eye contact and I don't want to talk about it.

Wait.

I open my eyes and look down at my dick. Mitch is sucking on it like a lollipop. Licking it and swirling it around in his mouth. Jesus, I can't think straight. I never would have thought that Mitch... of all people.

My breathing shallows. Mitch is squeezing the base of my shaft with his right hand and nibbling on the tip of my dick. God, it feels amazing. Without warning, I unload. I hear a little gag and then swallowing. I must have caught him by surprise. But he licks my dick clean. He swallows it like he hasn't eaten in days.

13

1996

The door buzzes. "Yes? Who is it?" I call into the intercom.

"Vyah! It's Jack! Your partner in crime."

"Go away," I snap. Lately, Jack and I have been cycling in and out of each other's lives. That's one of the downsides of living where you went to school. There's always somebody who remembers you doing something you wish you hadn't. Jack knows a lot of my secrets, since he instigated most of them. Sometimes I think I'm a willing participant and other times a dupe.

"Oh Vy, darling. Come on. I want to hear about the beach trip from last weekend." Jack whines as if he's some lonesome cowboy who has been running sheep across the big sky country without human contact.

Fuck. I wonder who told him about the beach trip. "Fine." I buzz him in. By the time I get to the door and open it, he's standing there with a shit-eating grin on his face. The Cheshire Cat is a pale second.

In college, we fed off each other's desires to be the center of attention. I knew at an early age that I was gay. Vietnamese culture may not have an actual word for the concept, but it exists. Coming to America, especially to the southwest corner of Virginia, painted Mother and the children as something exotic. We heard ourselves referred to as Oriental, as if we were furniture. There were very few Asians of any type in this remote corner. Since Dad was white, we lived on the all-white side of our street. There was some imaginary line that separated whites and blacks. Whoever drew that line did not count on Asians. It remained that way until the mid-70s. In this town, being yellow put you in a different category and outside of the normal white/black conventions. I thought this gave me permission to break expectations, even as I felt lonely and alienated from the people around me.

"Hey! Aren't you going to invite me in?" a bashful Jack says. It's all an act. His clothes mark him as a label whore. He's fashionable and gets offended if you don't recognize what he's wearing. All that trouble to make an impression, how dare you not recognize what he's wearing?

"Before you come in and have a seat, SIRE," I jest, "how did you learn about the beach trip?" There is a small part of me that doesn't want to know.

"Vyah!" Jack exclaims. "You know a girl never shares her sources." Jack thinks he's Truman Capote writing his next thriller on social conventions.

"FINE!" I declare. It won't be too difficult to figure it out.

I enter the living room and sit on the sofa. I hear the door shut and instantly Jack is next to me, leaning close to catch every morsel. The eagerness on his face is too much this early in the morning. This must be why people drink coffee. How else do you make it through the day?

"Well, well, well," Jack taunts.

I take my sweet ass time. I know Jack is not going anywhere. After Gordon was spirited away by his friends, I got to talking to Michael again. He invited me to go with him and Taylor to Rehoboth Beach. He had use of a house down by Queen Avenue, which is the unofficial start of the gay section, called Poodle Beach.

I give Jack a quick rundown of the horrid weekend—the binge drinking, the beach blow job between Michael and Taylor, our prolonged shower together, the morning denial that anything happened the night before, and the Sunday drive confession dealing with Jay. I tell Jack everything except about the herpes scare. Michael thought that Taylor gave it to him because he could visually confirm it by the bumps. He's waiting on the blood test. That's really none of my business. A person's sexually transmitted disease status should only be shared if confirmed, especially if you are sleeping within your circle of friends.

"So he's back with Jay. I didn't even know that he had broken up with him," Jack says. "And what the hell was Taylor doing giving him a blow job on the beach?" Jack's eyebrow arches.

"Sometime during your party and the beach trip, Michael broke up with Jay. He and Taylor went bar hopping to get Michael's mind off of the break up... or should I say non-break up. Well, later that evening, Taylor and he sucked each other off. Taylor came clean when I confronted him, but Michael couldn't remember the details." Since I left out the herpes 411, I can't tell Jack why Michael admitted something happened, since he contended that's when Taylor infected him. "I suspect all his drinking just makes him a whore," I spat.

"Dear. You obviously don't drink much. Alcohol does not make someone do something that they don't already want to do. Michael wants to be a whore and an angel at the same time. He wants to be both things just like that crazy single gay man versus monogamous couple thingy." Jack stands up. "People should be who they are, not some fake creation." Unless you're talking about your personal appearance, then Jack is your poster child for hair coloring, nail polish, labels, and spa services.

"The beach trip was a real eye opener for me," I say. "I'm not interested in being friends with Michael anymore. He's a flake and, worse, a fake. All the double talk just proves how loathsome he is," I say. Yet, silently, I tell myself that I wanted to be more than friends when I first met him. I can't seem to trust my own instincts around men I find attractive. They inevitably turn out unavailable for whatever reason.

I stare at Jack since I'm not getting an immediate response. I then notice that Jack is intently staring at a picture that's in an art deco, chrome frame. He turns, smiles, and walks back over to the sofa. He hands me the picture.

"Wow. Tim. I haven't thought of him in years. Are you guys still in touch?" Jack asks.

"Yeah, we're in touch. On and off. He still lives in Birmingham and he's still a lawyer," I respond.

"I remember in college when his best friend Buford and he took the train to D.C. from Birmingham, Alabama. Man, how he complained about the 22-hour train ride and how there weren't enough drugs to put him out of his misery." Jack smiles.

"I remember that Buford had a huge crush on you. You guys mimicked dogs in heat," I laugh. "Whatever happened between you two?"

Jack looks over at me and locks onto my gaze. "If I recall correctly, Buford saw me as the happy home-

maker, who couldn't HELP but take care of her man."
He drips with sarcasm. "I took care of him all right,
kicked him to the curb, especially when he commanded
me to move to Atlanta after school. Who the hell is he
to tell me how to live my life?"

I'm in possession of a slightly different version of
the story, courtesy of Tim, Buford's confidante. Jack
wanted to move to Boston but Buford's job was in Atlanta. Buford showered him with gifts to get him to
reconsider, but Jack wouldn't hear of it. He took the
position that Buford should move for love—his love.
When that didn't happen, Jack saw that as a sign that
Buford didn't really love him.

I'm not sure if I'd move for love. Hell, I don't think
I'd recognize love, especially coming off a false alarm
with Michael. "You kept talking about going to Atlanta a few times that year," I say.

"Yeah, I talked about going. But you actually went
to Birmingham for a week to see Tim during Spring
Break of our senior year. You were so in love it was
pathetic." Jack snorts.

"Something could have happened between us, if I
had been willing to move."

"Exactly my point! If Buford loved me, he would
have moved to Boston. You really didn't love Tim."
He pauses. "You didn't move for love."

I see that Jack is still debating whether or not moving for love is a test of a relationship. "Anyhow." I
dismiss Jack's criticism. "Tim's a great guy. He's kind,

intelligent, and funny. I just couldn't see myself living in Birmingham, so it's harder to see Tim as anything more than a friend," I finish.

Jack stares at me. I lock onto his gaze and in that moment my mind races back to Spring Break of our senior year, when Jack and I were best friends.

14

1982

"Hello, Vy." I instantly recognize Tim's voice over the phone.

"Hi Tim. I'm so excited to see you!"

"I'm the lucky one. You're going to spend your Spring Break with me here in Birmingham. I still think a place like Florida might be more exciting." Tim's a single child of an immigrant Italian family that migrated from New York City in the early '20s. His black hair is starting to recede and he's got a real man's build. His chest is firm; his stomach is a little soft; and his legs are solid from his daily five-mile runs.

"Yeah...but you aren't there." I smile so he can hear it in my voice.

"Young and cute. And already knows what to say," Tim exhales.

"I got your directions. I'll be overnighting with my grandparents in Wytheville on the way down. It looks like its half way," I say.

"You should arrive tomorrow then?" Tim asks.

"Yeah. I'm thinking around four or five in the afternoon. When I get into town, I'll find a phone and call you. Or, I'll show up at your house and if you're not there, I'll hang out on the porch."

"There goes the neighborhood," Tim smiles.

"What? Because some sweet young thing's hanging out on your porch? What would the neighbors say?" I laugh.

"How damn lucky Tim Marcoletti is," Tim jokes.

I head out early through the western part of Virginia. I've done this drive many times with my family since my father's kin live all throughout Southwest Virginia. Every time I see the sign for Pulaski, I get weird. I grew up in a house on a hill overlooking the town. I once read that one of the oldest rivers in America—and perhaps the world—cuts right through Pulaski County. The "New River" is its name. I often wonder why we call it new when it's actually very old and one of its sources comes out of a place called Boone, N.C.

My paternal grandparents live halfway between Pulaski and Boone. I always felt balanced here. Ironically, they also live halfway between D.C. and Birmingham.

"Hey, Grandma," I call out as I knock on the door.

"We've been wondering when you'd show," Grandpa responds as he opens the door. I expected Grandma since Grandpa is generally asleep by this time. It's about ten in the evening. The house is mostly dark.

"Sorry, Grandpa. I got a late start," I apologize. I put my overnight bag on the floor next to the love seat just inside the front door. The bag sinks into the beige shag carpeting.

"That's all you got, boy?" Grandpa asks.

"No. I'm just staying the night on my way to Birmingham. Thought Dad might have said something."

"Lonzy. Leave the poor boy alone," Grandma says. "Come here into the kitchen. I have cake." Grandma's got a sweet southern accent that's colored, enriched for living in the mountains.

I spy Angel Food Cake sitting on the table next to a bowl of stewed strawberries. If only they knew where I was going and what I was planning to do, it would have been Devil's Food Cake. I smile and help myself. I love the strawberries poured over the top. I'm hoping that tomorrow Grandma will make her famous cornbread.

"What are you going to do in Birmingham?" Grandma asks.

"Visiting a friend I met in college," I reply with a voice as sweet as molasses. Grandma can read and write on a grade-school level but Grandpa can't. He works the farms and the fields. That's the way his life has always been—tied to the ground. He always says there's no need for schooling. What would he need all that educatin' for? You just need a strong back and an even stronger constitution. Even today, he cuts the grass with a scythe. I tried that once, and thought I'd slice my leg off by the end of the day. All Grandpa did was laugh.

What I love most about my grandparents is their unconditional acceptance of us. When Dad brought home his "yellow" family, his seven siblings and countless cousins couldn't figure out why a white woman wasn't good enough. It didn't matter to Gramps, though. They said that Dad married Mother and that was good enough.

"You're always on the move," Grandma says. "You should think about settling down. Find a woman and start a family." She is genuinely expressing concern, especially since she feels that I'll end up alone unless I focus on doing something about it.

"I'm too young for that. I want to see the world first," I respond. Grandma started her family at the age of 14, having married a man four years her senior. They say Grandpa's Daddy was Dutch. He came over just before the Civil War and decided to marry into American-German stock.

After cake and some conversation, I go upstairs to one of the guest bedrooms. On the floor is a rug that Dad got in Japan. I marvel at the intricate block pattern of green, brown, and black leaves attached to twigs. It repeats itself over and over again, and in that simplicity shows the complexity of a repeating pattern. I hear that is how snowflakes are made. A simple pattern repeated over and over that creates a distinct snowflake like no other.

The next morning, the delectable scent of bacon fills the house. I drag my butt downstairs, wash up, and slink into the kitchen. Grandma is standing in front of the electric range. She's a big woman, much bigger than Grandpa's bony frame. I look around and notice that he's already gone.

"How late is it, Grandma?"

"8:30," she answers.

"Oh no! I overslept. I still have another seven hours of driving left," I lament.

"Here. Eat up first." She brings over a plate of soft, runny eggs, a slab of cornbread, and a side of potatoes. I love the cornbread. It's fried in a skillet on the stove and stone white, with no flavor except what you add. Of course, I shovel jam onto it and the rest of the family considers me a weirdo. You're supposed to eat it as part of a meal, like the way Dad does. He breaks it into chunks in a bowl, slices onions into it, and then pours beans cooked in fatback over the top. He then flips the mixture a couple of times in the bowl with a spoon and digs in. I like that, too, but I much prefer slicing the cornbread through the middle like a loaf of bread and then spreading butter and jam over it. When I order cornbread out, it's never as good as Grandma's.

"Where's Grandpa? I wanted to say goodbye," I say.

"He's helpin' your Uncle Toot clear land. He left at the crack of dawn. Took his Beloved." Beloved is what Grandpa sometimes calls his scythe, since it always got him work—even in the Depression. Grass needs cuttin'; land needs clearin'. He even got work cutting the grass along the Blue Ridge Parkway one summer.

"Bye, Grandma," I say as I wave to her. She stands on the porch smiling back. You can see two rockin' chairs off to one side—his and hers. The two usually spend their evenings chatting on the porch to passers-by walking down the street.

"Come back when you can!" she yells.

I pull out of the driveway and head south.

I'm excited to see Tim. Things aren't working out with Jack and his best friend, Buford, but I really like Tim. We made out and called each other a few times since that infamous train trip north. Buford wanted to do something different. He thought a train trip to the nation's capital after Thanksgiving and before Christmas was it. It never dawned on him that it takes roughly 22 hours to travel. He and Tim didn't even get a sleeper car so they were in the regular seats, round-trip. Tim said the train stopped everywhere that was a nowhere place. People came and went; the smell came and went; and the towns came and went. It was just too slow for Tim.

I pull alongside his house and make sure I can park on the curb. Sure enough, a sign reads, "Two-hour parking until six." It's all good. I get there at 5:30. I'm safe.

"Thought you were lost?" Tim smiles as he appears on his porch.

I laugh. "I got a late start from my grandparents. Your directions are great. I only got into a little bit of trouble making sure I was going the right direction on Highland Avenue," I explain. Tim lives in the trendy neighborhood of Southside. The bungalows and crafts-man houses dot the hills and surround a park just north of the thriving Southside social scene.

As soon as I get inside the door with my bags, we lunge for each other. I drop the bags to one side, and he kicks the door shut. His tongue instantly explores the inside of my mouth. We twirl towards the back of the house; the smooth wood floors practically slide us towards the bedroom.

Tim's room is sparse. A queen-sized, steel-frame bed rests in the center, covered in a white patchwork quilt. A single nightstand adorns one side of the bed, which includes a dull lamp and a stack of books. We side-step his six-drawer dresser with a twirl, all the while pulling each other's clothes off. I've got my pants and socks on but my fly is open and Tim is only in his boxers with his hard-on poking at the slit.

We break our embrace just long enough to strip the last of our coverings before mashing our bodies together again. We fall backwards onto the bed, rolling around and sucking face. I notice that Tim is pulling the quilt away from us and onto the floor, exposing the sheets. I guess he doesn't want to stain it.

I feel his hot mouth on my dick, while his hand pushes the foreskin down. "Ouch!" I scream. He freezes. "Just sensitive," I say. "Pull the skin back a little, then you can go to town on it." He smiles and hungrily attacks my head. I feel the coarseness of his tongue slather all over my bell end. I used to get hard-ons riding the city bus while wearing silk boxers. They would rub against the foreskin just enough to expose my head, which, being so sensitive, caused instant hard-ons. I love his licking from top to bottom and all around the shaft. I pull Tim up to me quickly—I don't want this trip to heaven to be a short one.

I kiss his mouth and suck on his tongue. I can taste myself on him. "Sit on my face," I command. He straddles me and lowers his ring down; I spit upwards and smear the mouth lube with my fingers as I spread his cheeks. My tongue probes the sides of the ring. I can smell the soap he used to wash—his hair is still damp along the edges. Good to know that it isn't sweat. With every thrust of my tongue I get a counterpoint moan. He rocks up and down as I suckle his ring.

He falls forward until he swallows my cock all the way down to its base. I let out a moan and give him warning before I shoot. He sucks the jism right out and spits it back on my dick, then uses his tongue to smear it all over the shaft. I can feel the warmth give way to coolness as it gets sticky and hard. He sits straight back up and turns enough to be next to me with his knees bracing my left side. He pushes his cock into my mouth and hits the back of my throat with his thrusts.

I grab it with my right hand and jerk it in rhythm with my sucking. I feel his head grow rock-hard and I know he's about to explode. I open my mouth and stick out my tongue, basically giving him the dentist's, "AAHHH." He shoots into my mouth using my tongue as a runway for his cum to slide into the back of my throat. I do not swallow but I do drain his load into my mouth and gurgle it back out so it drips from my chin and down the outside of my throat.

He collapses on top of me and kisses my cum-drenched face. He does a little finger painting, swirling the juice on his lips and spreading it over my throat and face.

"Now that is what I call a HELLO," I beam. I'm exhausted and exhilarated at the same time.

"I'm going to have a heart attack," Tim moans.

"Let's do it again," I challenge.

"You're going to kill me. I'm not as young as you," Tim pants. "Let's take a shower together and get clean." He moves off the bed but I reach up and grab his arm.

As I pull him close, I say, "Why don't we stay and get hard together?"

"Oye. Get the hell up," Tim asserts. He feigns disgust and laughs all the way to the bathroom. I can hear the water running. "Whenever you're ready," he cajoles.

We have sex every day of my visit. We never have it more than once a day, even though I'm horny twice a day. I decide to leave on Saturday and to drive straight through with no stops. The plan is to recover on Sunday.

With that knowledge, Tim wants to try out a new hip place on Thursday that just opened in the Southside. It's an Italian restaurant that sits on one of the corners facing the park, with a huge patio and excellent menu. I ask if we can go by foot but he thinks it's just outside of walking distance. Thursday night is going to be memorable. He is taking me to dinner and then to a club for dancing.

"Mr. Marcoletti," the hostess coos, "your table is ready." She beckons us to follow her to a dark corner of the restaurant. The tables are tightly packed. Good thing Tim got a reservation, or we would have been waiting for two hours.

I scan the mostly young, hip crowd. Only two tables out of 14 are occupied by a single-sex couple. All the others are mixed with good-looking, preppy Southern folk, all sitting down for dinner. We order and the food soon arrives. Tim is drinking his usual—a gin and tonic—and so am I—sweet tea. It's the best invention since Grandma's cornbread.

"So you like it?" an amorous Tim remarks.

"Yes. The food is wonderful and the ambience is just right. I bet when it gets warm enough and they open the patio, it will be great to do the al fresco."

"Well then, you will just have to come back," Tim grins.

As we are talking, a bright flash catches our attention. We turn in unison to the source. A waiter has just taken a picture of a smartly dressed young couple. Since the tables are closely packed, we're not that far away.

"That's Maggie," Tim comments.

"Maggie who?" I inquire.

"She's the daughter of an attorney here in Birmingham. I ran into him at the monthly American Bar Association meeting last week. He was beaming that his little girl had moved back to town. She'd been living in North Carolina for the last couple of years after graduation. He also mentioned that she brought home a fella. I assume that's him," Tim says.

I look at her date. He's gorgeous. I see their profile. He's got a perky nose and a great smile. His whole face lights up.

I hear the snap of Tim's fingers. "Down, boy. You're here with me," Tim says with a hint of jealously marring his playfulness.

"Oh puleaze," I mock back. "I'm not chasing after any straight boys. The gay ones are hard enough with their damage. I'm just admiring the scenery from afar. You're the one I'm going home with," I reassure. "Now. You'd better perform or I might have to rely on the kindness of strangers."

"You bitch!" Tim says, feigning lament.

"I've got to let some of this sweet tea go," I announce and stand up, looking for the restroom. I see it at the end of the restaurant. As I open the door there are two urinals, side by side—my dreaded configuration. There is no divider. I see someone's feet in the stall and take the urinal on the left. I figure if I start peeing before someone comes in, I'll be all right. If I don't start, I might have to wait until they are done or I'm alone. Pee shyness can be a real drag. Sometimes, I've had to step away from the urinal and go into a stall, if one is open. Thank god, I start to pee and know I am home free.

The door opens, but I don't care now that my bladder is already emptying. If he stands next to me it won't make a bit of a difference. I hear a "hmm" and then he steps up next to me. I look out of the corner of my right eye. And stop peeing.

It's him, Maggie's date. Oh my god. I can see in the reflection on the wall ahead of me that he's looking straight at me. He's got the most beautiful blue eyes. I start to panic because I think he is checking me out. I look down and take a peek. He's got a nice piece. I look back up and straight ahead. I see a smirk appear on his face. I'm busted.

I'm too nervous to move. The stall door opens and he breaks his gaze. He zips up and I can hear the water running. The door opens, I hear a shuffle, and then I'm alone.

Minutes later, I start to pee again.

15

My eyes focus on Jack—he is now hanging onto my every word. "I went to the most beautiful gay bar in Birmingham," I add. "On Thursday night, Tim took me to a club that had a raised dance floor and panoramic windows on two sides that overlooked the town. We had to buy a nightly membership just to get in."

"What else did you do?" Jack pries. "You were always so circumspect. You came back on cloud nine, you said the sex was great, and I always had the feeling that you left something out." Jack is good about reading between the lines; I think that's why he's so successful at picking up guys.

"I don't know what you're talking about, Jack." I express confusion, but have an idea of what he meant.

My lusting over a straight boy was nothing new, but for whatever reason, I always kept what happened in that men's room a secret, even from Tim. He did ask me about it since he saw the guy go in after me. I told him I was in the stall on account of me being pee shy. I don't know why I lied about that. It wouldn't have meant anything to Tim.

Jack decides to shift our conversation. "Anywho, we're going out to eat with this dinner club I know."

"Dinner club?" I ask.

"Yeah. It's a group of guys who meet on a monthly basis and eat at different restaurants across town. There's one happening right now at the Italian Kitchen on R Street. You in?" Jack's surprise announcements, I think, are how he gets people to go along with him; he gives you absolutely no time to consider the consequences.

"Sure," I say unsteadily. I'm not that enthused but it will at least get me out of the house.

We get there in about 10 minutes, and I recognize a couple of familiar faces. "Hello, Jerry," I announce as I approach the table.

"Hi, Vy. It's been a while. I hear you're running around with Michael."

"That's over," I say with a hint of finality that does not go unnoticed.

Jack is already circling the table for the perfect seat: the power seat, the metaphorical throne. It is always there and ready for those who are brave enough to take it. You can survey all those around you either blatantly or subtly from it. For every gay man on the prowl, single or not, it's the SEAT. I recognize it immediately and slip right into it. Jack gives me a scornful look and sits with his back against the door. Jerry is sitting across from me. I have a perch in which to see those who come in, those who walk past the window, and those who head to the bathroom. I'm next to the aisle so if I need to get up, I can do so quickly. You never can tell when you need to wash your hands.

"Do tell," Jerry prompts.

I'm not that eager to spill the tea. "Not much to tell. I think we're just on different paths. I certainly have no answers." I shift in my seat and try to change the subject. "Are you and Michael still hanging out?" The last time I saw Jerry he was still with Michael. I'm not too eager to be friends with people who are friends with Michael.

"Not really. Michael is someone I occasionally hang with. Taylor is my ex and is much closer to Michael," Jerry says.

"Taylor is your ex?" I express surprise, especially in light of what happened at the beach.

"Yeah. He wants to get back together. He called me yesterday and we're supposed to go to dinner Saturday night."

"Oh." Do I tell this guy whom I barely know about Michael's herpes accusation? It's not my business. "We

went to the beach last weekend. Taylor has some stories to tell."

"What do you mean?" a very curious Jerry asks.

"It's not really my place to say; just some friski-
ness." That' all I'm willing to disclose.

"What? Between you and him?" Jerry looks
shocked.

"No. Not me. You should just ask him about it."
Jerry eyes me suspiciously for the rest of the evening.
It's a drag to have negative vibes so close to me. But I
make do.

Jack and I trade barbs all evening. He's still upset
that I got the SEAT and Jerry warms a little once a
couple of cocktails are consumed. I love his sense of
humor.

He breaks into what he calls an Eastern Carolina
black woman. "Don'tcha come 'round here makin'
trouble. I puts you in your place. Don't get my neck
going." He mimics a neck roll. He loves himself some
black women. He does his imitation for the humor and
I detect no racial undertones. That's refreshing. I get
sensitive to people who seem only to relate to a color
as opposed to a person. I've been there.

"We should hang out some more," Jerry beams.
"There is an Arts Walk in Adams Morgan coming up
this Sunday. You want to meet up at two on 18th and
Columbia?"

"Sure." Why not? Jerry's a lot of fun to be with. He
doesn't take himself so seriously.

Walking home I've got Jack playing 1,000 questions. "So? Are you and Jerry going on a date?"

"No. It's nothing like that. I get a strictly friend vibe from him."

"Well, of course you do. He's single, handsome, and available. Not to mention, he's local."

"Screw you, buddy," I shoot back.

"Let me see here..." Jack says with an exaggerated lisp. "There's Paul in San Francisco that you met in a BATHHOUSE in Florida. You even went out there a couple of times. What happened that last time? Oh that's right; you met his boyfriend for the first time. Not only that, Paul wanted to fool around while his boyfriend was sleeping in the MASTER and you were in the guest room.

"Then there is Larry, who you met at a BATH-HOUSE in Dallas. At least this time, he lived in Dallas. Didn't he get drunk and then have no memory of what he did? Oops! That's a repeater. With MI-CHAEL.

"AND don't eeeeeeven get me started on the MARRIED men."

Already, there are enough vocal ups and downs to give me sea sickness. "Enough!" I yell through clenched teeth. "I don't know why I go after men who are unavailable. It's as if the one I want got away. And I don't even know his name. If I could solve that puzzle, I would."

The days blur by quickly and suddenly it's Sunday morning. I'm going to meet Jerry at two and that seems to be my entire day. How exciting is my life? I'm wired for stereo.

After setting aside the Washington Post, I hear the phone ring.

"Hello? This is Vy."

"Damn you!" I hear Michael's voice screeching at me. "Why the hell did you tell Jerry about the DAMN beach trip?" I can feel the anger coiling through his words.

"I didn't realize it was a DAMN secret," I reply. "Didn't tell him a DAMN thing. HELL. I don't even know why you're so DAMN mad!"

"Taylor—" Michael lets the pause slither around us as we stalk one another. "He called me yesterday in a panic because Jerry grilled him about the beach trip. Jerry wasn't taking any shit, and Taylor cracked. He confessed that he blew me on the beach. I don't remember THAT. Taylor said somethin' about an eye twitch giving him away. Jerry refused to accept the 'nothing happened' routine, and Taylor whimpered to me that he couldn't lie to Jerry. Jerry could always tell. I just want to be CLEAR. I know nothing about this damn blow job on the beach crap." Michael just spits this monologue right out.

"I saw it happen, regardless of what you remember. Anyhow, what does this have to do with me?" I push back.

"Funny that you should mention THAT," Michael shouts. "Taylor told me that Jerry went to a dinner club. GUESS who was there? YOU. YOU told him to ask about the beach trip."

"All I said was that Taylor got frisky and he should ask him about it." I can feel the killer viper coiling around my words as I spit them out. "Jerry told me that Taylor wants to get back with him. I just couldn't let him go in without warning. You are the one accusing him of giving you herpes. If it is true, then Taylor could give it to Jerry. My My My, how our wicked little circle spins." I'm laying down my own ground cover. I'm about to relive *The Exorcist*. Any minute now my head is going to spin and I'm going to vomit my words right out.

"You're an asshole!"

"I'm the asshole because you can't keep your dick in your pants; because you can't keep shitting where you eat; because you're such a nice and wholesome guy!" I vehemently shout back. There is enough venom in the air to poison all of D.C.

"Go to hell!" Michael slams the phone.

"Idiot. Buddhists don't have a hell," I say to a dead receiver. Sunday is already shaping up to be a bang up day. Now I get to see Jerry and find out what storm is brewing on his front doorstep. If he even shows, that is.

I arrive at the Belmont Kitchen and Jerry is already there, standing just inside of the awning. I called to change plans to meet up at a restaurant before the Arts Walk. I wanted a drink and figured that if Jerry was going to throw a hissy fit, then I could at least handle it on a full stomach. It would give me something to retch.

"How's your morning?" Jerry causally asks as we take our seats overlooking 18th. We're a few blocks south of Columbia Avenue with a multitude of restaurants on each side. I remember doing the diabetic waltz with a friend in this neighborhood, where we devoured six different desserts at six different restaurants in one night. Sugar highs are the best going up, but godforsaken coming down.

I'm not sure how to answer Jerry. What does he know?

"Good," I reply. Now all I have to do is wait for the inevitable car crash of "he-said, he-said."

"Thanks for the tip about the beach weekend," Jerry continues. "I cornered Taylor. At first he was cagey about what you guys did. But REALLY, a blow job on the beach? He should know he can't lie to me. We dated too long for him to think I can't read the twitches. When he said nothing happened, boom! There it was—the twitch just under his left eye. I knew as soon as that twitch did the happy dance that somethin' happened. Secrets? Puleazze."

Let's see if I can diplomatically find out if he knows anything about my actions. "So, what else did he say?" Oh for the love of God, what a lame question. Of course he'll know that I'm on a fishing expedition with a question like that. Stupid.

"What? That you were dick diving?" Jerry smiles.

I'm about to launch a mass offensive when I see the wink. Jerry bats those long, black eyelashes. I switch tactics. "What! Now I know you have a fish of a story. The only diving I'm doing is into murky, smelly waters that I can't wash off." I pause and make sure eye contact is established. "Even if it was communal." I wink.

"Oh, you SLUT!" Jerry cries in a mock, lilting voice that reaches for the rafters...and then he does it again. He bats his eyelashes like they are bull whips on crack. The whole look is pure mischievous chaos, Trickster Style.

"This can be the start of a great friendship," I exclaim as I raise my glass to toast to new beginnings and stale closings.

16

Present

"Can't we get out of the pool party? Gotta be better things to do on a Sunday afternoon," pleads Jerry. We're at our favorite lunch place—Café Luna—on P Street. It's the Saturday after last night's maniacal Cracker Jack ambush at Cobalt.

I drift away from the conversation like red balloons over an empty field. Oh fuck, I'm living the 99 Luftballons video; not paying any attention to anyone.

"Yo." Jerry smacks me on the left shoulder. "Talking here. Earth to Vy, you've lost your Major Tom."

I roll my eyes and pick up the avocado chicken sandwich. I take a bite and chew.

"Oh for crying out loud. What's gotten into you, Vy?" Jerry snaps.

"Funny you should mention the name, Tom." I give him a knowing stare.

Jerry looks puzzled. Then the light goes on. "Oh! Tom! The Belly Fetish Man!" Jerry yells out. The couple next to us turns and stares.

Tom, aka Belly Fetish Man, was the one who pushed me over the edge. He made me jump off the building known as the Tower of Babel and Married Men. I finally swore off married men after our encounter. I wonder if D.C., as a place, holds any magic for me anymore. As I sit here, I actually think that it's a karmic double whammy. Belly Fetish Man, BFM for short, came right after Cy, the married, high-powered partner at Arnold & Porter. Ah... Cy and his pretty boy looks, sharp wit, and cold steel-blue eyes. Didn't hurt that he could shoot gallons of cum. Never fall for a married man, though. They never leave—in more ways than one.

"Buddha Belly. Belly, Belly, Belly boy," Jerry mocks in a lecherous tone. He rubs his hands together like an evil scientist, just before the kill.

"You are so wrong, girlfriend," I laugh. "I wouldn't bring that up. My past should stay buried and lost."

"But Vy, BFM! That story kicks fiction to the curb, makes it pack its bags, and hitchhike out of town. You can't script something like that. No wonder you gave up married men," Jerry exclaims.

"If BFM had a section in the library, it'd be under True Crime Stories. First, I fell for Cy and then rebounded with BFM. It's one shocking crime after another. One steals my heart and the other steals my sanity. I'm amazed I'm not committed to a white room with Men-in-White as my altar boys." I sigh.

I watch as a grin spreads across Jerry's lips.

"The whole thing with BFM was so weird. He came onto me based on research he had done on Asian male anatomy. It turns out some Asian males have a "pouch" just below the bellybutton. When he saw that I had one, he couldn't help himself," I explain.

"What serial killer could? You know how they are committed to their fetishes," Jerry laughs.

"All he wanted to do was jerk off while snuggling with my belly pouch." I shudder at the memory. "What's worse is that my fate decided to use it as a lesson."

I bow my head.

"Truth is stranger than fiction," Jerry says.

"Yeah. The next day I got an invitation to go see Falsettos, a play about a married man leaving his wife for his gay lover. I was placed on the waitlist as number eight, which the receptionist thought was weird, since they rarely ever went above number five. When they called my number, an usher directed me to my seat—the last one in the house. Lo and behold, as I was sliding over toward my seat, I looked down and into the eyes of BFM! I ended up sitting two seats over—right next to the crazy man's wife. Kill me now," I chortle.

"Wow," Jerry exclaims. "I still can't believe you didn't plan that, Vy."

"How could I? I was dumbfounded through the entire play. I felt my fate laughing at me like some cosmic joke I wasn't in on."

'Did you ever see him again after that?"

"Not really. I blew off his request to spend Memorial Day on his boat. I think a few months later we passed each other on the street. Seriously, in Buddhism, the number eight is significant. It's like my religion was telling me to get on the right path, NOW. I know without any doubt that fooling around with married men is only going to curse my many lives. The worst thing about Tom, outside of his belly worship, was that he was a rebound from Cy, the one I actually fell for. One stole my heart and the other stole my mind." I shake my head wearily and glance down at my plate. "I was taught early in life that there is a Path. Sometimes one can see it; sometimes one is pulled alongside it; sometimes one thinks there isn't one. But there is always a Path. It's up to us Buddhists to know the Way."

17

Present

"Hey, Gordon," I hear as I place the receiver to my ear.

"What's up, Tommy?"

"Do you still need me to cover the rentals this weekend?"

"Yeah, man. I'm heading out to D.C. as soon as I finish dusting."

"Okay, Okay," Tommy laughs. "I'll hang up so you can finish playing house maid. Have a good trip."

As I hang up the phone, I realize that I'm still holding one of the frames. As I place it back on the bookcase, I notice it's the picture of Maggie and me at that restaurant in Birmingham. I can't help but laugh at her 80s hairdo. Sheesh, was it that long ago?

"Hon. Would you come in here and help with this curtain rod?" Maggie yells as she balances herself on top of a wooden stool.

"Coming." I traverse the living room and notice my junk sloshing around inside of my gray boxers. "Isn't it late to be doing this?" I ask.

"I know. But I can't stand seeing this rod crooked any longer," Maggie replies.

"What do you think?" I ask.

"Better. Yet…" Maggie pauses. She paces to and fro in front of the window, and then side to side like a pendulum. "Not sure. It looks straight but there might be a bend in it."

"Hon. You're obsessing over this. Let's go to bed." Staring up at her tight body gets me frisky, so I sweep my left arm around her waist and pull her close.

"What has gotten into you?" Maggie exclaims. She allows herself to be pulled towards the bed. I ignore her and unclasp the back of her black dress, which she shimmies out of and lets drop to the floor. She rubs up against my gray boxers in nothing but her pink panties; then little Gordy pokes out as if to check the weather. Storms are never too far away.

I plop onto the edge of the bed and spread my legs for her to kneel before my altar. I enjoy playing the fallen Baptist. I feel her hot breath race down my shaft and the twirl of her tongue work itself back up. Man she's good.

"Hon." A puzzled look flashes in Maggie's eyes as I grab her and lift her onto the bed, plant her on her back, and with a quick hip roll, spread her legs.

"Dammit, Hon. No," Maggie growls and twists violently away from me. "You know that if we are going to fuck, you enter from behind. No pussy."

"Fine!" I push her face down, butt up. I start poking her but she keeps squirming. I hook my hands onto her thighs to steady her and get ready to plant. "FUCK!" I scream as I feel an intense pain in my groin. She kicked me in the nuts.

She turns around and covers herself with the sheet. "What the crap has gotten into you, Gordon?" Maggie demands. "You know that I have to be relaxed for that. And that doesn't just happen, you prick."

"Dammit. I'm not the one who wants to be a virgin on her wedding night," I spit back at her.

"That's it. I'm going to Daddy's." She throws some clothes on and grabs an overnight bag before marching towards the door.

"Wait. Please wait," I implore as I stalk her naked around the house. "I don't know what's gotten into me."

"You need to sleep this off and we can talk in the morning," she snaps. And with that, Maggie disappears out of the kitchen door. I hear the car start and fade away.

Damn, Gordy. You freaked. Fucking her is supposed to make you believe you're still a man. Still in control.

I grab some booze and mix up a gin and tonic to get through the night. I dread our talk in the morning.

"Are you okay?" Maggie asks as she enters the house through the kitchen door.

I'm sitting in my sweats, eating a bowl of Froot Loops. I didn't actually hear her enter. I didn't even hear the car. I'm nursing the one too many from last night. "I'm sorry," I say. "I'm not sure what got into me." I push my forlorn look around my face.

Maggie lets out an exasperated sigh. "We need to talk."

Shit.

I push my eyes up to meet the words that every man dreads to hear. She's beautiful and I'm screwing this up.

"Okay," I say and push away from the table. I look right at her, waiting for her to begin. I really don't have anything to say. I already said I was sorry.

"What's happened to us?" Maggie sadly asks. "In college, we dreamt of living in Berlin for a few years and hiking around Europe. But that never happened. We're in our careers and living in Birmingham. Now we seem to fight more every day."

"I don't know. I never thought I'd end up in Birmingham. Who knew I'd be working in a property management firm and you'd end up as a lawyer in your dad's firm? Maybe we just grew up?"

"Gordy, I don't think that's it. When I showed up at Daddy's crying..." Maggie starts.

I cut her off. "What! I didn't mean to make you cry." I want last night as a do over. I still can't believe I lost control. She wasn't ready to screw, and I should have listened.

"I was crying because I was upset. You making or not making me cry is not the point. Daddy tried to calm me down. But he asked me one simple question that made me do a lot of thinking last night."

I can't imagine what that could be. I stay quiet. The silence builds and I can hear the birds landing on the feeders. The seeds ping the deck floor in a steady rhythm, like raindrops.

'Daddy asked me why we aren't married yet," she drops.

"But..." I protest.

"Look, I know that I'm the one who said to wait awhile. But I still need to understand why we aren't married. God, you are a handsome man and my daddy thinks the world of you. I think you won his respect, which I didn't think I'd ever live long enough to see a man do. I've always been his little girl. But we still aren't married and we've been together for over seven years." She grabs my hands and with tears in her eyes she continues. "I don't think our love is big enough to overcome whatever it is that's between us."

I nod, trying hard to convey that I understand what she's saying. "Hon. I love you. Last night won't happen again. You'll see." I squeeze her hands to stop me from falling into an abyss.

"I know you love me. And I love you. I just don't think we are on the same path. You know I'm a practical girl. I remember how freaked you were when I said to enter me from behind. You sat on the bed, shell-shocked that first night. I coaxed you into me. I only had to do that a few more times."

I remember how that had puzzled me. I always associated anal intercourse with homosexuals.

"You know I want to be a virgin on my wedding night," she continues. "That's always been important to me. I think it's all the Sunday School brainwashing about being a virgin on your one special night, that first night as husband and wife." A quick look of disdain spreads across Maggie's peaches-and-cream complexion. She doesn't like following orders and she always viewed the roles of husband and wife as equal. "But soon you warmed up to doing the anal. Sometimes I'd think a bit too warmed up. Except for last night; it's like you had something to prove. And Hon, it wasn't for me." She lays it all out.

"I think I got horned up and wanted the front," I counter. I see that she is not buying it. Her brow is knit and she's considering her next gambit.

"Isn't Mitch your old college roommate? Why do you whisper his name in your sleep?" Maggie asks.

Upon hearing Mitch, my entire world shatters, like china thrown onto a marble floor. The shards slide across the stone, scratching the veins, and turning the beautiful floor into a minefield. "What about him?" I ask, a bit too forcefully. I realize I might have said too much.

"Hon, we're four years out of college and you still whisper his name in your sleep." Maggie's brown eyes meet mine. "And, until last night, you really didn't want the front. I've been tempted to let you have it. Yet it doesn't feel right." She looks away into the distance.

"I think we're over-analyzing this," I reply. "I got horny. I wanted you in the worst way." I want off this topic. What is she accusing me of?

Maggie walks over to me, bends down and places a gentle kiss on my lips. She then places her right hand on the top of my shoulder and squeezes. It feels like she's trying to convey pity. "Goodbye, Gordon. I'll come by later with Daddy and some men to move my stuff out." With that she turns her back to me and walks out the door.

I sit in the kitchen, staring out the window, wondering what the hell that was all about. We're not on the same path? What path? I scratch myself and sit for a while longer. I too won't be here. To hell with her and her path crap.

18

"Bro', there're other girls," Tommy announces as he hauls the last of the trash bags out of the rental unit.

I look right at my brother and ponder what he means. A meteor strikes me in the back of the head; I realize his is referring to Maggie. It's been almost a year since I moved back from Birmingham. "Don't know who you're talking about," I lie.

"Ah come on. You know exactly who I am talking about!" Tommy exclaims. "You've been depressed ever since you got back. There are other girls. Hey, I hear Mary is back."

Mary had a crush on me all throughout high school. I've practically known her my entire life. "Not interested," I say as I shake my head. "We've got a few more units to hit today. Let's focus on that," I add.

"Whatever. Tryin' to help," Tommy says, slightly wounded. He wants to play big brother. Sometimes I think he's trying to make up for not looking out for me as big bro'. When I was discharged from the hospital, he was all torn up inside when he saw me bandaged and limping around.

The rest of the day blurs by. The family owns a number of rental units throughout town, and the end of semester is a hellish time for my dad. Our biggest source of renters comes from the university. It's great to hear every year that they want to expand enrollment but not build enough dormitories. All that time in Birmingham wasn't wasted. At least I'm putting the property management skills to use.

"Son, this came for you today," Mom says as I come into the kitchen. I decided to move back home until I figured out where I want to end up.

"Thanks, Mom." I take the letter, ascend the stairs, and head to my room. I place the letter on the desk and strip. I've got to wash this rental grime off of me. How can people live like that? Some of the places are going to require demolition before we can rent them out.

After cleaning up, I pick up the letter and sit on the bed. The letter is from the Army. I wonder what they want? The meteor that hit me in the back of the head is nothing compared to the crater the letter opens up inside of me.

"Announcement. The Reunion of Charlie Can Company. Fort Leavenworth, Leavenworth, Kansas. Saturday of Labor Day Weekend."

I can't believe it. I thought everybody in my company had died! Damn... somehow I feel that it would be easier than dealing with living buddies. I shudder to think of what state they are in now. What a hellish ordeal it was over there... Even now, the ambush, and everything that came after, is fuzzy. The only real memento I have is this tattoo on my left shoulder and I can't even remember how I got it. I've been thinking of getting rid of it but I always seem to back out at the last minute.

A couple of days before the reunion, I tell Mom and Daddy about the invite. I can see the concern on their faces, afraid of what I might remember when confronted with others who were involved in the horror. I'm a bit apprehensive about going but feel that I need closure. Maybe I'll even get a few memories back.

"Sir, the reception hall is this way," a young, freshly minted female GI says. She leads me into a large banquet hall decorated like the Fourth of July. I haven't seen so much red, white, and blue since my injuries. I smile at my morbid joke.

I sweep my eyes across the room and see older guys with a bunch of children running around their legs. They must be the unit slammed with the babysitting chores.

Suddenly I feel a slap on my back. "I'll be damned! Gordy from the mountains of North Carolina survived the fields of 'Nam! Hot damn!" Stunned, I turn around and meet the eyes of a rakish, fit man. At his side, he's got a younger man in tow.

Stunned, I stare at him, mute. The guy must sense my confusion, so he continues. "It's Brady, from New Hampshire," he calmly says with a wide smile.

Oh my god! Brady, my best buddy! I remember him getting hit by a dozen stingers before I crawled away towards the water. "I...I..." I sputter out.

"It's okay. Sit and talk with us," Brady soothes. "It's a lot to take in when you're talking to Ghosts."

"I'm sorry. I really thought I was the only survivor, because I woke up alone on the transport." My voice is knee-deep in melancholy.

"You would have been if not for the lieutenant." Brady noticed my puzzled expression, so he continues. "Lieutenant Minh. We all thought he had deserted us. Turned out he was actually conducting a wide survey for any Việt cộng in the area. He left us in the village to teach us some respect. He just didn't figure that we Americans could be such huge assholes when we have guns and a can-do attitude. We were supposed to wait for his return. He didn't think we'd be so stupid as to leave without an escort. Hell. We showed him!" Brady laughs.

"He came back?" I ask, dumbstruck.

"Hell, man. Most of us wouldn't be here today if he hadn't." Brady steadies his gaze on me and lowers his voice. "We thought we lost you, buddy. The guys couldn't find your body when it was time to go. As for me, I was on a stretcher looking like Swiss cheese. I still have the scars." He proudly pulls his shirt open to show me an old bullet wound, now covered in scar tissue. "I still can't lift my right arm very high above my head. Docs say that's a small price to pay for being alive."

"Yeah, I have a few myself," I add. I glance over at the younger guy again. He's quiet. He's a fairly handsome guy—in good shape and clean shaven. I'm drawn into the brown eyes when I feel Brady's hand gently slap me across the face.

"Get your own," Brady laughs. "This is John, my boyfriend. We live in Portland now." Boyfriend? Or a boy who is a friend? I mull it over in my head.

"Yeah," Brady says, amused by my silence. "You heard right—boyfriend. I realized I was gay once I got past 'Nam."

"Glad to meet you, Gordon," Johns says, extending his hand.

"Glad to meet you, too," I respond and shake his hand. I turn to Brady and see that same smug look that he had when singing the praises of Vietnamese women. "Did you always know?"

"I dunno. Hell, in 'Nam, I did my fair share of whoring around. Maybe then, deep down, I was trying to convince myself otherwise. My road to enlighten-ment came when I was doing physical therapy in Bos-ton. This orderly was just a little too friendly. Every day, I noticed his touches, his eye contact. Then one day he admitted he had a crush on me. Well. Not one of my prouder moments. I yelled back that I ain't no fag, and if I had the strength, I'd clock him. Poor guy was shocked. Shit-scared. He couldn't get out of the room fast enough. So he stopped coming around. Over the next few days, I kept thinking about it and won-dered why I was so warped with rage."

"Did you ever see him again?'

"Funny you should ask," Brady replies. "He was my first boyfriend. After I cooled off, I went looking for him. A few months later I found him in another part of the hospital. After my outburst, he had transferred to another unit. He was scared shitless when I came up to him, so I quickly apologized and asked if we could talk. I told him it could be anywhere he wanted. We met up at a diner near the hospital and I slowly came out with his help."

"Mind if I ask how you guys broke up?" I ask, eye-ing John.

"It wasn't anything dramatic, like when he first came on to me. Once I got comfortable with who I was, I realized I wanted to go west and live on the Pacific Coast. Up to that point, I'd always lived on the East Coast. I thought it was time for a change. Well, Todd—that's the orderly's name—didn't want to leave Boston. So we broke up. Funny, he didn't want to move for love because I was in love with him," Brady says and then winks at John. "A few guys later, I met John and I couldn't be happier." A big grin spreads across Brady's face and he stretches over and kisses John on the cheek. I flush red.

They both look at me and burst out laughing. "He's a much better Frencher," John admits.

"I don't give a damn what anyone in here thinks," Brady laughs. "I survived 'Nam."

The two men rise from their chairs. "We are going to mingle a little bit more. I feel like shocking more of our former comrades-in-arms. Make sure you say hi to that guy over there in the wheelchair. That's Big Mike. He survived 'Nam, too. Just not his legs."

"Oh my." I look over and then back to Brady. John is already moving towards the other end of the hall when Brady stops and comes back.

Brady lowers his mouth close to my ear and whispers, "By the way, if you want to walk on the wild side, that private over there by the bar, he's been lusting after you all night." As I turn towards Brady, he's already shimmering away. My head is reeling. I get up and head towards the bar. I really do need a drink.

"Gin and tonic. Make it a double," I beg.

"Some stiff drink there, sir," says the guy who's supposed to be lusting after me. How does Brady know these things?

I turn, smile, and hold up the drink. "It's what I need right now." I gulp it down and order another.

"By the way, my name is Mitch." Whoa. Stop everything. Did he just say his name was Mitch? My mind briefly flashes back to my college days with my old roommate. This new Mitch notices my silence and prods me to speak up.

"Are you enjoying the reunion?" he asks. A broad, warm smile sweeps across his face. I'm losing it. He's shorter than me and the thick, wavy black hair, cream complexion, and deep blue eyes start doing a number on me. I see all these Ghosts come rushing towards me, haunting my every move. He did say his name was Mitch.

"Yeah," I say half-heartedly.

He slides a napkin with his name, address, and phone on it. There's a quick map drawn on it, showing how to get there from the base. It looks pretty easy to follow. "When you're done here, come over for a nightcap. I've got the place all to myself and cold beer in the fridge. Anytime." He smiles and disappears into the crowd.

Before I can react to the unsolicited invitation, I feel a bump against my left leg. I look down and see Big Mike in his wheelchair. "Heya, buddy! My god you're a sight for sore eyes. Brady said you're here and

I couldn't believe it." Big Mike is beaming. He'll always be Big Mike—jolly as hell, no matter what life takes from him. I share some small talk with him and we exchange contact information. I stay another hour before heading to Mitch's place.

I knock on the door. It opens and standing before me is Mitch, wearing only white boxers and dog tags. He's got a tuft of black hair between his pecs. I step through the threshold and hear the door shut. We don't say a word.

I feel his hot mouth on mine and the force of his body springing towards me, pushing me against the front door. His tongue is licking the back of my throat and his hands are clawing off my clothes. I reach up and grab the back of his head, forcing the exposure of his Adam's apple, and plunge my hot lips onto his neck. If I were a vampire, I'd have tasted blood.

He forces his head forward and into my exposed chest. I feel the swirl of his tongue on my nipples and the quick nibbles around the base. My pants hit the floor and I slip just a bit, but Mitch is there to catch me. I'd already come out of my loafers when we hit the front door.

He pulls my raging hard-on out of my boxers and leads me to the bedroom. I'm turned around and pushed back onto the bed. Off come the socks and then the boxers. My legs are kicked wide open and I feel the roughness of a tongue on the base of my nuts. I feel warm spit sliding over my crack, and fingers massaging the open hole. I'm not ready for that. I sit up and set Mitch on top of me.

I force my tongue into his mouth and wrap my arms tightly around him. I can feel his squirming body against mine as we begin to roll on the bed, back and forth. With him on the bottom and his back pressed into the mattress, I lick my way down his chest, belly button, and to the top of his pubic hairline. I stare briefly at his shaft. All those times in college when my ex-roommate, Mitch, blew me, he always had some preconceived explanation for his actions, like drinking too much.

Looking at new Mitch, I plunge his cock into my throat, until I feel the head hit my uvula. I refrain from gagging, sucking hard and forcefully. "Whoa," I hear Mitch say. "A little more licking, less sucking." Hearing the directions, I pull his cock from my mouth so I can lick his shaft from the base to the top, again and again. I grab the shaft in my right hand so I can stroke it while I nibble on it. A river of spit slides down Mitch's crack. I decide to follow it with my tongue.

I probe his ring and dart in and out of it. I hear Mitch moan and feel him spreading his legs wider apart, so I insert my index finger and then my middle finger. His sphincter relaxes to take both fingers deep inside.

"Fuck me," he pleads. He grasps a bottle of lube and a condom from his bedside table. Just hearing those words makes my cock harder than ever. I slide on the condom and lube it as quickly as I can but I don't think either one of us needs lube at this moment. I aim my shaft and slide it in.

Feeling the sphincter clench around the walls of my dick, I almost shoot my load. I thrust and thrust, harder and harder, rocking forward and backward, picking up speed. I'm mashed down on Mitch, mingling my sweat with his, our tongues fused together. Then, I feel a rush of warm, sticky juice just below my belly button. Our friction is enough for Mitch to shoot a load. I'm close to losing it.

"Come on my face," Mitch gasps into my ear. I pull my head up. Then, I pull out, swipe the condom off, aim, and shoot my load as instructed. A river of hot cum coats his right side like paint on a wall, drying as it slides down his forehead, cheek, neck, and upper shoulders. I shudder as I feel his mouth back on my cock, slurping up the remainder of the jism. My eyes roll backward as the ecstasy takes hold, then focus on this man's face, now wet and sticky.

Mitch rolls off the bed and throws me a towel. I wipe off and can hear the water running in the bathroom. I lie down in the bed and then a few minutes later I feel him crawl alongside of me. I hook him under my left arm and we both pass out together.

When the sun smacks me awake the next morning, my first thought is: "Oh god... where am I?" I then see the note on the pillow next to me.

"Great night. You're one hot daddy. Would love to do it again. Have an early morning call. Pull the door shut and it locks automatically. By the way, you never gave me your name."

I grab my clothes and simply write on the bottom of the note, "Gordon."

19

Present

Jerry really hates the idea of going to Michael's for my birthday party.

"But it's my birthday..." I whine.

Jerry cuts me off with "...and it's your turn to cry, Ms. Lezy Gore," in his customary deadpan delivery.

"Ha. Ha," I mock back. "We'll just make an appearance, then disappear. Sound good?"

"How about we say we did and find a better place to celebrate your Big 4-0," Jerry shoots back.

Jerry's right. We could shaft Jack and not show. But I'm curious to see what Michael's been up to. Since our friendship crashed and burned, I haven't really heard from him. "Aren't you a bit curious at least?" I ask.

Jerry just stares at me. "Yeah."

"I knew it," I exhort.

"Don't get all Ms. Mighty with me," Jerry says.

We decide to walk to the townhouse and once we enter the front door, Jack swoops in on us. "It's about time!" he exclaims. "I thought you guys shafted me." Jerry and I make eye contact and grin.

"Well, we're here. Let's get a drink for Jerry," I muse. "Where's the poison?"

"Outside on the deck," Jack responds as he leads us out through the kitchen. We make it to the outdoor bar setup, get our drinks, then work our way over to the far side of the deck. I turn to my left and see HIM at the same time he sees me. Damn. I can't turn away now.

"Hi. It's Vy, isn't it?" the gorgeous man says as he approaches me.

"Yes. Gordon, right?" My reply comes out as a question.

"Yep. You're looking good," he says before introducing the guy to his right. "This is Craig, by the way. I'm staying with him and his partner, Tom." Off to the side, Jerry is suppressing a giggle. I shoot him a dirty look. "What's so funny?" I inquire.

"Nothing, just an inside joke. Hey Craig, I see you a lot at the gym." I desperately try to push the conversation away from Belly Fetish Man.

"You're the guy who wears those great looking shirts. Like the one you've got on now. You must buy two of anything you get. I'm a size double large," Craig says.

I'm not sure if Gordon's friend is being serious, so I let out a nervous giggle. "Yeah. I see you all the time," I say. "We've just never actually spoken. This is my best friend, Jerry." I pull Jerry into the spotlight. "I'm glad we finally get to meet. Now I'll know someone else at the gym I can talk to," I say.

"Yes. Add another man at the gym you can talk to, Ms. Social Butterfly," Jerry mocks. "It's already taking twice as long now to finish a workout."

"He's exaggerating," I say. "It doesn't take that long at all. He'd know that if he'd come a bit more often." I grin and the group laughs. With that Jerry grabs Jack and they disappear into the house as if running for cover.

I turn my full attention like a watchtower spotlight on a yard full of criminals. "Gordon, last I remember, you were getting a German Master's degree, right?" I look into those icy, blue eyes that fleck with color in the light. He's lost more hair and he's keeping it short. The Cesar looks good on him.

"Yeah. Good memory. I finished up about a year and a half later and then went home to Boone."

"North Carolina?" I interject.

Gordon nods. "I didn't stay in D.C. as I thought I would. The high country was calling me home. It's beautiful in the mountains."

"You should join us for dinner at my house," Craig says to me. "You'd get a chance to meet Tom."

"Sure," I reply, since I never turn down a dinner invitation. Thankfully, the workouts have helped me keep my figure. Mother and Minh have become rounder since they discovered double bacon cheeseburgers. Ngoc is like me, though: still slim.

"Come by around seven to 1421 Corcoran. Do you know where that is?" Craig asks.

"Yeah. I live at 1423 R. We're practically neighbors," I smile.

Out of the blue, Jack and Jerry reappear with that cat-caught-with-canary look on their faces. "It's time to go, Vy," Jerry and Jack giggle in unison.

"What did you guys do?" I exclaim.

"Tell you on the way." Jerry grabs my arm and the three of us rush out of the party.

My heart breaks to leave Gordon so abruptly but I'm soothed by the dinner invite. We say our quick goodbyes and out the door we go. On the way to the metro, I demand, "What the hell is going on?"

Jerry sheepishly says, "I asked Michael if he had caught any STDs of late."

"What the fuck?" I screech. "What possessed you to do THAT?"

"He was lording over me about how he treats his boyfriends with respect; how he finally let Jay go because it was time to move on. He then gamely introduced us to his new boyfriend, Gary. So I asked if Gary had been checked for any STDs. You should have seen the look of death on Michael's face. The best birthday celebration you've ever thrown, Vy," Jerry laughs.

I shake my head. Michael competes with Jerry at everything. I'm sure that Jerry took the opportunity to settle some old scores. In many ways their lives are parallel in structure: both are from small towns, both have children, both have been married, both work for the same company and have the same job, and both are gay. That's a recipe for similarity breeding contempt.

"You should have seen it," Jack laughs. "Gary was completely surprised, like a deer caught in the headlights on a dark country road. He's probably wondering what the fuck we're talking about. Michael started gabbing on about how we always tease each other. Then Jerry let out another stinger."

"Oh my god, what did you say now?" I'm smacked. I'm sure there are only a few people on this planet who know that Michael had a herpes scare. It turned out to be nothing when the blood tests came back. So much for visual inspection.

"Well..." Jerry starts and bats his eyelashes. "I said to give Michael a few more drinks, then the whole party could gangbang him, and in the morning, he wouldn't remember it, or at least claim he couldn't remember it. You should have seen the look on Gary's face as he turned to Michael for an explanation." Jerry is giggling like a Catholic schoolgirl gone bad.

"You guys are so BAD," I say as we skip back home. We recount the day's adventure for clues of our impact.

I can't help but wonder about tomorrow night's dinner as the metro train pulls us out of the 'burbs. I reflect on my good fortune of running into Gordon. Our encounters are way too short but I get a huge charge when I'm in his presence. I can't think straight, which is all well and good since I'm NOT.

I hold my finger down on the button to speak into the condo's intercom system. "Hi, Craig? It's Vy."

"Come on up," a disembodied voice commands.

The door opens to Craig with a big smile on his face and a tight, printed t-shirt. He possesses one of the largest chests I've seen on a guy, but it isn't monstrous. His legs are nice and lean as well. If you put both halves of his body together you'd have a martini glass. Looking at him now, I see that image is apropos, since there's a martini glass in his left hand.

"Come on in," I hear another voice call out from inside the condo. I step past Craig and see Gordon sitting to my right and another guy approaching from the dining room.

"I'm Tom. Welcome," he smiles. "I hope you're not allergic to cats. Abby is running around here somewhere. She lets us stay with her when we're good. Can I offer you anything to drink?

"Club soda. Straight," I gamely smile.

"Just club soda?" a perplexed Tom asks.

"Yes. No alcohol, please."

"You don't drink?" A chorus of mildly surprised voices sings out. People who drink always seem surprised that there are people who do not drink. It's like they've come across a new species of human.

"Well, more for us, I guess," Craig shouts as he raises his drink and gulps down the last of it.

"You've joined the wrong crowd, my friend," Gordon says.

"So it would seem."

Tom is a tall guy, slim and trim. His striking feature is his bald head and blue eyes. He speaks with an easy, low register.

"If anyone's still interested, food's ready," he says with a grin.

We take our places at the table, and I find myself sitting next to Gordon. I can feel the young schoolgirl crush rising up. I learned a long time ago that when dining at a friend's house, there is no SEAT, although I sometimes catch myself looking for one.

'How do you know Craig?" Tom asks. Whenever a single gay man comes into a couple's sphere of influence, there's always a hint of suspicion around him. I always wonder if it's just the nature of being guys, like we're all Alpha dogs or something.

"Well, we officially met at Michael's pool party. But I usually see Craig at the gym and the occasional party. By the way, weren't you guys at the Art for Life dinner last month?" It's best to get this out and over with so there are no more fishing expeditions. Even though Craig and I have never done anything together, I see him as an attractive guy. The fact that he notices what I wear tells me there's an interest. That interest could be for friendship, but it's more likely that he wants something more.

"Yes," Craig pipes up.

"How long are you staying?" I ask, turning to Gordon. His eyes are so blue... like clear, open skies. I swear I see flashes of lightning when I look into them. I have to steady myself.

"I'm leaving on Sunday. It's time to get back to the family business." I can tell that Gordon is looking right back into my eyes. I wonder what he sees?

"Gordon's family owns rental properties all over Boone," Craig adds, sweeping his arms in the air for emphasis. I notice Gordon's demeanor shifts and he becomes a bit guarded, as if some piece of private information just got free from his control.

"I'm sure that can be quite intense," I say. I look at Gordon to offer him a chance to close off the subject.

"It can be. There's nothing much to it. My brother handles things when I'm away. I'll pick it back up on Monday," Gordon replies.

All during dinner, the four of us do the dance of disclosure. We share what we do for a living, what is happening in our lives, and what cities we've visited. I learn that Gordon lived in Berlin and still visits it regularly. Craig is enamored with London and Tom is content to stay in D.C. for now.

Gordon proves to be delightful. He makes me feel so comfortable in his presence. He tells me all about his university days, about a girl he dated—Maggie—and about a couple he met in Berlin.

Soon the dishes are put away and we bid farewell to one another.

"I'm getting ready for bed," Tom says. "Stay as long as you want, Vy. I mean it." He leaves the living room and heads down the hall. I suddenly see a Siamese cat shoot out from under the living room couch, chasing Tom before he closes the bedroom door.

"Be right behind you," Craig adds. "If you guys want to talk more, please do. You won't be disturbing anyone." With that, Craig exits down the hallway.

Wow. It's Gordon and me. Alone. I smile.

"They're a great couple," Gordon says. "I stay with them when I'm here in D.C., and I let them stay with me when they come down to Boone. You should come down with them some time."

"That might be fun. I remember growing up in the mountains..." I pause to pull out a memory that I don't want to share, "...in Virginia. It was an idyllic time. I was a teenager, carefree, and the war seemed so far away." With that statement, I realize I've said more than I wanted.

"War?" Gordon exclaims.

The room gets small very quickly. The air seems to hold its breath, waiting for the sound of thunder. I want to kiss Gordon, not talk about the past.

"I want to kiss you," I whisper. I don't give him time to respond—I reach out with my hands and grasp his face. In one motion, my mouth touches his and we both spring to our feet. Our bodies mash together. I caress the back of his head and push my tongue into his mouth. I want to kiss him so hard as to take his breath. I squeeze my arms around his torso.

Gordon smells wonderful. I feel for his nipples and begin to pinch them, then reach for a handful of his ass.

"We gotta stop," I hear Gordon breathe. I break contact immediately, confused.

"I don't want the guys to come in and catch us," he says.

I realize that we are standing in the threshold of the living room and hallway. Who cares if they catch us? Is this some sort of excuse?

"Okay," I say. "But I feel so... connected. You're incredibly attractive."

"You're a good-looking guy, too," Gordon responds.

I press my body against his, pushing him back into the living room. I suckle on his ear and wedge my leg between his and we pirouette onto the couch. I can feel my hard-on pressing against his inner thigh. Our lips are locked and our tongues are dancing inside each other's mouth. I suppress the urge to rip his clothes off and pull his pants down.

What is it about this guy that has me losing control? He's got me all turned inside out.

Suddenly, the both of us hear a noise from the bedroom.

"Whoa," Gordon says. "We've got to stop. I really don't want the guys to catch us."

I don't understand why Gordon is so afraid that we're going to get caught. What is the worst thing that can happen? I'm all worked up. I want this guy so badly even a blind man can see it. "Okay," I say, resigned. "I'd better go." I begin collecting myself for the walk home.

"I want to see you again before I leave, Vy," Gordon says. "I think we are going out on Friday. Whatdya say?" I hear a sense of longing hidden within his words.

I'm totally confused. I blurt out, "Sure." Why the hell did I do that? I just want to get away from this embarrassing scene. I feel so connected to Gordon. Now my body aches because I'm leaving. My mind races with confusion by the mixed signals, and my spirit falls from grace by the loss of intimacy.

In a blink, I find myself outside on the street, running home. My world blurs behind me as my breathing quickens. When I hear the front door of my condo shut behind me, I slide to the floor with my back bracing it. Tears streak my face like meteor showers across the sky. I taste something sweet and ripe in the back of my throat that now leaves me fallow. I hug my knees to my chest and wait for dawn. I meditate on these feelings, hoping that they desert me.

20

"Hey Vy, come by the house around 6:30 and we'll head out to JR's. Afterwards, we'll pick a restaurant along 17th, like the Italian Kitchen." I stop Craig's message on the answering machine, not sure what to do. I'm embarrassed about what happened the other night. It's been three days. Thankfully, I haven't actually run into any of them. Especially Gordon.

I take a deep breath and dial Craig's number. It goes to voice mail.

"Hey guys. I'll be there at 6:30." I'll show and see what happens.

When the door opens, Craig greets me with a big, warm smile, beckoning me into the living room. A couple of other guys I've seen around town are here as well. I don't immediately see Gordon but I know he's here.

"Hey, Vy."

There he is.

Gordon enters the living room from the hallway, clutching a drink in his left hand. He sets the drink down on a side table and approaches me.

I go to embrace Gordon and give him a quick kiss on the lips. Just a peck, like I did for Craig when I entered. But Gordon turns his face right, and I end up pecking his cheek. The movement catches me off guard but I go with the flow. "Good to see you," I say before taking a seat diagonally from him. I see that he isn't really making eye contact with me. I feel stupid. Monday night gets farther out of reach as the moment expands. I hear a song in my head that there's more between 2nd Avenue and 5th Avenue than three blocks, I tell ya'. I hear Secondhand Rose come to life. I definitely feel like I'm on the outside looking in.

Vy is cute tonight, wearing a gorgeous, striped blue shirt. I can't get myself to make eye contact with him. I want to, but I need some time to pull myself together. I'm afraid that I might lose control. I couldn't let him kiss me on the lips—that might start something that can't be controlled. Craig's got his D.C. friends here and I'm a bit out of my element.

"Let's get going, guys," Craig says with a smile. "Does everybody have a drink?" His eyes scan the room for agreement. Ever since he got the industrial margarita machine, it's been Mardi Gras every weekend, except there's no giving up for Lent.

"Where's Tom?" Vy asks.

"He decided to visit his family in North Carolina this weekend," Craig replies.

"Oh," Vy says. I see his face crinkle around his eyes. I'm sure he's thinking it's a bit strange to leave your husband with a group of guys, especially gay guys, drinking. You never know what Odyssey can transpire and what stories will be passed around and around. Sometimes myths are much more telling than the real-life events.

We pass through Dante's doorway at JR's, an S&M bar. "Certainly jammed here tonight with a lot of faux models," I shout to no one in particular. I look at Vy, and he's nodding in agreement. "I really hope Craig doesn't want to stay long."

Blissfully, it's a short one-drink minimum. The pre-drinking sloshed us, and now hunger drives the party. We can smell the meat in the air. We push out onto 17th street, a gaggle of men laughing and beating their drums. Our revelry pushes us down the street like a tidal wave pushes water inland. We crawl over pedestrians and fill the gaps in the sidewalk. Eventually, we manage to snag a table on the Italian Kitchen's patio.

Vy's smile lights up his face. I wonder what he finds so amusing. I notice his eyes scanning the people walking by. Sometimes I think I see recognition, disgust, happiness, sadness, and lust. I like the idea that Vy is a what-you-see-is-what-you-get kinda guy. His emotions paint across the canvas of his face, illustrating his inner being.

"The Summer Fest party in the mountains is coming up," Craig tells us after swigging his beer. "Our house won't be rented, and there's a hot tub."

"Hey Vy, you think you'd go?" I grin with a hint of mischievousness.

"I've never been to Boone before," Vy replies. "I did spend my teenage years in the Virginia mountains, though. Sure." He looks right into my eyes. I swear I see flashes of lightning in his pupils. The other two guys seem caught up in their own conversation, and are oblivious to Vy and me.

"You'll like it. It's a great town with wonderful people," I say.

"Tell me, Gordon, what's it like for a single gay man in Boone?" he asks.

I try to divert the question. "People are very friendly. The moment you meet them, they seem like long lost friends."

Vy tries again. "Yeah. But what's the dating scene like?" He's now smiling at me, trying to look coy.

"It's a great place to live. Right near Boone, about eight miles up the road is Blowing Rock. There's a gorge that'll take your breath away. The houses there are actually planted into the side of the mountain and hang off the rock. No backyard, just straight out views."

"Okay. Wow," he says. "Not sure if I'd want to look out the back of my house and see no land. I've practically got no footing now as it is. I can't imagine living off a rock. Talk about no playing in the backyard."

Vy's got the most expressive brown eyes I think I've ever seen. I enjoy talking to him. I like the way his eyes crinkle when he laughs. I should just enjoy and let myself go. Luckily, there's always a drink around like this yummy gin and tonic.

Before long, a couple of hours have slipped by and I get tired. As we all get up, Vy says, "It's time for me to go."

"Really? You're not going out clubbing with us?" I'm astonished. I don't know how Vy put me in such a relaxed state. I just want to soak it all in and now he's not going with us. "You've got to come to Summer Fest, then," I blurt out.

"Well..." he replies, and then looks over to Craig.

"Kewl," Craig says. "For sure you should come with us to Summer Fest. Tom and I go every year. In fact, you can ride with us."

"Okay. I'll go." Vy says this like he's giving in. Regardless, I'm glad he's coming.

I take my chance and hug Vy, now that he's within striking distance. He completely relaxes into my arms.

It feels so good I don't want to let go. It feels like it's been forever since we kissed. I squeeze to make sure I'm awake.

"Don't forget, you're coming to Boone," I whisper into Vy's ear.

"Yes," he responds. I hang onto Vy until I feel the air push us apart like some jealous lover. I think I might've held on a bit too long. I wish he would stay out with us. But it's best not to open that can of night crawlers, I admonish to myself. Oh my, it looks like the group is already down the block. I'll have to run to catch up. Now I know I held on a touch too long.

21

The Summer Fest weekend comes up fast. We decide to leave at about seven, right after rush hour. I hate the idea that it's seven hours away. I have to burn two vacation days.

"Thanks again for the invite, Craig," I say as we speed down the highway into the high country.

"No worries. Glad you could make it, Vy," Craig responds.

"Where's Tom?" I ask. "I thought he was coming?"

"He's at a family event back in North Carolina."

Hmm. I've noticed over these last couple of months that Craig and Tom have been jostling with relationship spikes. I hear whispers through the scene about marital difficulties. Personally, I think they make a great couple. I hope they can pull each other out of whatever quicksand they are sinking into. I hear that slow motions can overcome the pull, while thrashing around just hastens the sinking. I find myself staring out into the darkness. Craig puts on a mix CD of the latest dance music. Nice to bring along the club as we hurl into the back woods of undeveloped territory. The rhythmic beats lull me into a deep trance, and it doesn't take long for me to nod off.

"Little one, what catches your attention?" a solemn voice asks. It is carried by the heat trailing off the jungle floor.

Startled, I turn and say, "Great Thầy, I beg your pardon." I bow and then continue. "From here, the temple's garden wall frames the jungle."

"That catches your attention?"

"I cannot see anything, it is so dark," I reply. "Mother says there are too many dangers to walk about the grounds outside of the village."

"Your mother speaks from experiences that may not be on your path," Great Thầy says. He notices that I am puzzled. "Walk with me."

I dutifully walk a half step behind him, out of deference. Everyone seeks his guidance. Some do not speak; others say very few words; and some talk and talk.

From what I've witnessed, he always meets them with a sense of serenity, and speaks few words.

We walk in silence for some time. I notice that we skirt the edge of the village and take a path that leads to the river. It's dark. Only the smoothness of the path tells us we're on it. The stars are pin lights crowning the full moon.

"The moon graces us; you see what she sees," Great Thầy says. "Does she tell you what you see is dangerous?" he inquires.

"Great Thầy, the moon does not talk," I say. I notice that he smiles.

"All around you is illusion. Only the light here..." Great Thầy touches his head and then his heart, "...shines truly enough to guide you through the dark and dangerous paths." He then slips into silence.

The jungle's noises are amplified by the soft patter of our footfalls. Some make me jump and others are unrecognizable. Soon, the sound of the river drowns all else out.

"What do you see now?" Great Thầy asks as our toes touch the water's edge.

"I see blackness across the river. I see water moving in that direction." I point to the left of me. "I see the reflection of the moon."

"What else do you see?" Great Thầy gently pushes me.

I don't know what he means. I stand at the water's edge and hear its roar. I see the direction in which it pulls itself, the moon looking down, and nothing on the other side. The darkness seems to have taken a life of its own. I know that the jungle and its dangers are over there. But what does Great Thầy want to hear? I ponder. I notice that we will not move until I answer. We have been here long enough for the moon to have peaked and it is now sliding down under the canopy. I sweat anxiety, for I do not know the answer.

I blurt out, "I see the water moving in this direction; I see the moon is already sinking; I see nothing on the other side of the river." I hope that what I say is correct.

"Hmmm," Great Thầy says. He turns from me and moves back up the path towards the village.

I run after him and plea, "Were those the correct answers?" I'm on the verge of great embarrassment that I don't live up to Great Thầy's expectations.

"You seek my approval?" Great Thầy gently reproaches.

I am concerned that all I'm doing is dishonoring Great Thầy. "I am sorry," I say in a quiet lament.

"You are sorry, now?" Great Thầy again gently reproaches me. "You seek answers on the outside in the world of illusion."

I ponder what he says. I feel a lesson has been shared and I don't understand it. Then I suddenly hear a stick crack and I jump back, raising my hands.

The slam of the car door smacks me awake. I jump. "Whoa," I say.

"Sorry. Just stopped for gas," Craig says. "All done now."

As I adjust to my surroundings, I examine the truck stop. We must be close to Troutville, Virginia.

"What were you doing? Dreaming?" Craig asks as we pull back onto Interstate 81.

"I was dreaming about the Great Thầy."

Craig throws me a puzzled look.

"He was the head Buddhist monk of the village I lived in—in Vietnam. One night he and I hiked from the village to the river. I learned a lesson that took me many years to understand. He was like that. He'd enlighten you towards a path and then it was up to you to go forward, backward, or sideways."

"I don't know much about Buddhism," Craig replies. "I grew up Southern Baptist until I fell off the wagon and decided not to get back on." We both laugh.

"Well, that night on the way back, I got a huge fright," I continue. "It was dark in the jungle—only the moon lit my way. All of a sudden, I heard the sound of cracking twigs. I thought it was a wild animal charging us, but soon learned that it was Mother. She had gone out looking for me."

"Really? How old were you then?" Craig probes.

"I was 14. Later, I learned that Mother gave Great Thầy a scolding for taking me out to the river that late at night. She reminded him how dangerous it was." I laugh at the thought. "Mother was always trying to protect us. She still does today, even though I'm 40 years old. I don't know about you, but in a Vietnamese family, children will always be children in the eyes of a parent."

Craig laughs. "What was the lesson?"

"Oh, that we live in a world of illusion, and it is impossible to seek truth from it. The only truth is the truth that is." I smile at Craig's quizzical look. "In order to find the path to enlightenment, one must meditate and essentially become one with all that's around you. Only through quieting the mind can one become aware of one's intrinsic truth. That intrinsic truth leads one through the world of illusions, which is the province of Desire. It's Desire that causes suffering. You can find no answers or approvals in that world, which happens to be the world of our senses. Buddhists seek to break the chain of rebirth to achieve a state called Nirvana, which is absolute cessation. The only way to do that is to turn completely away from this world. I like to call it the state of total oneness. There's a debate of what exactly it is."

"Interesting," Craig remarks as we drive through the New River Valley.

We turn off Interstate 77 at Route 221 and head south. If you head in the other direction, that's where my adoptive dad grew up and where his kinfolk still live. Unfortunately, my grandparents are no longer among the living. They're resting in the family plots on one of the mountains at Foster Falls.

We arrive at the rental house as the car clock shouts three in the morning. I help unload our belongings and then crash. I figure I'll be back in the land of the living in time for dinner. I'm not counting on making the first two meals of the day.

My first day in Boone is uneventful. I wake up at four in the afternoon, and have a quick meal after I learn that dinner won't be served until nine. I'll never make it to dinner without a snack. I might start eating people, I'm that hungry.

As Craig and I are seated at the restaurant, a blond guy approaches us. We rise to meet him.

"I'm Skip," the man announces. That will be easy to remember since he seems to skip as he walks. His blue eyes are showcased in a pair of multi-colored fashion-forward frames. His blond hair is cut to mid-length to allow the bangs to be pulled behind his ears. His fair face is sprinkled with freckles and his mannerisms are a mixture of preppy and dandy. You'd expect Buffy to be waiting outside in the Beamer station wagon. My bad...He is Buffy. I later learn that he drives a Beamer station wagon.

"I'm Vy," I respond. We then circle and hug before taking our seats. I ask the first question of the evening. "What do you do here?"

"Not much. I run a small gift shop in Blowing Rock," he replies.

"Blowing Rock?" I ask. "We're supposed to go there tomorrow afternoon and then have dinner. I'm excited about seeing the houses planted into the side of the gorge."

"Trust fund baby," Craig whispers in my ear. I smile. Skip eyes us suspiciously. Before anyone can say anything, Gordon is being led to the open seat.

"Hey guys," he says enthusiastically. The four of us hug him before he sits to my right. "I trust the drive down was okay?" he asks.

"Until Vy here had a nightmare," Craig laughs.

"Not a nightmare," I exhale. "I dreamed about something that happened while I was still living in Vietnam."

"Oh, do tell," Skip says.

I relate the Great Thầy's lesson for all to hear and explain a little of Buddhism to provide context.

"I've always wanted to learn more about Asian cultures," Gordon says. "I've spent time in Berlin and traveled around Europe. I haven't done any travel in Asia except for that stint in the Vietnam War."

"How long were you there?" I ask.

"Briefly. I was there for less than a year."

I couldn't imagine Gordon fighting in the war. I'm dumfounded and just stare at him. He occasionally makes eye contact, smirks, and then looks away. I want more. "What did you think of the country? Where were you stationed?" I probe.

I have Vy's total attention—not like he hasn't already been watching me like an owl. "I remember it being very different than the mountains, with its thick green canopy, the swarms of insects, and stalking heat that strips moisture from your skin. That heat is unrelenting, like a living, breathing monster. There is no heat like that here. It took me a couple of weeks to adjust." I feel the memory of it licking my neck like a long lost lover.

"How old were you?" Vy asks.

"19. I got to the country in late '73 and was out in April. There was all that noise about the Paris peace talks, which of course meant nothing in the end."

"Good thing that ambush came along and got your ass out before the Việt cộng wiped away the South a year later," Craig adds.

No! I mentally scream. "Let's not talk about that tonight. I'm sure Vy does not want to revisit the war, especially on his first night in Boone," I implore.

Skip shouts in agreement. "Yeah! Let's leave the war talk outside for now." He downs his drink and makes eye contact with the waiter. "Bring another round of drinks for everybody."

22

"Are you ready to see Boone and Blowing Rock, Vy?" Craig jokes as I come down the stairs of his rental house. The house sits on a ridge that overlooks a bright meadow ringed by condos and other houses. Farther up the ridge is another home.

"Okay. I don't figure it'll take long. The towns don't seem all that big," I say.

"Yep. We'll head into Boone, pick up Gordon, and show you around."

"Great," I reply. Gordon is going to spend the day with us. I like the idea. I'll have a chance to ask more questions about his time in Vietnam. My heart sank when he changed the subject last night.

We pull up to a ranch that sits at the end of Elm Street. It's unassuming, but has two driveways—one leading to a carport, which I surmise leads to an entrance through the kitchen, and the other leading to a garage/basement. The front door is approximately in the middle of the house.

"Come in," Gordon says through the screen door.

We enter the house and I immediately realize it's much like Gordon—unassuming on the outside and built solid on the inside. The kitchen is an open design that bleeds into a dining area with a back door that leads out to a deck. The living room, attached to the kitchen, is decorated with solid wood furniture. I notice the sparseness of the room. I think the design is more of a practical nature than anything else. Craig told me once that although Gordon is financially secure, he lives a very low-key lifestyle.

I walk towards the bookcase at the far end of the living room and scan the shelves of photos. My attention halts on one picture of a couple sitting in a restaurant. I gasp.

I turn to see Gordon in jeans, a non-descript shirt, and baseball cap.

"What's up?" he asks.

"Is that... Maggie?" I point to the picture and look at Gordon. He's speechless, his eyes wide and his mouth open.

"Hey guys, what's up?" Craig interjects as he enters from the kitchen. We both turn.

"How do you know Maggie?" Gordon asks, dumb-struck.

"I don't know her. I was at this same restaurant in Birmingham with a guy I was seeing. He knew Maggie's father because they both practiced law and served together in the local American Bar Association," I say. "I remember the dress with its shades of red, my favorite color, interplaying with the blue and orange pattern."

"It can't be," Gordon breathes. "You're the guy in the bathroom."

I nod with a wide grin.

"That picture was taken years ago," he offers.

"I know. I was a senior in college," I reply. And then I see it. I open the glass cabinet door, reach in, and take the picture out. I take a small step towards Gordon, who's now being shadowed by Craig.

"What?" Gordon asks.

"There. To the right of you. It's Tim and me!" I laugh.

Gordon takes the picture from me and examines it closely. He blinks a few times, and then slowly looks up at me. He's stunned.

"What a small world?" I say.

"Amazing!" Craig exclaims.

We decide to get off the topic, since none of us have any more words to describe our incredulity. I eventually break the silence.

"Let's see Boone and Blowing Rock," I announce. I take the picture from Gordon's hands and replace it on the shelf. "Craig, what's the play for the day?"

"Well." Craig refocuses on the here and now. "I thought I'd show you Downtown Boone and then Blowing Rock. We can hit some of the scenic areas while connecting the dots."

"Dots are exactly what I would call Boone's downtown," Gordon laughs as he picks up his car keys. "Ready when you are."

We eject from the house. It takes a whole 15 minutes to see Boone and 10 minutes to see Blowing Rock from behind the car window. The lifestyle differences are quite extreme between the two towns. Blowing Rock is definitely wealthier while the other is working class. Yet, I like the university area of Boone.

"Are we heading back to your house before the big, gay dance?" I ask Craig as we finish up the tour of Blowing Rock's Main Street.

"Yes. We'll freshen up and then meet Skip at the Bistro before we head to the lodge," Craig says. I notice Gordon nodding his head in agreement. We drop him off and I watch him disappear into his ranch. I still muse about our crossing paths in Birmingham.

23

What a day! I'm still getting over the fact that Vy and I crossed paths in Birmingham. I only thought D.C. was the place we had in common. Vy seems so out of place here out in the back woods, especially around all the scenic areas we visit. I like the way he looks out at nature, as if examining it from behind the glass of a nature preserve. It must be surreal going to high school in Pulaski County. I can see why he left as soon as he could. He's an urban guy like me. Boone's small. I know how Vy must feel coming here. When I came back from Berlin for that year abroad, it took quite a while to re-adjust. I thought I would go mad in Boone. I still remember the day I told my parents that

I was going to Germany for a year when I got back from the army reunion.

1984

"What's all this talk about living in Germany?" Daddy asks as we sit for dinner. Both my siblings have already left the house, so I am one on one with Dad. It's a little intimidating, especially with Mom watching so intently.

"It's been a passion of mine for some time since college. Maggie and I planned to go right after graduation, but after a couple of years in Chapel Hill, I followed her to Birmingham instead. I think now is a good time to go," I say.

Daddy sits back in his chair and nods. "Since you've been back from the reunion, you've been a bit off. Too tightly wound, as if something set you off."

"You might be right about that—it's quite the sight to see buddies I thought were long dead. I think it might have stirred up a few things. But it's nothing I can't handle." I am not about to spill the Mitch adventure.

"Dear. You've had your share of excitement. We're a little concerned that you'd be so far away," Mom interjects.

"I'm not just showing up in Germany. I'll be a part of UNC's year abroad program as an alumnus. The credits I earn can be transferred to a graduate program. I've always thought I might get a Master's in

German." I try to say this with enough conviction so Mom won't be too concerned.

"Still. I'm not comfortable with you just up and leaving," Daddy says. "I know you're a grown man, but a man who has been through a lot."

I know Daddy is referring to 'Nam. Yes I'm still haunted and have dreams both surreal and nightmarish. I can't let them think that they need to take care of me for the rest of my life. "I looked over the study abroad program and I can start the first of January. That means I'll be home just after Christmas. It's just a year," I say confidently. "Besides, I speak enough German to get by."

"Maybe, Dear..." Mom turns to Daddy. "It'll be all right. The college program provides structure and..." she turns her dark green eyes onto me and lowers her voice, "...you'll call if you need anything."

"Yes, Mame," I say, and with that I know I'm Berlin bound.

A month goes by before I meet the creatures responsible for opening my world to new possibilities in Berlin. I'm in the student center and it's packed.

"Hello. Mind if we sit here?" asks an Asian man with a tall German guy in tow. They are both classic versions of their racial groups. The Asian man is short, with black eyes and black hair. He has to be no more than 110 pounds. The German is taller than me, about six feet, blond and blue-eyed. They make a striking couple, if that is what they are.

"Nein. Bitte, setzen Sie," I say using the German I spent years in school learning. It takes a few weeks to get the hang of it again. You can tell I am not a native speaker.

"Where are you from?" the German probes.

"America," I reply.

"Ooh," the Asian coos.

"Name is Gordon," I say and extend my hand. The Asian guy grabs it and then stares at it, turning it over and over. Not sure what he's looking for as he continues to study my hand.

"Man of many talents. You use your hands, yet I sense you don't need to do so," he smiles up at me.

"You have to forgive Lok," the German says with a grin. "He sometimes gets very psychic. By the way, my name is Ulrich." He takes my hand away from Lok, shakes it, and gives it back.

"No problem," I say with a suspicious glint in my eyes. I'm thinking *freaks* when Lok stares at me with disgust, abruptly gets up, and walks away.

"Did I offend him?" I ask. I hope the six-foot-tall German isn't coming after me.

"No," laughs Ulrich. "Lok is as Chinese as they come. You'd think Germans have French manners compared to some of the Chinese. It's the years of living under communist rule. Anything that smacks of the bourgeois is considered an affront to the state."

As if on cue, Lok reappears with a tray of food. "I'm famished," he announces. "Here." He shoves the tray under my nose. "Eat."

Bossy is all I can think of at the moment. I see they're watching me, so to be polite I take an apple. "Thanks," I say. I see they're still watching me. "So... are you at the university?" I ask in a reserved manner.

"I am," Ulrich states. "Lok here is creating chaos all over Berlin."

"I'm an artist," Lok says in a condescending manner.

"Of?"

"Abstracts." Lok gives me the evil eye for daring to ask. How dare I not know what he does.

"Surrounded by Philistines. That's why the artist's life is so DEMANDING," Lok declares in the most pretentious voice I've ever heard.

"Don't mind him," Ulrich grins. "He's not that bad once you get past the bluster." He looks at Lok and I sense an electric charge pass between them. I think they're a couple.

"Anyhow. You're cute. I like your blue eyes and thick curly hair," Lok declares. "I forgive you."

"Now that we have taken care of that," I say, my voice rich with sarcasm.

"Hey," Ulrich beams. "We're hosting an exhibition of Lok's work tonight, then a private party. Why don't you come?"

"Yes. Please come," Lok says in the most vampish manner outside of a two-dollar hooker. I feel like a john.

"Well..." I begin. Granted, Ulrich is at the university—so he claims—and Lok is just a cute freak.

"We won't hear otherwise," Ulrich finishes for me. "Here's a special flyer with the address and the all-important stamp that will get you into the showing. You'll be with us and we'll head to the private party."

No harm in taking the flyer. "Ok. Thanks for the invite," I say as calmly as I can.

"We hope to see you there," Lok hisses. It's like talking to a viper. His black eyes shoot right through me. The hair on the back of my neck stands up, and I break out in goose bumps. I definitely feel like prey.

Later, as I am looking at the flyer, I see that the exhibition is from 10 pm to 12 am. Things happen late here. Clubs don't get started until midnight. Witching hour seems to flash like a starter pistol. People rush to get things done before the sun rises. I'm intrigued. What's the worst that could happen? I survived 'Nam.

"Darling, look who I dragged in," Lok announces to Ulrich as he pulls me into the gallery space. "Fresh meat," he adds as a coda.

"Hey," I say to Ulrich, taking his hand. The room is one large post-industrial space, with hardwood floors, exposed plumbing and rafters, and a few holes in the wall. There are maybe 20 to 30 guests milling about,

looking at columns lined haphazardly across the room
with large abstract paintings hooked to the center. I do
mean hooked, right through the center of the painting
and into the column.

"What do you think?" Ulrich asks.

"Some of these paintings are out there. What's up
with the hooks in the center?" I casually ask.

"The hooks are part of the painting. If you buy one,
you get the center part of the column and then you
can install it wherever you like," he explains.

"Do they sell?" I ask, since I cannot imagine why
anyone would want one of these harsh abstracts with
hooks in the center.

"He's sold 10 out of the 30 here," Ulrich states with
pride.

"Really!" I try to hold my surprise in. I'm not much
of an expert in this type of art, hell, any type of art,
but these paintings are $2500 a pop. Wow.

"Is it time for the after-party, darling?" Lok asks,
bored.

"Dear, stop being so melodramatic. The party will
be there. Just a few minutes more and we can go."

"Come with us," Lok says to me as we exit the
space. He ends up selling 18 paintings and it's considered a good night. He does these showings every two
months so as not to saturate the art scene, as Ulrich
explains. Ulrich is getting his Art History degree.

I tag along because I'm curious about this after-
party and why it seems to brighten Lok every time he

talks about it. He keeps saying that it is a special affair for discriminating men.

We get to the front door of a non-descript row house on a side of Berlin I've never heard of. It's close to the Berlin Wall. We arrive a little after one in the morning.

With Lok in the lead, we storm the door and into the building. Standing transfixed, I let my eyes scan the room. There are more men than I can count, but they break into two main groups: whites and Asians—or, as I learn a bit later, the wheat and rice crowd.

"Darling Loky, what took you so long?" a mild-mannered Asian slinks over and exaggerates his vowels as he speaks.

"The show just kept going on and on. I did everything to push everyone out. Ulrich here demanded that I stay and entertain since I was the guest of honor." A mildly subdued Lok bats his eyelashes for effect.

"Poo. The Banana Boat Party is just about to hit full steam," the guy says.

Ulrich nudges me in the ribs with his left elbow and whispers, "If you get uncomfortable, let me know and I'll get you out of here."

What on earth is he talking about? I soon learn what this Banana Boat Party is all about. My first clue is the white guy in the far corner of the room, leaning over and blowing an Asian guy. It's a sex party for gay whites and Asians. I'm getting dizzy; I'm not sure if it's the alcohol I've been drinking since the exhibition, or the stuff I'm downing right now.

"Also, watch out for the edibles on the table. You don't really know what chemicals are baked into the batter," a conspiratorial Ulrich again whispers into my ear. It's a gentle warning. I'm riveted to where I am standing. I so appreciate these bon mots, since this North Carolinian country boy is in way over his head.

I suddenly notice Ulrich isn't standing at my side. Instead, both white and Asian guys are buzzing around me, trying to make eye contact. I feel flush and I avert my gaze. I start moving, thinking that the prey that moves has a better chance of surviving than the prey that waits to be devoured. I round the corner and stop cold in my tracks. The house has several small rooms that lead into each other, without a central hallway. There are more men back here in the labyrinth than up front. I discover where Ulrich and Lok went.

As I look into one of the interconnected rooms, I see Ulrich, nude as the day he was born, bobbing up and down on some Asian guy's dick. He's bookended with a nude Lok, standing to his left, and a nude white guy, standing to his right. He's already swallowing Lok's dick down to the base. I watch him spit it out and turn to swallow the white guy's dick. He's taking turns on the popsicles. I sense they know I'm watching. I can't avert my eyes.

In slow motion, I see Lok smile and move towards me. "Hmmm. You like?" he whispers in my ear, just a fracture of a second before I feel his tongue slither into my ear canal. I feel my eyes roll into the back of my head, flash-freezing on Ulrich's grin as he slurps on the guy's shaft.

"This is a private session," I hear Lok rasp to faceless shadows in the doorway. He shuts the door and locks it. "It will be okay. We take good care of you. This couple we know very long time. Clean," I hear Lok tell me as if he's in a tunnel underwater. I turn and look into his black eyes and feel my pants hit the floor.

I shudder as I feel Lok's tongue probe my hole and pinch it between his teeth. There's a chair that I brace myself on. My knees feel weak and wobbly. It's getting harder for me to grasp air. I look up and see Ulrich standing in front of me with his massive dick inches from my face. I feel his hand cup my neck and my mouth opens wide. He slides his uncut dick deep into my throat until I feel it push against the back. I nearly lose it when I feel the hot mouth of the other Asian guy suck my dick. The white guy stands side by side to Ulrich so I can take turns. I hungrily let myself go. I then jerk straight up into Ulrich's tight, firm torso in response to Lok sliding himself inside of me.

I'm reeling from the sensation of having a guy inside me. I feel the pressure building and this intense contraction as I work to accommodate him. My breathing grows ragged and heavy. The sensation is too much and before I can say anything I unload into the Asian

guy's mouth. I can hear him spit it out and say something off-handedly about not being warned. I want to
say I'm sorry but I can't think right at the moment.

A realization pops into my head. Is Lok wearing a
condom? I grow tense and start to twist. That seems
to signal Lok to pull out. I nearly collapse forward, but
when I turn I see Lok is wearing a condom. I relax.

"We'll finish and you can take your friend home,"
says the smiling Asian who just got a mouthful. "I
think he's had enough excitement for one evening."

The images blur by. I see Lok mostly takes the top
and Ulrich the bottom position. That I'd never suspect. The other couple is more versatile. They flip and
flop with equal abandon. I watch the three of them
unload into Ulrich's mouth. I watch him swallow.

Just the memory of Lok and Ulrich has given me a
wet spot. That year was a wild one. After the two took
me in, they showered me with experiences of hard-
hitting sex, drug-induced concoctions, and no-holds-
barred pleasure trips. Not to overstate things, but my
year in Berlin was an eye-opening experience.

Vy reminds me of Lok and Ulrich. He moves with
the grace of Lok and has the common sense approach
of Ulrich. It's going to be fun dancing the night away
with him. I better get ready or I'll be late.

24

Back in D.C., I tell Jerry all about Boone, a place that has been at the edge of my life since Pulaski. It's like a seesaw in which the seats are Pulaski and Boone, my grandparent's place is the fulcrum, and the New River is the board that connects it all.

"It's a working class town with a well-to-do population eight miles down the road in Blowing Rock," I say. They have a university there, Appalachian State, or ASU. It's small but they have plans to increase enrollment."

"Yeah, but what about Gordon?" Jerry exclaims. He cuts through the bull.

"What's there to say? I don't think he's dating. And even if he is, I'm not sure if I'd be on the plate," I whine. "I saw him Friday night, Saturday, and Sunday. We left Monday morning around seven. It was a hellish drive, but thankfully, Craig drove. The trip really is too long for a car." I shake my head and use my hand to dismiss an imaginary servant.

"What's next?" Jerry inquires.

"Ironically, I'm heading back down with Craig in October to get his rental house ready for winter. I hear it can be pretty harsh up there," I share.

"What! Dear. DO you have a fever? What are you doing going back?" Jerry demands.

"I know, I know. It all started with our Sunday night dinner. We were just shootin' the shit back and forth, laughing at everything and anything, when in one of the pauses, Gordon got this really serious look and stared right at me like he was looking through a sniper scope." I pause for dramatic effect. "He asked me to come back to Boone. I didn't know what to say. I sorta made a face and said, 'Sure.' With that opening, Craig piped in that he was coming back in October to get the rental house ready for winter. And just like that, I'm coming back to Boone."

"The girl doth protest too much, I do declare," Jerry mocks.

"Oh, stop!" I cry for mercy and then sheepishly add, "I also agreed to go to the New Year's Eve party."

"What?" Jerry howls. "Wait! Aren't you going to your sister's in New York City?"

"I was." I avert my eyes from the daggers being hurled in my direction. "Don't hate me...because I'm beautiful," I implore. I then switch to a more catty persona. "Yo! You're taking your kids to Disney World for the holidays. So, if I recall correctly, you're leaving me all alone during suicide week."

"Please. Don't go to martyrdom just yet," Jerry shoots. "You were invited."

"I know. I do appreciate the offer, but it's not my cup of tea." I reach over and pat my best friend's hand.

"Now, tell me how the New Year's Eve party invite happened?"

"Well, Skip mentioned that one of his friends, a party planner, is putting on the show. So he asked everybody to go to support his friend. Naturally, I told him, 'Sure.'"

"You and your damn 'Sure's,' always getting us into damn trouble. The last one got us into Michael's pool party. Yuck!" Jerry coughs out like he's hacking up a fur ball.

"You had fun calling Michael out for his two-faced behavior," I interject. "I see that smile. Don't go batting your eyelashes at me, darling."

"Wait," Jerry says. His eyes are fixed right between mine. I hold my breath. "By the time you take the October trip, you'll be going back for the party. You could've used that trip as an excuse to say yes to Gordon's question, yet you didn't." Jerry's eyes narrow. "What aren't you telling me?"

"I don't know what you're talking about?" I can see Jerry isn't buying it, but the truth is I don't know what he's getting at.

"Hmmm, Mr. Vy. You can pass that Ms. Innocence with others but not with your best friend," Jerry says.

"I really don't know what you're talking about," I repeat. "After dinner on Saturday, we went to the big gay dance at the lodge. That was it."

"What happened at the dance? Did you guys dance?" he probes.

"Yeah. We danced to quite a few numbers. Gordon's got the same dance style I have. It's lots of fun having him as my dancing partner."

"Hmm. What words were exchanged between you two?"

I don't like where this is going. I can't quite put my finger on it but I know Jerry is pushing me into a trap. "Well. He said that he's a one-man dancing machine," I say with a smug smile.

"One man, like he only dances with one man at a time?" Jerry asks as he snaps the trap shut like a confident hunter.

"He did say that he is a one guy-at-a-time type of person." I hedge my bet.

"Knew it. You think you have a shot with him," Jerry declares. "You're so programmed. It's like you're on autopilot; you and your unavailable man syndrome.

Really. It should be listed in the Diagnostic and Statistical Manual of Mental Disorders, with your picture front and center." He pounds the nail.

I don't know what to say. We sit in silence for a bit. "I'm not sure why I go after men who are unavailable. It's a broken record I play over and over," I limply say. "It doesn't matter if they're geographically undesirable; in a relationship, gay or straight; workaholics; messed up on drugs; gay but not out; or the ever dreaded straight boy who's friendly."

Jerry studies me for a moment. "You're in a pattern. We just have to break it. You won't be able to say yes when the right one comes along if you keep focused on the wrong ones in the here and now."

"I know," I respond weakly. We end lunch and I walk home, thinking about all the truth that Jerry managed to spill onto the table. He sees things more clearly than me, especially when it comes to dating. I get all tied up in the probabilities, and distracted by the possibilities.

When I get home, I see the letter. I read the sender's address—it's from someone named Ken. Why does that name sound familiar? I tear open the letter and freeze.

Dear Vy,

I hope that you are well. Wondering if you would like to get together for dinner? Call me. Let's do this soon.

Sincerely,
Ken

Ken? I wonder if it's the same guy from the Georgetown gym, after all these years. We first met 21 years ago, when I was 19. We talked over the years but then lost contact about 15 years ago. Could this be him?

I dial the phone number listed on the letter, and a voice I barely recognize answers.

"Hello?"

"Hi. It's Vy," I cautiously respond.

"Vy! It's great to hear from you. So you got my letter. I wasn't sure if you'd respond."

"I was curious if the Ken I remember is you. It's been over 15 years since we last spoke," I say.

"How true," he responds. "I thought of contacting you sooner but never got around to it. The medical practice takes up all my time."

"I understand—no hard feelings," I respond.

What about dinner?" he asks. I hear a hint of longing in the question.

"Sure. I wouldn't mind catching up," I say with just a hint of concern. The last time we had dinner, we ended up fooling around.

"Come by the house on Saturday around six. Do you remember where I live?" I can hear the anticipation in his voice.

"Sure. If you haven't moved."

"No. Same place," he confirms.

After we hang up, I wonder if it's a good idea to open this can of worms. Jerry is right. My "Sure's" can get me into a lot of trouble.

On Saturday, I arrive outside of Ken's row house in an exclusive Georgetown neighborhood. It's painted in the same blue as I remember from 20 years ago. I wonder if the house still looks the same on the inside. When I first visited, an interior designer had just redone the house. He essentially gave her a blank check. I'm hoping that in all these years he might have updated the place.

"Come on in," a friendly, older Ken says as he opens the door. He's gained weight around his midsection and still has a pear-shaped body. His brown hair is cut shorter. He's okay-looking for a guy in his 60s.

"Thanks," I say and enter his home. As I scan the living room, I confirm that nothing has changed. It's just aged.

I vaguely remember having dinner in his kitchen's breakfast nook, which was kind of sad, really. As I follow Ken to the kitchen, I suddenly realize that we are going to eat in the same breakfast nook, 21 years later! When I take my seat, I try to hide my smile. Ken prepares the dinner, which is essentially what we had long ago—chicken and vegetables. Amazing what I recall once I get here. It's a recreation of a moment in time.

"How's the chicken?" Ken asks once we begin eating.

"Good. I think this is the same meal we had the last time I was here."

"Last time you were here was special. I thought we could see about having that again," Ken replies.

Not sure what he means so I watch him carefully. As we eat and fill in the gaps over the last 15 years, he asks if it's ok for him to drink a beer. I say yes. I also don't want Ken waiting on me, so I get a Ginger Ale. I notice when I open the fridge door that the entire middle shelf is stocked with bottled beer.

As we sit and talk, his leg gently nudges mine. It's like a gentle footsy play under the table. I hope he doesn't expect a repeat of what happened at the end of our last dinner.

After the eighth beer, I think what courage he's looking for is found. It seems that six beers is the magic number, the one that will allow him to take our conversation to a place he wasn't able to take it until now.

"The time you came over for dinner was very meaningful to me. I'm sad that you were here one moment and then gone the next." Ken's trying to keep his emotions in check. I can see his eyes watering.

I remember that night 21 years ago in which one thing led to another after dinner. We found ourselves upstairs, giving each other what I consider to be very quick blow jobs. I remember that we both finished ourselves off. He did have one arm draped across my shoulder when I brought myself to my own climax, just like he did for himself. Once we came, I got up, washed off, and said my goodbyes.

That moment is done, forever frozen in amber. I now see that it haunts Ken as a moment that miscarried before it came to term. I stay quiet and let him continue. He's having difficulty expressing a primal need.

"Stay the night," he quietly requests, full of hope and anxiety.

"I don't think that's a good idea, Ken," I respond kindly. Thankfully, I already told Jerry that I would meet him at JR's. That gives me strength.

"Dammit, Vy! Stop being so damn polite!" Ken howls. "Tell me to fuck off and be done with it." His need overpowers his body as I see him twitch.

I grow quiet. I realize that when I am faced with strong emotions, I retreat into a wall of politeness. It's how I can withstand the onslaught of emotions and not lose myself. Without it, I would be caught in the undertow of others' emotional wakes. "I think it's best for me to go," I say as straightforward as possible and stand up. I move towards the front door, and when I look back, I can tell my desire to leave calms Ken.

"Please," he laments. He gets up and closes the space between us. "Just stay one night. We don't have to have sex. I just want to wake up next to you... just once," he pleads. I can see the look of longing and abandonment swirling across his irises.

"I'm sorry, Ken. I've got to go. My best friend Jerry is waiting for me." I say this as evenly as possible. I feel the need for distance. His request isn't so unreasonable if I think of it in terms of helping another human being become unstuck. I think my Buddhism is clouding my judgment. I can't unstick him from time.

"Just, please consider it," Ken softly repeats. I shake my head, unable to speak, and walk out the door to meet Jerry. I can feel Ken's teary eyes glued to my back as I disappear into the night.

"How did your date with Ken go?" Jerry asks when I meet him at the restaurant entrance.

"Oh my. It wasn't anything I expected. I need a drink," I announce. I order a beer and take two swallows, then set it back down. That's all I need to calm my nerves. I can see Jerry's eyes go wide.

"You don't drink anymore!" Jerry announces with concern.

"I know. And these two swallows are already affecting me. I can feel myself blushing," I confirm.

"Tell me, what happened?" Jerry takes me away from the bar and over to a corner with fewer patrons. At least I can look out into the alley to gain perspective; I do feel like I was playing in the gutter. What was that quote about always making sure you're lying face up?

"I told you about Ken—he's a guy I've known since college," I say. "We met while working out in the gym. One night, I accepted a dinner date with him. It was the only time we ever did anything outside of the gym. He was already in his 40s when we met."

"Okay," Jerry says, trying to encourage more disclosure.

"The first time he asked me out, I went to his house for a dinner date. He made it seem like we would be going out, but instead he cooked up a simple chicken dinner, and we ate in his dingy little breakfast nook. The same thing happened tonight. He cooked me dinner, essentially the same dinner minus the salad. The first time he invited me, we..." I pause to find the right words. I know Jerry won't judge me but it's difficult to share youthful indiscretions now that I'm an adult. "...we ended up in his bed."

"You didn't do that again, I hope?" Jerry asks, horrified.

"No," I interject. "He wanted me to, but I said no. The first time, we just gave each other quick blow jobs. The encounter lasted less than 20 minutes. I remember thinking that it was a mistake and cursed myself for letting it happen."

"I bet you said, 'Sure,'" Jerry chuckles.

"Bitch!" I exclaim and grab my heart for dramatic effect. "Anyhow." I ignored his obvious insight. It probably was a "Sure" that got me into that situation. "When we finished, I was outta there. To me, that moment was complete. But for Ken, it was an unrealized moment. He's been holding onto it ever since. I don't think he has seriously dated anyone in the past 21 years. Just now, he wanted me to spend the night so that he could wake up next to me. He assured me that he didn't even want to have sex." I look right into Jerry's eyes when I say this.

"Oh my god. What are you going to do?"

"Right now? Nothing. I'm not planning on staying the night. I don't know what would happen if I opened that door. Would one night be enough? Or would that just increase his demands? I would like to help him get past this 19-year-old, idealized version of me that he's captured in amber. The Buddhist part of me wants to help him get unstuck," I clamor. "I don't think I'm that compassionate, though. The thing that grabs me by the throat is that we never dated. We never did anything that amounted to dating. We talked at the gym and I had dinner with him that one night."

"And you sucked his dick and jerked yourself off," Jerry reminds me in his gentle, sarcastic voice. I just shoot daggers into his eyes.

"Fine, we had sex. But it wasn't great—we barely sucked dick. We jerked our own selves off."

"You got under his skin and festered there like an open sore," Jerry says.

"Yuck. What an image!" I throw back. Still there's much truth in what Jerry says. Somehow a stuck moment was created in Ken's mind and he's nurtured it for the last 21 years. I certainly understand pining away for a guy. I know I've done that enough times to feel unclean in the morning.

"Shake it off," Jerry encourages. "You can't help what's done. You certainly can't take credit. And you shouldn't. He chose to fixate on that moment. He'll have to unstick himself."

"You're right," I agree. I can't be responsible for his actions. Unfortunately, I know that this is going to turn over in my head a few million times before I let it go.

25

"Explain to me why you guys eat so late?"

"It's only nine," Skip quips in Her Majesty's tone. He can be quite hysterical when he wants to, or just plain mean.

"What's the big deal, Vy? We like to hang out," Gordon interjects. I look over and he smiles at me.

"Hanging out is fun. It's the eating at nine that's killing me," I protest.

"You'll have to forgive the city girl. She gets cranky when her blood sugar drops to the floor," Craig smiles.

"Least it's not her panties," Skip barks.

"Ha. Ha." I roll my eyes for effect. I've eaten with these guys enough that I'm sensing a pattern. We eat late and then drink till whenever.

"Hey, Craig," Skip coos, "is the hot tub working at your place?"

"Yeah," Craig confirms.

"Let's take the party there!" Skip exclaims.

We all agree, especially me. I've got to get up and move around. The food is just sticking to the sides of my stomach like grease down a drain. I feel the reflux stirring. Of course, before we arrive, we make sure there is enough booze to alter our states completely.

"I don't have a swimsuit," I announce and then turn to Craig. "Do you mind if I free ball it?" I look right at him as I notice Gordon out of the corner of my eye.

"No. But I'm wearing my swimsuit. Got these love rolls to pull tight," Craig proclaims.

I ease into the hot tub in my birthday suit glory. Skip is across from me in his underwear, and Craig is to my right in his swimsuit. Gordon is in his underwear, and about to get in when he says, "On second thought, I think I'm going to lose the shorts. Hope you guys don't mind."

"I'm stark naked. I'm in no position to complain," I reply.

"Okay," he says, removing his underwear. As he enters, he turns to me and gives me a full frontal.

Interesting. I've been wondering what Gordon looks like under his clothes. I like his hairy body. His chest hair is trimmed evenly and a nice piece hangs below the belt. I wonder what it looks like hard. It's interesting that we are the only ones naked.

Soon the heat and alcohol takes its toll. We all agree it's time for bed. Craig wants the other guys to stay and leave in the morning. He says he doesn't want us drinking and driving, plus we can all eat breakfast together. We will finish the last few tasks, eat lunch, and then head off to D.C.

I watch Gordon walking around the room, naked, as if he is looking for something. His body looks even better under the room lights; as it shines down on his tight body, it accentuates his strong torso. As I put my underwear on, I figure out what Gordon is looking for. Privacy. He's gone over to the far side of the room near the bathroom and is using the door to shield from prying eyes as he puts on his underwear. I wonder if the act of putting on clothes is somehow intimate to him. I see Skip approach him. I wonder what he wants? I can just make out a few snippets. I think I hear the word "tattoo."

"What is that on your left shoulder?" Skip asks in a concerned voice.

"Just a tattoo I got in 'Nam," I reply. "I never liked it."

"You've got the money. Why dontcha remove it?"

"Well, I had wanted to, until I spent a year in Berlin. I was running around with this couple, Ulrich and Lok, just hanging out. Great guys." I pause as I jostle into my shorts, and then continue. I wish Skip would have given me a moment before coming over here to talk. "Lok is an abstract painter. He saw my tattoo and admired it. He told me that a Master must have done it because it's complete, yet belongs to a set. He thinks there is a twin to it and if found, the set will reveal itself as something more."

"Really?"

"I just thought Lok was full of shit. But as I studied it, I noticed that it forms the shape of a cat in silhouette. Lok is convinced there's a twin. He just feels it. Ulrich always said that Lok was psychic about certain things."

"Wow. Let's show the other guys," Skip reaches for my arm.

"No!" I flinch. "Let's not and let's drop it," I say in a very low voice. The tattoo is private and I generally don't strut around naked showing it off.

"Okay. Okay. No need to get so serious about it," Skip protests.

Soon we all retire to different corners of the rental to sleep the night off. It's late and the booze is finally kicking us down. I actually want to cuddle next to Gordon. I've thought a lot about our kiss and the door it opened between us. I could feel his soul touch mine, yet now I get nothing. I often ask myself, was that my own mind playing tricks on me? It felt so real that I could taste it, touch it, and feel it. Sometimes when we hang out, I try to get close—but not too close. Now I'm sleeping under the same roof and can't help imagine him breathing next to me.

The next morning after we finish getting the house ready, we start packing up the car. "Hey Craig, on the way out of town, do you mind swinging by the university?" I want to do a quick drive by, just to look around," I say.

"Oh. Thinking of moving here?" Craig replies. Thankfully the other guys have long since left. It's just us.

"Well. I told you that Boone isn't that much different from where I grew up in Virginia. It's in the mountains and it's small. It's a nice place, but I'm not sure if I could actually live here," I explain.

"Okay," Craig smiles. I don't think he actually buys everything I say. It's okay because I don't really know what I'm doing.

While still thinking about last night, I pull up to the rental, remembering that Vy watched me all night. I enjoyed the way he looked at me. I can't encourage him, though. He lives seven hours away. He's a big city guy and would never settle for a place like Boone.

26

"Hi. My name is Vy Mueller. Is this the Appalachian State University Graduate Admissions Office?" I ask.

"Yes, sir. How can I help you?" a warm voice responds.

"I want an application to the Master's program in Education," I say. After I hang up, I am assured that a package is on its way.

"You did what?" Jerry exclaims. "What are you doing? What's happening with you?" He sniffs the air like a bloodhound on the trail of a criminal, and scans my body language for clues to my sudden psycho behavior.

"I got the package from the admissions office to-day," I protest. "It's not like I've applied."

"But why even get it unless you're serious?" Jerry counters.

"The whole business with Ken is throwing me off." I mount a bigger defense. "He took a moment in time and built a gilded cage around his heart with it. Now I'm back in his life. He wants me to help free his spirit. He's called me a couple of times already, begging me to come over." I trail off and look into the distance. We are sitting on the sidewalk, watching the denizens of 17th go about their business on the catwalk. "There's a part of me that wants to help him. You know, unstick him from THAT place," I impart.

"Vy, you can't help that. Some people get stuck. You really don't know what it is that captivates him, since you guys haven't really spent much time togeth-er. You said that you met at the gym, and talked in between reps. You talked for how long? 15 to 20 minutes max? Then you had dinner one time, staying three to four hours, tops."

"I hear what you're saying. I just wish I could help him leave me, or, more precisely, the idealized image of a 19-year-old me," I add, wistful.

"You really can't. He took something and built it into what it is today, his own private Idaho. He sounds like he has some void that he's trying to fill." Jerry pauses to gather his wits. "Vy, what are you going to do if you try to help him and it doesn't work? It will only get weirder. Then what?"

I sit in silence as I ponder Jerry's words.

"What is this truly about, Vy?" he finally asks.

With that question, Jerry has stabbed me in my heart, my longing, my fears. "I'm afraid I'll end up like Ken," I whisper. "Trapped in a what-if, what-might-have-been, what-could-be moment, waiting to exhale. Maybe I've missed my chance for love." I look back over the street through the moisture clouding my vision. The sun is banking towards the west, reminding me of my family's plane trip out of Vietnam, out of the turmoil into a new land that would soon add a new father.

1974

A strange man, "Ted," hands me an opened green can. I look into this mess of noodles and brown chunks. I turn to Minh and Ngoc and grimace.

Upon seeing my face, Ted smiles. "Food," he says in Vietnamese, and then makes a motion of putting his fingers into his mouth. We don't move. He picks up a strange-looking thing with a handle and four prongs. He stabs into the can, pulls out a chunk and puts it into his mouth. "Mmmm. Good," he grins. Then he stabs into the can and pulls out another chunk. With it clumped on the strange thing, he moves it up to each of our mouths. "Go on. Good for you," he says.

He keeps waving the food in front of us. I get curious and open my mouth as he slides the utensil inward. I gently clamp my teeth onto the thing and scrape the chunk off. I slowly chew. Not so bad, but not very tasty. When I take another bite, Minh and Ngoc try it. If big brother can do it and nothing bad happens, then they can. We end up finishing the can, but do not want any more.

He opens another green can with a brown thing inside. He smiles as he pulls it out. "Look here. It's a brownie. Yum," he says. He breaks it into smaller chunks and gives us each a piece. I see Ngoc place it in her mouth and smile. Minh and I do it next. It's sweet and very dry. It makes us thirsty.

I see Minh grab Ted's arm with his left hand urgently, and then jump up and down. Ted recognizes that Minh needs to go potty. He leads him to one side of the plane towards a small door.

"What was that?" I ask Minh when he returns.

"Bathroom. Ghost made me wash my hands before I left," Minh says.

"Why?" Ngoc asks.

Minh shrugs his shoulders.

"You don't think Mother will die?' Ngoc asks with a worried look on her face.

"No! Mother would never leave us. Not with Ghosts around," Minh replies. Minh is younger than me. His anger simmers on the surface. How would he know? I wonder. I don't say anything because I don't want Mother to have empty eyes.

"Here are some blankets. Sorry, no pillows," Ted says. We just look up at him, confused at his words. We each take a blanket and lie on the floor next to the bench against the wall of the plane.

We awaken when the plane starts shaking around. Ngoc and Minh start screaming.

"Hush," Ted soothes as he hugs us together. We don't know what is happening and why the plane is bumping up and down. Once the rattling stops, I realize that the plane has touched down.

We disembark from the back of the plane, holding onto each other's hands as tightly as we can. We keep our eyes riveted on Mother, who is lying on a bed with wheels. We hurry to stay close.

The sun stabs me in the eyes as we emerge outside. We're moved towards the back of a vehicle with a big door swung open. They roll Mother to the back of the vehicle and she disappears inside. The door closes, yet we are still outside. Once the vehicle starts pulling away, we scream and run toward it in an attempt to catch up. Ted grabs Ngoc and me, but Minh is quicker. He keeps running. Another man appears and tackles Minh to the ground.

"Safe!" Ted says in Vietnamese, pointing at the retreating vehicle. "Your mother is safe." Minh is brought back to us and told the same thing in Vietnamese. I look over the deserted landing strip and see the Ghost we brought being wheeled into the back of another plane.

We're taken to a small apartment near the hospital where Mother was taken. It's a couple of days before we can go and see her, and Ted stays with us in the meantime. His Vietnamese is awful. We have to ask him to repeat himself many times. He doesn't hit the tones correctly, so he ends up saying a lot of nonsense.

"Mother!" we exclaim as we rush into the room and surround her. Our tears of joy flow at this happy reunion. Mother, too, is crying.

"I thought I'd never see any of you again!" Mother exclaims and grabs each of our hands. The doctors are amazed that she survived so much blood loss. Ngoc climbs into bed and lies next to Mother, snuggling up as close as possible. The rest of us sit at the foot of the bed. I notice Ted watching us from the far end of the room.

Then I see it. The realization hits me like wild lightning dancing above the jungle canopy during rainy season. The invisible thread that connects Mother to this Ghost pulsates. It is a look that they silently give one another. When did this moment happen? Mother was fighting for her life. When did she have time to become close to this Ghost? I can't believe it but it is true nonetheless.

I'm going to have a Ghost Dad.

"Hey, Vy. Whatcha thinkin' about?" Jerry asks, snapping me out of my melancholy.

I wipe the moisture from my brown eyes. "I was thinking about the time I realized I was going to have a new father—a white father. Mother later told me that she was attracted to the softness in his eyes and his attentiveness. She fell in love with him when she realized how much he cared for us." I smile. "From that day forward, she moved with him, following her new love to wherever he traveled."

"That's such a romantic story," Jerry remarks.

"Yes, and it's all true," I say, then focus my eyes on Jerry intently. "You're my best friend, Jerry, and I respect your opinion. But I'm going to apply for the Master's program." I feel Jerry's concern vibrate across the table as a physical object. His face contorts like a carnival clown without the makeup. I quickly add, "I know you think I'm on a fool's errand. I probably am. Mother left Vietnam and found a new life with a man she deeply loved. I know that I'm being a hopeless romantic. I just need to try it, to surround myself in a new place with new possibilities. I think D.C. is not the place for me to find love. And, I've always wanted my Master's. It won't be a complete waste if nothing else happens besides getting my degree."

"Are you going to say anything to Gordon?" Jerry asks. His tone is stern.

"Not about him being a reason for doing this. From what little I've experienced, he's not in dating mode.

He's gone out of his way to squash any hint of attraction beyond that of friendship. As of now, it feels like the kiss we shared was an aberration," I say with disdain. Somehow the window that had opened with Gordon has slammed shut on my fingers. The moment I noticed Mother and Father's connection matches the moment of my kiss with Gordon. I understand Ken's plight; how a moment can be still-born when it seems ready for birth.

"You don't think he'd be suspicious?" Jerry asks.

"No. He will be. I'll tell him I'm simply interested in getting my Master's. And, why not Appalachian State University? ASU's program is highly rated and close to where Father's family is from."

"Hmm. The best laid plans of mice and men," Jerry harkens.

"I'm thinking if I'm there, I can react if he goes into dating mode. If he does, then I'll know if I'm his type," I muse.

"And what if he never enters dating mode, or you're not his type? What then?"

"I'll have a Master's degree and I'll move away," I state. "Anyhow. This is all speculation until I get accepted. I sent in my application a few days ago. The program starts next fall but I can take up to nine hours of classes prior to admission and apply them to the program. It's pretty sweet."

With that comment, we finish our meal and bid each other adieu.

Part Two

Tigers swimming together in time

27

Winter hits the rest of autumn pretty hard with its freezing temperatures and gray skies. By the time Craig and I leave D.C. for the New Year's Eve party, the countryside has become a frigid, icy place.

"I can drive," I state.

"No worries, Vy," Craig replies. "Just sit back and relax, and think about the party. It's going to be a blast."

I nod my head. I don't ask why Tom isn't with us. I don't want to put Craig on the spot and I don't want him to feel obligated to answer.

"Do you ever think about making Boone home?" I ask.

"Not right now. Not much to do there. People arrive for the weekend and then poof. In-season is really the only time there's life on Mondays, Tuesdays, or Wednesdays. There's really only two seasons: winter for the skiing, and summer for escaping the heat. The turning of the leaves is starting to create a mini-season, but it's still a ways off," Craig elaborates. "I think I enjoy big city life too much. I'm still figuring out how to live in London without going broke."

"I love London," I exclaim. "Walking around Piccadilly Circus and Trafalgar Square were my favorite spots. I also enjoy the English accent. It transports me. A cute bloke could damn-well read the telephone book to me and I'd be taking off my clothes right then and there," I laugh.

"What about Boone, Vy?" Craig asks. "Would you be able to live there?"

"Well, I'm going to test that," I say, keeping my answer as cryptic as possible.

"What do you mean?" Craig arches an eyebrow.

"I got accepted to Appalachian State University's graduate program. I'm going to get my Master's of Educational Media in the fall. My plan is to move there in time for summer school. I can take up to nine credit hours before the start."

"Wow. When did you decide this?"

"Well, I've always wanted my Master's degree, and I liked what I read about the program at ASU. I grew up in the mountains on the Virginia side. It would be like going home again."

"You know that you can never go home again," Craig says. "Is that the only reason?" His voice is full of accusation.

"What do you mean?" I reply innocently.

"You know what I mean. Did you meet anyone in Boone or Blowing Rock?" Craig has angled into shark-infested waters. There seems to be a feeding frenzy building.

"Outside of Gordon, Skip, and Gordon's friend... what's his name?" I ask.

"You mean Jeff?" Craig offers.

"Yes," I quickly respond. "It's nice to know some friendly faces. It's the icing on the cake."

Craig shakes his head with a smirk. "You should ask Gordon about places to live. He's got all that rental property and he must know practically everyone in Boone." Craig then drops, "He likes you."

He likes you, I silently repeat to myself. What does that mean, exactly? As a friend or as someone more than a friend? I wonder. I throw back, "I like him, too," to see what sticks.

Nothing. I wonder if Craig's testing me. I wonder if Gordon said something about the kissing. I don't think so, but I don't know. I turn my head and look out the window into the darkness. Soon, the headlights will be eaten by unlit highways. Hurling forward, I shiver in my mind as I ponder what it will be like to live in a place both unfamiliar and strangely familiar. Out here, the sounds of nature are the deafening noise, especially for big city girls, especially for those who think they have the right to everything, especially for those who know the rainbow ain't enough.

After we get settled in, the next day Craig and I bundle up and head to the lodge where the New Year's Eve party is shaking. The one delightful detail not shared is that it's GAY.

Once we arrive, I notice Gordon speaking with some friends. I approach him, and we wish each other a happy New Year.

"Good music!" he shouts to me.

I smile back as I think about the drive last night with Craig. We had traveled down the interstate of my life, connecting my past, present, and now, it seems, my future together. I'd never guess how much this mountain spine has profoundly factored into my life. Could this be the feeling that people call "home?"

I decide it's time to dance, and Gordon quickly joins me. Our bodies instantly go into sync mode. I look into his sky blue eyes and smile. He smiles back and gyrates to the music. I admire that he stays on beat. He may look straight, but his dancing shows that he's got too much rhythm for a white boy, especially one who grew up in the mountains. He's getting awfully close. I can practically lick the hairs on his arms and chest. I wonder what he would do if I moved in for a taste of those lips.

I like the way Vy dances. He lets his whole body go. I watch his hips lock and drop, his arms cast spells, and his feet step out in angles to his torso. I'm close enough to see the sweat and smell his scent, and those lips... God, how I want to taste them again. I could shift my head forward and do the lip-lock. No. There're too many witnesses, even though this is a gay dance. The lodge is almost in the middle of Boone and Blowing Rock. Most of the guys here are weekenders.

Suddenly, Vy slides right behind me, planting his crotch firmly into my ass, and placing his hands on my hips. Together, we simulate fucking.

I drift momentarily away with this delicious feeling. But reality comes crashing into me, bringing me back to earth. What the hell am I thinking, simulating fucking in public? I better shift this around. I spin and plant his leg between mine. We then pivot around, mashed closely together. I can see the heat emanating off Vy's body. My sweat is mixing with his through our clothes. I see guys taking off their shirts and exposing their chests. I would love to do that.

"Enjoying yourself?" I whisper into Gordon's ear.

"More than you could know, Vy," he whispers back, sending goose bumps up and down my body.

"It seems that there are other guys who want to dance with you, Gordon. I can see the lust dripping right off of them," I coyly say.

"I'm a one-guy-at-a-time type of guy." Suddenly, Gordon breaks away and asks, "Do you want a drink?"

"No. I'm fine. I still have the Ginger Ale that Craig brought me." Gordon nods, and I watch him saunter off to the bar.

I find myself alone at the corner of the dance floor. Couples are still twirling around me, writhing to the music in a sensual tango. There are no lesbians here, but a few straight women. I decide to break and take a drink.

The far end of the dance floor overlooks an expansive view of the plateau that the lodge sits on. If you relax your eyes, you can survey the top of the valley and trace the gentle slope of the mountain at the far end. The sunrise must be spectacular from this view. Even in the dark, with lanterns posted around the grassy ledge, the view is gorgeous.

Out of the corner of my eye, I see Gordon coming back with a drink. He and Craig love their drinks. I've never seen them drunk but I've sniffed the smell of teen freedom in the air around them. "Another Gin and Tonic?" I ask.

"Sure is," he smiles. "Are you enjoying yourself, Vy?"

"I am. You're right, by the way. The music is good," I say with a grin. Then I decide to drop the bomb. I hope the collateral damage isn't too much. "I'm moving to Boone to go to graduate school," I declare. I brace for impact.

"I know. Craig told me," Gordon replies.

I shake my head, confused. "He did?" Well, that's annoying. This is my news. I wonder why Craig jumped me.

"Yeah. He wanted to see if I could help you find a place. I'd love to," he offers.

"That's very kind of you," I say. "I don't want it to be a bother."

"When do you want to do this? Some months are better than others, depending on the move-out times."

"I was thinking in February," I reply. "Is that too late?"

"It might be too early. Craig also mentioned that you wanted to settle in before summer session."

"Yeah," I respond. So Craig told him that, too. What else did he say? How did Gordon respond? Questions keep popping up in my head like serial killer Jack-in-the-boxes.

"Come back in late February or early March. It'll be cold and we may have snow," Gordon says.

"Oh great, SNOW?" I exclaim. I keep forgetting that mountain winters can be brutal and long. I hope that won't be the case while I'm up here.

"How long will you be here?" Gordon asks.

"The program is a year and a half. I'll see where I'm at when I'm done."

"You never know," Gordon smiles. "You might fall in love with Boone and never want to leave."

I wonder if that could possibly be true.

28

I still can't believe Vy is moving to Boone. Urban lights burst all around him, casting shadows over everything he does. I like that air of cosmopolitanism that hangs like scents of lavender across the mountain passes. With him, I always seem like I should be eating at sidewalk cafes, riding bikes along city streets, and dancing in jazz bars.

"Hello? Is this Gordon?" a familiar male voice asks over the phone.

"Yes. This is Gordon."

"How the hell are you!" shouts the voice.

I still can't quite place that voice. "Great. And you?" I ask, and wait for an introduction. It's like I should know him.

"You don't know who this is?" the voice declares with a hint of reproach.

I'm starting to get annoyed. "No. But you do sound familiar," I say nonchalantly.

"It's Mitch, your old college buddy."

I'm stunned. It's been quite a while since we last talked to each other.

"Hello?" Mitch adds.

"Sorry. You caught me by surprise," I say. "It's been a while."

"Who would have thought 20 years later? It all seems like a blur," Mitch says with a hint of astonishment. "I called because I'm going to be in Boone tomorrow, meeting at the university's development office. A client I represent wants to leave a sizeable donation. I'm here to finalize the paperwork. I remember you telling me how much you loved Boone and thought that by now you might be back."

"How true," I concur.

"Hey, I want to see if you're available for dinner. I'd like to catch up. My meeting is late and I'm not driving back to Wilmington until the morning," Mitch says.

"Yeah, that would be great. We can catch up and it'd be good to see you. Just tell me where and when," I offer.

"Wonderful. I'll come by and pick you up."

"You don't have to go to the trouble."

"No trouble at all," he replies. "How about 7:00?" I swear I can hear him smile.

"Okay. I live at 124 Elm Street." I provide him with the directions. I'm not really sure what to expect. It's been a long time.

Waiting for Mitch stirs up a lot of conflicted feelings. After that first night he stumbled into my room, we made it a regular thing for him to blow me. I never let on to the other guys. It was awkward the first few weeks, but then we fell into a regular pattern. When the other guys were out, he'd get a bit drunk and "lose his way" to his room. Next thing, I'm feeding him a load. Then, he'd suddenly remember where his room was. Towards the end of our senior year, he dropped the drunk bit and started up a blow-n-go program. He'd go in spurts. He'd want to suck me off every weekend and then nothing for a few months. I just let him do it. Around that time, Maggie was still letting me butt fuck her.

"Hey there," Mitch says when I open the front door. He's aged gracefully, with chiseled lines and silver temples. He's a bit soft around the middle and like me he's lost most of his hair on top—just sideburns and stubble in an irregular pattern cut to the scalp. The jock look, he still commands. There's an easy gait as he walks in.

"You're looking good, Mitch," I say.

"You're the one looking good. You've kept your shape much better than me. Family life does that. Bonnie and the two boys keep me quite busy, but eating on the run is what's keeping this..." Mitch grabs his belly, "...growing. I've started running to see if I can stop the middle-age spread. There's always some young Turk fresh out of law school who wants to be big swinging dick." He smirks.

"Thankfully, I work for myself," I reply. "I'm my own boss and there are no up-and-comers looking to steal my spotlight."

"Being a partner helps keep some of them at bay. But you still have to do the performance reviews and select who gets to wear the brass ring," Mitch says. "I'm starved. Where to?"

We both decide to go into town, to a place I love— the Wild Onion. After dinner, Mitch has a look of satisfaction written all over his face. He just oozes contentment from his pores.

"Food's wonderful," he says. "I'll have to keep this place in mind if I come back this way."

"Maggie and I used to come here. I always liked it more than she did."

Mitch nods. "I'm sorry about Maggie. You guys seemed so much in love."

"Thanks," I reply. "I actually followed her all the way down to Birmingham where her old man is a top attorney. We never made it to Berlin together, but I did get the chance to live there for a year and then a couple of stays throughout the years. I made really good friends with this couple, Ulrich and Lok. I even got a Master's degree in German from Georgetown University."

"That's great news," Mitch beams. "I met Bonnie in law school. We got married right after graduation and then the boys followed. She does part-time legal work for another law firm in Wilmington. She's a top notch real estate attorney. She's so good that the firm allows her to work part-time."

"Ah, the sweet life," I note.

"What about you, Gordon? Did you meet anyone after Maggie?" Mitch probes.

"No. Not really," I protest.

"Good lookin' guy like you, single? Hard to believe," Mitch muses with a slight challenge. He's probably thinking I'm hiding something.

"What can I say? It's hard to land this whale," I smile. "We should be going. You've got a big drive ahead of you tomorrow."

"Yes." Mitch stands. "I've enjoyed catching up. We should do better keeping in touch."

"That's a good idea," I reply. As I stand, I get a bit woozy.

"Hey. I think I better drive," Mitch says. "How many drinks did you have?"

"I..." trail off and work hard to focus. "I think five or six." The realization hits me between the eyes. Not sure why I've been drinking so much of late. Come to think of it, I've been drinking five to seven drinks every time I go out now.

I hand Mitch the keys, and we head to my place. The drive home is quiet, and soon my eyes grow heavy.

"There you go, buddy, back on your sofa," Mitch says and I snap awake.

"Already home?" I call out from the haze my head is lost in.

"Yeah," Mitch laughs. "Are you okay?" He sits beside me and drapes his arm across my shoulder. It feels comfortable.

I gaze up into his dark brown eyes and remember the good times in college. Mitch always put me in a good mood when he was around. His blowing me was icing on the cake.

Mitch leans forward and I taste his lips. I can feel my tongue and his dueling in our mouths.

We wrap our arms around one another and fall between the sofa and the coffee table. I feel my skin cooling as my clothes are removed. Mitch is as hairy as me, but he's got more silver in his chest hair. I nibble on his tit and lick the space between his pecs. I feel my legs go wide and his tongue instantly probes my ring. I'm in pure ecstasy. My sphincter lets go and I can feel his fingers inside me. With my legs bent over my head, his tongue and fingers dance inside my ring. God, I'm about to lose it. Pre-cum is oozing between my belly button and joy stick. I nearly black out when I realize that Mitch is deep inside me, riding me like a stallion on the Pony Express, desperately evading Indians to deliver the mail. Going postal is what my mind and body are doing. My college buddy, my married college buddy, is fucking me blind. To hell with this. If anyone is getting screwed, it's him.

I lock my legs around his grinding hips, then flex my back and twist him to the ground. His cock slides out of me. I'm kneeling above him, having pushed off. I see that he is face-down and his ass grinning back at me, so I split his cheeks apart with my hands and spit at the bull's eye. I watch my spit dribble down his crack. Using my fingers, I massage the moisture around and into his ring.

"Whoa, Tiger!" Mitch exclaims. He grabs something from under the sofa, arches back, does a torso twist, and grabs my cock in his hands. I feel a slippery mess cover my cock and something sliding over it.

"Be gentle," Mitch whispers as he kisses the rug.

I have no intention of being gentle. I mount Mitch as if he's a bitch in heat. I slam it inside him. I hear him yell and I push his face deeper into the rug. I set my hips to grind into his and jackhammer the side-walk. I feel the blood pounding in my face. I see a river of sweat running down my torso and splashing all over his backside. My breathing has become ragged and shallow. I dig my nails into his ass cheeks and plant a big thrust until I shoot the moon.

Mitch twists and kicks one leg over my head and I can see his heaving chest. I look down at my limp dick. It looks strange. The whole scene looks strange. He does a sit up and locks his lips on mine for a moment. As he goes back down, he hooks his right hand behind my neck and pulls me face forward. I open my mouth and his dick suddenly spikes me. Before I can come off his shaft, he's unloading everything he's got into the back of my throat. I spit most of it out but some feeds me.

"Hey, buddy. It's my time to go," a voice says, startling me awake.

"What?" I stammer. I'm stark naked on the living room floor and feel crust on my lips, chin, and neck. I sit up. I lock eyes on a fully clothed Mitch, now standing at the front door.

"Last night, you were an animal," Mitch grins. "I haven't been fucked that hard in God knows how many years. It's like you wanted to tear me a new one. You almost did, Kiddo."

"I...I..." just stammer. The bang of the drum is still ringing between my ears. It's hard to concentrate. Thoughts abort as I try to grab them.

"Don't worry—we were safe. Even though I don't let guys come inside me even with a condom on. Consider yourself lucky," Mitch beams. "I'll keep in touch. Thanks for everything, Gordy." With that, he swings the door closed and is gone. A few minutes later, I hear the car start and drive away.

What the fuck happened? I sit up and scan the living room floor. I see two spent condoms on my left side. So Mitch carries condoms and lube with him. I don't expect to see him again. His farewell sounds too much like a "Let's do lunch" request. You just know that'll never happen. Wow. I remember him screwing me and then me mounting him, but that's about it. I better clean this mess up. I need a long, hot shower. I don't think I'll ever be clean again. I really didn't want to go there with Mitch again. We've gone from blow buddies to asshole buddies.

Asshole buddies—Brady's favorite phrase. Guys didn't think they'd have sex with other guys, but it happened. The phrase, asshole buddy, describes the "non-gay" sex that men have with other men. It's viewed as charity work, a helping hand for when women aren't around. Well, that's how we justified it. There was one cardinal rule, however, with asshole buddies: no intimacy, because that would be too faggy. Sex is what men do. Relationships are only between members of the opposite sex. How funny, now that Brady is in a gay, committed, monogamous relationship in Portland. He has gotten quite far from that battlefield.

29

"Thanks for coming over to help me pack," I say to Jerry as he enters my one-bedroom condo. It's now cluttered with boxes and piles of my stuff. My life has been taken apart, piece by piece, and re-assembled in makeshift stacks waiting for something, anything, to happen.

"Of course! You're my best friend. Even though I think you're crazy for moving to Boone. It's in the middle of nowhere, Vy," Jerry observes.

"I know. But I think I need to take the chance. I'm scared that there might not be that many more. What's a place if not for the people? I've been living here for like, forever, and I still haven't found the one. Why would that make a difference? I think a shock to the system might help break me from my habits and routines. Anyhow, the worst thing that could happen is if Gordon didn't want anything to do with me. At least I'd still get my Master's."

"No," Jerry replies. "The worst thing is that nothing happens and no degree."

"True."

"And if you want to break old habits, why not stay and move to another neighborhood?"

"I think I need more than just a neighborhood change," I counter.

"Okay." Jerry admits defeat. He looks around the space. "Hey, you are not de-cluttering enough! I see lots of stuff with 'Goodwill' stamped on them. Do you need all these books, magazines, clothing, furniture, paintings, and all these knick-knacks?" He sweeps his arms across the room like windmills in Holland.

"It's tough to let things go," I reply. "I've got so much emotional baggage associated with them. Every time I see my stuff I can't help but think I'll wear it again; or I'll sit down and read that book again; or I'll need that again because it'll solve a problem." I smile and survey the stacks taking up residence in the room.

"Aren't you looking for a fresh start? Hard to do that when you're weighed down with your past," Jerry says.

"My past?" I exclaim. "I do declare, you're besmirching my reputation, you hateful, hateful bitch!"

"Ha. Let's see if we can't divide these piles in half."
A glint of mischievousness sparkles in Jerry's green
eyes. I grow concerned.

Eight hours later, I remove half of what I am taking
to Boone to the yard sale and giveaway pile. Some
things Jerry pries out of my hands, over my death
grip. I clutch some items so hard I think I bleed. He
keeps telling me to let it go, let it go, like a child's lull-
aby.

"So, when are you house shopping?" Jerry asks. He
then quickly adds, "...with your new hubby?" A wicked
serial smile pops onto his face.

"Bitch," I say with a hint of amusement.

"Well? What's the 411?"

"I take a week off," I say, "starting next week. I'll
drive down Saturday and be back the following Sunday. I'm staying with Gordon."

Jerry's eyebrow arches up. "You're what?"

"I know, I know. But it should be fine. Gordon isn't
going to ravish me, dammit. But I'm going to look
damn good in everything I drape over my body. I want
him to see what he's missing." I strike a few poses.

"You go, Madonna! Give 'em your like-a-virgin routine," Jerry howls.

"I do hope there ain't snow," I remark.

"It's late February in the mountains. If there's no
snow, it's going to be colder than a witch's tit," Jerry
laughs.

"I hate the cold. The things we do for the hope of love," I offer up to whatever old gods might still be listening to humanity's pleas for salvation.

The week goes screaming by like a banshee in search of vengeance. I'm flying solo. The seven-hour drive practically kills me. I start the appreciation chant for Craig who drove all those times. As I get closer, the sky thickens into concrete slabs, and chunks of white pummel the car.

"You made it, Vy!" I exclaim as I open the door. The poor guy is covered in white powder.

"I thought the drive would be the death of me. Not only is it snowing but it's freakin' cold," he whines.

"Come in and warm up. I'll help you get your stuff in a bit," I offer.

"That's kind of you, but I'd like to get it now so I won't have to go out in this again today."

"Okay," I say. I fetch Vy a black jacket and brown, dusty boots. Before I close the door behind him, I see how high the snow has fallen—it's already six inches on the ground, and the weather report calls for another six.

"Anything else?" I ask as I help Vy carry his bags to his room.

"Just another bag and that's it. Would you mind locking the car after you get it?"

"Okay. I'll see you back inside."

Gordon moves with a spring in his step. I've noticed how he practically runs everywhere we go, as if airborne. There's a *joie de vivre* in his demeanor. I find it engaging and intoxicating. He's sometimes a big kid, whereas I'm so serious all the time. I'm drawn to his carefree persona, which radiates outward and burns away indecision and doubt. I'd like to live that way, out loud, to be heard, to be outside conformity, to be a maker of joyous sound. This must be how it feels to be found.

I'm too tired for evening small talk and beg off to sleep. I notice Gordon stays up and conducts his work in his home office. He tells me that he doesn't mind. I mentally note how solitary this feels, even though I know he's as much of a socialite as I am.

"What are you looking for in a rental?" I ask Vy as we sit around the table for a quick breakfast. He has been up for at least a couple of hours. I normally don't meet the day until after 9:00 AM.

"I'd like it to be within walking distance of the university and hopefully living around an older group of students. I remember being an undergrad and all the noise I caused. A place with other graduate students would be ideal."

"That rules out most of my stuff," I laugh. "I rent to a lot of undergrads. I may have a place or two but they are a bit farther away. People who take them tend to be professionals rather than students walking to school." I look into Vy's brown eyes and wonder. I'm surprised that he's actually moving here. I know he says it's for school, but I can't help thinking there's something more. "Much of what is available, especially around the university, is geared to students. There's not much architectural panache," I say with a hint of irony.

Gordon couldn't have been more right. Over the next few days, all I see are drive-in motels masquerading as apartments. I hate the idea that you have to go through the bedroom to get to the bathroom. I especially despise that floor plan.

I sit next to Gordon as we drive through one of the mountain passes that pretends to be a road. I look into the darkness and wonder why I'm here. Nothing I see is remotely desirable. I appreciate Gordon going out of his way to show me around town. I didn't think it would be this hard to find a suitable place. I am suddenly reminded of my early life in the States, when we first moved to the mountains. I remember how hard it was to find a home then. Nothing felt right. Nothing was Vietnam.

"Hey, Vy. What's the matter?" I ask, concerned. I see a couple of tears sparkle as they roll down Vy's cheek. That seems to snap him out of thought.

"Nothing," he says abruptly. "I'm just thinking how hard it's been to find a place. I didn't really think it would take this long."

"We'll keep looking until you find a place you feel at home in."

"Thank you so much for doing this, Gordon. I don't want to be a bother."

"No problem," I assure him. "What is it that you don't like? Do you have an idea of what you want?"

How can I tell Gordon that his town lacks aesthetics? The lack of design is killing my spirits. There's nothing to satiate my culture-hungry body. The one man who lights a fire within me isn't even in dating mode and scarcely notices me beyond a friend. Blowing Rock provides a cultural milieu but it's for wealthy weekenders. I am so far from that ideal, that I participate as a social bystander, like a homeless person looking in.

The silence fills the space between us. I see the snow picking up intensity out the window. I hear there's another five inches coming. Hey, Mother Nature, there're already 12 on the ground, you can stop now! I silently scream. She must be in a foul mood.

"It's hard to pinpoint..." I say finally. "Most of the apartment buildings remind me of my family's summer vacations, when we piled into the station wagon for cross-country road trips and stayed in roadside motels. The places you've shown me so far didn't feel like homes but motels for lost families. I also despise the bathroom entrance from the bedroom. I don't want visitors going through my sleeping space to pee or shit." I feel like that last comment was a bit too harsh.

"Wow. You really are taking this seriously," Gordon remarks. "But now I have a sense of what you're looking for. I might have a place we can check out. I'll need to call the owner. She's a family friend. I'll find out if her place is still available."

"Thank you," I say. "I don't mean to be so difficult."

"No problem," Gordon says.

Suddenly, I feel the car jerk to the right as the back wheels begin moving ahead of the front wheels. I see Gordon turn the steering wheel into the direction of the slide. The car pitches and begins to twirl. All I can think of at that moment is my life ending on a cold, dark and lonely mountain pass. This Disney ride makes me sick. In a desperate bid to stay on the road and not go off into the ravine, Gordon hits the accelerator and spins the wheel in the opposite direction, causing the car to lurch off the road. We slide to a stop facing the wrong direction, but at least we're in a ditch on the mountain side and not down the ravine.

"Are you okay?" Gordon asks, panting.

"If you count the fact that I'm about to shit myself, then yes," I respond. I draw in my breath to stop hyperventilating. I hate the cold and particularly ice. Some of my worst accidents took place when I hit ice patches. I can hear the back tires spinning as Gordon gives the car gas. He's rocking the car from forward to reverse to get some traction. "Should we hike to someone's home and see about calling a tow truck? I have AAA," I offer.

"No. I'll get the car out of the ditch," Gordon says a bit forcefully. He then hops out of the car and pops open the trunk. I step out to see what he's doing. "We mountain folk rely on ourselves to get out of jams," Gordon proudly announces, pulling out a snow shovel and a bag of cat litter. "We're self-sufficient."

Okay. I've hit a nerve. I watch Gordon dig a space under the back tires and fill it with the cat litter. He's going to prove just how self-sufficient he is...at my expense.

"Hey, would you drive the car forward on my mark? I'm going to push it from behind to clear the ditch," Gordon explains.

"Sure," I respond. I hear the signal, put the car into drive, and hit the pedal. I can hear the tires spinning but feel no traction. I stop and stick my head out the window.

"Dammit!" Gordon yells. "Vy, when I give the signal again, I want you to go in reverse." He walks to the front of the car, plants his palms on the hood and gives me the signal. The back tires just spin. "Dammit. Fuck," he yells to the heavens.

"I don't mind walking," I gently offer. I see he's getting hot under the collar. He wouldn't be out here if it wasn't for me.

"No!" he screams. He immediately calms himself down. "Sorry. But I know we can get out of this. This isn't major."

"Okay," I calmly remark. I decide to keep my mouth shut. Asking for help in Gordon's world must mean he's helpless and I get the feeling he'd rather die than admit that. I hope I don't freeze to death while he figures that out. I see Gordon digging more space between the back tires and spreading more cat litter. He is now laying down a blanket behind the tires.

"On my signal, in reverse," he commands and moves into position. He gives the signal and I punch it. The car lurches backward and Gordon hits the snow face first.

"Oh my god! Are you okay?" I run to Gordon who's looking up at me, covered in black slush.

"Hot damn! We did it," he exclaims. "We're out of the ditch and back on the road."

I can hear the smugness in Gordon's voice and the triumph of his self-sufficiency. We pile back into the car and off we go. I'm never so grateful to be pulling the covers over my head.

The next morning, we decide to eat a simple breakfast: cereal with assorted fruit. I made sure to bring soy milk for myself. Some of the things I take for granted in the big city would leave me high and dry here.

"Vy," Gordon says.

"Yes?" I look into Gordon's eyes, wondering if I'll ever find a home. It's already Friday. I've barely recovered from the near-death experience last night. No more Disney mountain rides, I mentally shout.

"Before you leave on Sunday, we'll find you a home," he announces. "I got in touch with the family friend about her place and it's still available. We can take a look at it this afternoon. It's a bit farther of a walk to campus but not much. I'd say 15 to 20 minutes."

Great, I think. When there are icy death traps and snow banks at every turn, a walk in the park will do me good. I can practice staying warm while the frostbite starts at my tips and works itself to my center, like lethal ivy covering up stone and brick for all eternity. I smile back. Gordon is doing his best and I'm despondent.

The afternoon arrives on the sun's back. Most of the roads are cleared and the snow mounds are piled high to the sides. It reminds me of the frozen version of Moses parting the Red Sea.

"The apartment is in that house?" I ask as we drive up to a two-story bungalow.

"Yep. When Sue bought the house a few years back, she divided it into three apartments. To get to the one she's got available, you enter on the south side. It's kind of cool that she put entrances to the north, east, and south. North and south share the back while east has the front," he explains.

"That's interesting. I like it because it doesn't remind me of a roadside motel." I flash a devilish smile towards Gordon.

The bungalow puts me in a better mood. "Plus, you get two parking spaces," Gordon continues. "Other guests will have to find parking on the street. If they live in Boone they'll have a parking decal. Anyone else will have to fend for themselves."

We step inside and find ourselves in a mud room that leads into a galley kitchen with an eating nook, opening to the living room. There's a half bath under the stairs, which lead up to a large bedroom with huge windows facing west. Even now, the sun is banking west and radiating the bedroom splendidly. The apartment is large—its square-footage probably takes up half the back side of the building. This must have been a grand residence in its day. It has many odd angles, surprising nooks, and architectural flourishes.

I swing my arms around Gordon, pull him in, and give him a big hug and a kiss on the lips. "As long as the rent isn't outrageous, it's a done deal," I say with enthusiasm. "You've done it!" We stay embraced for a couple of extra moments before we separate. He feels so good pressed against me.

"I thought you'd like the place. The rent is quite reasonable and Sue is willing to make it work. You're a friend after all," he contently remarks.

"She doesn't have to give it away," I protest.

"Dontcha worry about that. She ain't givin' anything away," Gordon laughs.

After the paperwork and money exchange hands, I pack my belongings and prepare to leave Gordon's. "Thanks for everything, Gordon. I couldn't have done it without you," I say.

"No problem. I'll even help you move in. Just let me know when. Who would have thought that when I asked you if you would return, not only would the answer be yes, but you'd actually be moving here," he beams. "It feels good knowing you and I will be close. I can tell that we are going to have some good times together."

With that thought, I knew that I had made the right decision to come.

30

"That's it Jerry," I say. "The truck's loaded. Thanks again for driving the car down with me. That saves me from getting a car hitch."

We are standing on the street in front of my condo building. I decided to rent the place until I'm sure where I want to live. The property management company's cleaning crew arrives tomorrow. They'll take care of everything for a nice 15% of the rent.

"I'm doing this all for you," Jerry wistfully says. "I still can't believe that you're moving. My best friend is on some wild hunt for the elusive Mr. Fox." Jerry rolls his eyes.

"I need to follow this path and find out where the journey takes me. Plus, you'll meet Gordon," I say with a hint of mischievousness. Jerry is hurt that I'm leaving. Our friendship sustains us. We've been through quite a lot over the last few years, especially all that rot around Michael. I'm sad to even think about us being apart.

"Oh goody! I can meet the man who's stealing my best friend," Jerry exclaims.

"I'm sorry. Your friendship means the world. This must be taking a toll," I gently add with a hug.

"I want you to be happy. If he hurts you, I'll cut the bitch." I can hear Jerry's thoughts turning like gears as he considers the likelihood of Gordon hurting me.

"If the truck is all locked up, let's head to my house," Jerry says. "We'll eat, reminisce, and be on the road at the crack of dawn."

The crack of dawn shits us out of bed. We float the Colombian coffee cartels, considering the amount of java injected into us. We laugh how we need intravenous hookups to stay awake. Our seven-hour journey down the yellow brick road takes nine before we roll in.

"Nice place. I like it," Jerry comments. "So it's actually a triplex and not a single person's home?" As Jerry tours the space, I can see him cast an adoring gaze over the façade.

"Yes," I respond. "My entrance is on the south side. I'll go pull the truck closer and you can park in that space over there." I point to my very own parking space—a luxury I didn't have in the city. It's the small joys that can add the steam to your walk.

"It looks even better inside. It feels like a residence and not a sterile apartment," Jerry pipes as he wanders around. I can hear him walk upstairs and do the twirl, making sure he grabs a quick peek. I wonder if he is looking for bodies.

"Thankfully," I shout in agreement. "Most of what I saw reminded me of roadside motels where my family would stay on our cross-country vacations. Yuck. You drive your car right to the front window of your room. Of course the hallway is the outdoor balcony. I found it all quite depressing," I add.

"You're too Cosmo for most of this," Jerry replies.

"You're right. I think Gordon caught me crying on that apartment hunting safari," I confirm.

"Ah, Vy. It can be so disappointing leaving civilization."

"Hey there," Jerry and I turn toward Gordon's voice. He's brought Jeff and Skip along with him.

"Hey, guys! Great to see you!" I exclaim and hug them. As we break, I reach over and pull Jerry closer. "This is my best friend, Jerry. I'm going to miss him terribly. He's a great guy. He helps me out when I've lost my way. He's the voice of reason when he's not leading me off a cliff." I smile. Best not to cry right now, I tell myself.

Six hours later, all the boxes are stacked into the apartment. I'm glad that someone else decided to climb those stairs to put the boxes labeled, "boudoir" into the master.

"You've got quite the number of boxes," Skip says. "I should send you my chiropractor's bill. You've got enough stuff to last the end of the world."

"This is only half of his shit," Jerry mocks. "Be thankful I got him to get rid of it or you'd be movin' it. Poor boy has an awful hard time letting stuff go. And it's not always stuff, if you know what I mean."

"Stop spilling my tea," I command, light-hearted. The other guys roll their eyes. "These guys don't need to know that I'm a hoarder."

"Did you say whore?" Jerry laughs.

"What are your plans for tomorrow, Vy?" I ask, trying to deflect the kidding around at Vy's expense. I see relief blooming on his face. I get a kick out of watching his emotions surface, do a vogue, and shimmer away.

"I plan to return the truck and then show Jerry around. You guys interested in meeting up?" he offers.

"Let's meet up for lunch and I'll tag along, if you don't mind."

"I won't be able to join you boys," Jeff chimes in.

"I can join for dinner, but not lunch," Skip adds. "I need to be at the shop."

"By the way, have you been upstairs, Vy?" I ask.

"No, not yet... why?"

"There might be something you missed when you were here before," I smile. We follow Vy up the stairs and into the master bedroom, me with a devilish grin on my face.

"Oh My God!" I exclaim. During the entire move in, I never once went upstairs. As I enter the master, I am shocked to see a full bedroom set with mattress, box spring, frame, headboard, side table, and six-drawer chest. The only thing missing are the sheets. I look back to the threshold as the guys pile in.

"You like?" I hear Gordon say in a seductive, playful voice. He's wearing the biggest shit-ass grin I've ever seen.

"Yes!" I beam at Gordon, wanting more than ever to kiss him full on the lips.

"I remember you saying you weren't moving your bedroom set," Gordon explains. "Sue was sending this set to storage so I asked her to leave it for you. It's one less thing to buy."

I can't help myself. I spring into Gordon's arms and plant a kiss on his face. He blushes and then I blush. The other guys' eyes arch and a few sly grins appear. "I'm caught up in the moment," I say in my defense, but it is impossible to counter the snickering.

Jerry and I hit the sack early and sleep practically until lunch's doorstep the next day. Thankfully, I found some old sheets in a closet, so he and I share the mattress overnight.

As we wait for Gordon, I see Jerry smirk.

"What's all this about?" I inquire.

"I'm just remembering yesterday when you decided to shove your tongue down Gordon's mouth. You see a bed and you go commando," Jerry laughs.

"You bitch," I smile. "As I said, I was caught up in the moment."

"Of course you were, Blanche," Jerry deadpans. "Should I leave and give you a private moment when he gets here?"

"Stop it. You're so BAD!" I exclaim in the most exasperated manner I can muster. I did let my emotions run away. Usually, I can keep my passions locked down. Gordon's habit of getting past my defenses is like a slow trickle of water. It seems inconsequential, but the constant exposure wears the rock smooth.

"Howdy, guys!" Gordon announces, and then spots the relief on my face. "Sorry I'm late. I was checking in on a neighbor who's having a tough time."

"What's wrong?" Jerry asks.

"Nancy has a disease that makes her bones brittle. She's trying to hang on so her grandchildren will remember her," he explains. "She's afraid that they are too young to create fully, realized memories of her."

"That is so sad," I say. "She wants a touch of immortality through remembrance. That's so Vietnamese. You gain immortality through your family. They carry you with them into the future."

"The disease has progressed rapidly, rendering her bed-ridden. She must be very careful. Anything could cause her bones to break. I couldn't stand to be in that condition," Gordon says. "Put a bullet in my brain if I ever can't take care of myself."

"Well, she's trying to hang on," I add. "As you say, she wants her grandchildren to remember her, even if it means they remember her bed-ridden."

"I never want that to happen," Gordon repeats, shaking his head. "NEVER. EVER. EVER. If you won't put a bullet in my brain then you can't spend my money keeping me alive." Gordon's sudden outburst has us all perplexed.

"Sorry," he says, calming down. "I get worked up when I think about being an invalid and having to be taken care of."

I look over at Jerry. We make the connection to a comment I made about Gordon's need to be in control. We let the moment build a castle of silence, allowing Gordon to gather his wits. He takes a sip from his gin and tonic.

"What are you guys planning for the rest of the day?" Gordon finally asks in a much calmer tone. The gin has taken the edge right off the top.

"I'm thinking of showing Jerry around," I answer. "You know, do the tour of Boone, Blowing Rock, and the Blue Ridge Parkway. Care to be our tour guide?" I smile. Please say yes. I like having you around.

"Ok," he replies. "I like showing off the high country. Of course there isn't much. But what we have is what brings people back. If you're not careful, you'll move here, like Vy," Gordon says, and winks at Jerry.

"There's no fear of that happening," Jerry laughs, "unless you have something in a size 9." I kick him under the table.

"Ready if you guys are?" I interject as I see Gordon making the connection. He smirks.

"Let's see what this place has to offer, even though the main attraction could be right in front of you," Jerry deadpans and I catch Gordon looking at him with a puzzled look etched across his brow.

"There're surprises everywhere," I exclaim to distract Gordon from the innuendos that Jerry is tossing around. I sweep my arms out and across the air, skywriting an imaginary message. I send a look of bedevilment straight through Jerry like whalers harpooning their prize.

"Yes, surprises and attractions throwing themselves at you," Jerry jeers back. He's having a field day. It's like recess time at school for him.

Gordon is hard at work deciphering the coded language, looking to figure out the combination. He keeps darting his eyes from Jerry to me, me to Jerry. I should have known that Jerry couldn't help himself. It's too easy, like taking candy from a rug rat, or shooting a rifle into a barrel of fishes. You get what you want but with a lot of collateral damage. Jerry is rubbing in his disapproval of me leaving. I hope he comes around at some point.

"Jerry, when are you heading back?" Gordon asks Jerry. He wants back into this conversation.

"I think we're leaving tomorrow?" Jerry replies and looks right at me.

"Yeah, we're leaving tomorrow right after lunch. I come back on Tuesday. Thankfully, classes don't start until next Monday," I answer, right on cue. The intervention short-circuits Jerry's put-Vy-in-the-hot-seat syndrome. I'm sure relief spills across my face and Gordon picks it up. I notice that he has been paying close attention. I often wonder what's going on behind his blue eyes.

"It's been great fun showing you guys around," Gordon says, hopping out of my car. "I like getting the chance to play tour guide."

"We enjoyed having you," I say and then realize that must have sounded like a double entendre. A smirk explodes on Jerry's lips. Even Gordon is having some fun with it, with that oh-my-god look. I feel the heat rise in my cheeks.

"Look at that. A red sky at evening. Isn't that sailor's delight?" Gordon says, smiling. He's laughing at the red in my face, I'm sure of it.

"Yes, I think that's a sailor's delight," I concur, ignoring the potential meaning behind his words.

"Sailor. Did someone mention a sailor?" Jerry struts his chest out and blows his body bigger. "Oh. You're just tryin' to get a rise." We all laugh.

"Hey," Gordon says. "I want to let you know I can't make dinner. Tell Skip I'm sorry but duty calls. I have a couple of rentals that are misbehaving and I've got to put a stop to it before it gets out of hand." Gordon keeps his eyes steadied on me as he says this.

"Oh. Damn. Sorry that you won't be joining us, Gordon." I show a bit too much disappointment. I've certainly got Jerry's keen attention.

"Don't worry, Jerry," Gordon adds. "Skip will show you a good time." He then hugs us both and bids us farewell.

"There goes your future ex," Jerry deadpans.

"What an awful thing to say." I punch Jerry in the shoulder in a mock fighting stance.

"Ouch! Watch yo' self, bitch. I'll cut choo."

"Serves you right." I further press the point. "I don't think he even sees me like THAT. We'd have to date first before we'd be exes," I ruefully add.

"You're right. I don't think Gordon is in dating mode. I'm not sure why you guys ended up kissing that night."

"I don't know either. For the briefest of moments, I think I made it past his defenses. Afterwards, a moat, a wall, a guard popped up, cutting me off at the pass.

I'll never be able to get that close again." After a moment I blurt: "I'm not sure why I'm here."

We ride in silence to the restaurant.

"There you guys are," Skip says. "Where is Gordon?" He does a quick scan around the restaurant as if we're hiding Gordon in our pocket. As he sits at our table, he shakes his hair and pulls the bangs over his ears.

"He couldn't make it," I say with a hint of sadness.

"Duty calls," Jerry interjects. I smile at Jerry. He does lay the fire down right where I need the most cover and protection. Truly a special friend, I'm going to miss him. Hold it together, Vy, or you'll start crying here at the table.

"Work. You'd think the world would end if he didn't immediately handle whatever shit the rentals throw at him," Skip says. "I'm not the only one to suggest that he keep more regular hours. The way he does it, he's always on. He gets up in the middle of the night, especially weekends, to shut off parties. He answers his phone immediately; says playing phone tag just makes things take longer. The invention of the cell phone has made him a 24-hour schlep."

Wow, I think Skip's sporting major frustrations with Gordon. I wonder where that's coming from. "How's your day been?" I ask to change the subject.

"Fine. Shoppers in this town really need some manners. I like the French way. When customers enter a store, they actually say hello to the shopkeeper."

"Who would have thought that the French would have better manners than us?" Jerry opines as he winks at me.

"Some things the French do better," Skip dismisses. "Enough shop talk. How was hanging out with Gordon? Did he show you what makes this place special? And believe me, it's not the people."

For a quick moment I think he's serious. Then I realize that's just how Skip phrases his barbs. "You did decide to hide out here," I drop.

"Yes! Do, tell us how you ended up here?" Jerry jumps all over it.

Skip's eyebrow arches and he slowly turns his head with as much disdain as it will support. "Oh, waiter! More drinks. Bring me a double." He grins impishly. I suddenly get the feeling that we are about to travel down the rabbit hole.

Jerry is sitting on the edge of his seat, waiting for Skip to spill his tea. Skip is milking this for all its worth. He'll wait until the moment ripens before sharing. He loves to make sure the audience is about to get up and walk away, or scream in anticipation.

"When I was in Charlotte, I was out of control. I drank my way through one party after another. Some of the worst things I did, someone else will have to tell you about them. I don't have the brain cells to recall

all the chaos I caused. In one of my last lucid moments, I remember thinking: if I don't leave, I'm going six feet under."

"My. My," Jerry remarks.

"So," Skip continues, "I packed up, sold everything, and moved to Blowing Rock. Now I run a little garden gift store there. It keeps me off the street. I just drink now." Skip salutes his drink. "I've found some modicum of peace here."

"Are you dating anyone?" I ask, since I'm going to be here a while and the object of my affection that brought me here is blind to my feelings. I'd like to know how a single gay man copes with Boone's dating life.

"It sucks. All you've got are weekenders and couples fishing for thirds. Singles that you want to date are endangered species around here. You'd be struck by lightning before you stumble upon an eligible bachelor."

"Isn't Gordon single?" Jerry throws out. I can't believe Jerry just went there. I shoot him a nasty, dirty look before I smile at Skip. Yet, deep down, I'm glad he did.

"Single, yes. Dating, I don't think so. Then again, that would be a question for Craig." Skip drops the atomic bomb right in the middle of the table.

"Craig? He's got something to do with this?" I cautiously proceed. The mushroom cloud is blocking my view and my insides are liquefying.

"Well," Skip lowers his voice, "you've got to promise me that this stays here, okay?"

"Okay," we both affirm.

"I think Craig and Gordon are having a thing. I've confronted both of them and they deny it. But every bone in my body says otherwise. What upsets me the most? Craig says I should consider dating Gordon, but he knows damn well that Gordon's not available. I feel played. The only person I feel sorry for is Tom." Skip scorches the earth with his longing and pain. I see Skip would consider Gordon, but he must feel like a cast-off from a play that he's not even allowed to watch from the audience.

The next day we drive back to D.C. I seriously question why I'm moving here now. Jerry is mostly quiet. He offers me his sympathy and hopes that getting the degree is enough. I reminisce on the interactions I've witnessed between Craig and Gordon. I conclude that they do act like a couple. I notice Gordon drops everything when Craig's around. He answers his calls and always returns them if he misses one. Craig is behind the wall I want to be behind. Since my need comes on strongly when I'm in Gordon's presence, I wonder if it blinds me to the non-verbal indiscretions passing between Craig and Gordon. All I know for certain is that it's going to be a long year and a half.

31

"Hey Gordon, are you around?" Craig asks as he walks through my front door. "The door is unlocked."

"Craig. Good to see you. How was the trip down from D.C.?" I warmly greet him as I enter the front foyer.

"It sucked as usual. It's too damn long," Craig moans as he hugs me. "Have you seen Vy lately? We haven't talked all that much since he moved in." I can hear wistfulness in his voice.

"Not really," I answer. "I thought I would, but except for a couple of drive-bys, I haven't seen him at all. When he got back from D.C., I saw him once over the weekend for lunch. Then, school started and pretty much nothing. I figure it's the adjustment. It can't be easy coming from a big city like D.C. to a small town like Boone," I acknowledge.

"I'll send him a message that I'm in town. Maybe this weekend we can all get together and hang out," Craig says with hope shining through the pauses.

"I'll let him know that you and an old army buddy, Brady, are in town this weekend," I offer. "Vy told me to let him know the 411 and he'd make it."

"Brady?" Craig wonders aloud.

"You know, Brady and his partner, John. I've mentioned them to you. They live in Portland, Oregon. I told you about that guy, Mitch, who I met after Brady picked him out of the lineup. The reunion of Charlie Can Company turned out to be a pivot point in my life," I explain. "I finally got some of the guys to come out to the East Coast. They should be arriving later this evening from Charlotte. By the way, I have you in the other guest room. I'm giving the larger one to Brady and John."

"What? I'm being kicked to the curb?" Craig laughs. "I see where our friendship ends." He then hands off two of his bags to me in the foyer. He's traveling a bit heavy this time.

"Spoiled, aren't we?" I smile. "Be thankful I have room for you or you'd be down at your house kicking out the rental this weekend." I drop off his bags in the smaller guest room and ask, "Why all the bags?"

"I'm staying through the following weekend when the house isn't rented," Craig explains. "I can move over there next Thursday. That lets me take care of some repairs and fix-ups that I've been meaning to do for a while."

"Is Tom joining you?" I ask, wondering how he's going to respond.

"No. He can't get the time. As you know, as long as there is a phone, I can work from pretty much anywhere."

"It's been too long since Tom's last visit," I add. "Where does he go now?" I watch for clues as to whether Craig is going to give his answer straight or bent. I'm never sure of the pitch, even though he expects me to catch the ball.

"He mainly hangs with his family in the eastern part of the state. If not there, he heads to Provincetown in the summer. He doesn't like Rehoboth Beach; it's practically D.C. with sand. The last time we went, you might as well have stayed in D.C. The only other flavor is a Philly contingent mixed in for good measure."

I nod, deciding that he's telling me the truth.

"What do you have to drink?" he asks.

"Whatever is in the upper cabinet and the freezer," I offer. I decide to continue pressing him about Tom. "So Tom hunts new grounds? What does that mean for you guys?" I watch Craig like a barnyard owl who has spotted a field mouse.

"It sucks," Craig says as he makes a gin and tonic. He takes a couple of swigs before continuing. "The last couple of years, we've been dancing around the edges of a box, which neither of us wanted to get inside or stay outside of. We'd need a team of lawyers to split us apart. We're trying to make the relationship work. It just flows and ebbs."

"What happened between us was a one-time event," I offer as a defense. I can see Craig looking right through me. We both momentarily flash to the night when one thing led to another. We had initially messed around but never had any actual sex, until...

We were out doing our usual drinking, a little eating, and then more drinking. As a lark, we went skinny dipping in my hot tub. We were laughing and carrying on, and then it happened. Our tongues were darting in between our mouths and our raging hard-ons were dueling with each other as we mashed our bodies together. In quick succession, I bent Craig over the side of the tub, spread his cheeks with my tongue, probed his hole with my finger, and then speared him. We were unsafe but we've both tested numerous times since and are thankfully negative. I shot my load all over his ass and then he gave me a facial. When we finished, we washed up in the hot tub and collapsed into separate beds.

"Tom confronted me about our shenanigans in the hot tub. I thought we were discreet that evening," Craig laments as he looks to his feet. "Someone must have told him. Someone must have seen us." Craig makes eye contact with me. I know he thinks I may have inadvertently said something. I've never brought up the subject.

"You know, some of that evening is missing," I say, focusing us on the central issue. While banging, we were tightly enmeshed in each other's hold. We would never have known if someone else was around, spying on us. Hell. We did it outside in the open. There's no telling who saw us. A year later and it's still casting ripples.

"All water under the bridge," Craig remarks with a touch of sadness. There's a forlorn air tinged with nostalgia hanging between us. He emphasizes his mood with a shake of his head. "The irony is that we put together rules for a narrow opening in our relationship for extracurricular activities, either together or solo. Yet, this event is the equivalent of a nuke. I don't really understand why this upsets Tom so much. We've been together for more than 20 years. Relationships like ours have ups and downs. I sometimes wonder if ours has finally run its course and demands a new path with new players, new beginnings and new endings."

A knock at the door interrupts Craig. We both look at each other. I realize its Brady.

"You look great, Gordon!" Brady exclaims as he hugs me and Craig. "This is John, the love of my life," he says to Craig when they pull apart.

"You guys have anything else for me to carry?" I inquire when I notice only two suitcases.

"Nope," John says. "We travel light. I hate checking bags and then waiting at the carousel of doom, wondering if the bags make it in one piece, multiple pieces, or no pieces at all."

"John's practically a Nazi about it," Brady says. "Since we are only here through Monday, John refuses to even consider an extra bag."

"You know it, Hon," John smiles. "We would have to be gone for more than a week, and even then, we'd have to seriously consider if we really need it." I look at Craig who just rolls his eyes.

"Hey, follow me," I say. "I'll show you your room." When we get to the end of the hallway, I motion them to the left in the larger guest room, the one that shares the same wall with the master.

"Guys, I'm going to bed," Craig announces. "Tomorrow night's dinner should be fun, if everybody shows. You guys are going to have a great time here." And with that, Craig melts away.

I notice Brady and John eye casting. "Our friend, Vy, moved here for grad school," I say, guessing at their unspoken questions. "But we really haven't hung out. He's gone MIA. He did mention, though, that he'd join us if he can get away from his studies." I hope so. I miss talking to him. We always seem to have a lot to say to each other. I bid the couple goodnight and retire to my office to wrap a few things up before bed.

The next day is filled with conversation, as Brady and John fill me in on their West Coast life. I admire the give-and-take in their relationship. I swear they light up like Christmas trees when they're around each other. I find myself telling them all about Vy, the big city boy who grew up in the Virginia mountains.

"So where is this mysterious Vy?" Brady asks as we wait for our dinner.

I look at Craig and then back to Brady and John. "He hasn't called to say that he isn't showing. He's not the kind of guy who flakes out without warning," I say.

"Are you guys still waiting on one more?" a young female waiter asks.

"Maybe we should order appetizers," Craig offers and then orders himself another drink.

As the appetizers appear, so does Vy, as if the food conjured him up.

"I'm sorry," he says, "I left my cell phone at the apartment and then got caught up with one of my professors." He looks sincerely flustered.

I didn't mean to be late. But there's a part of me that didn't want to come and see the accused. Why do I really care? It's not like Gordon promised me anything. He's practically gone out of his way to show me there's nothing more than friendship. If Craig wants a side dish with Gordon, then who am I to say anything about that? That's between Craig and Tom. Now that I'm here, I've got to put all that aside and enjoy myself. Just remember to breathe, Vy.

"Glad you could make it, Vy," Craig exclaims. "I've missed our talks." I can hear a hint of remorse within that comment. I too miss our conversations, just like I miss Gordon's. I can't have any distractions, though. I'm here to get my degree and then move on.

"Good to see you guys," I smile. I then turn my attention to the couple. "Hi. I'm Vy," I say and extend my hand.

"My bad," Gordon interjects. "I should have introduced you. This is Brady and his partner, John. They're staying the weekend. I've got a full house."

"It's a pleasure meeting you both," I remark as I sit down and order an iced tea. I then help myself to the nacho appetizer. "How do you know Gordon?" I ask. I'm looking to have a quick dinner and then beg off because of school.

"Oh, we go way, way, way back," Brady chuckles. I see John rolling his eyes. He must know this story. "We're asshole buddies that reunited at our platoon's reunion some years back."

"Brady!" I hear Gordon exclaim. "You've got to explain that REMARK." I smirk at Gordon's angst.

"Don't get your knickers in a knot," Brady says, dismissing Gordon. "In 'Nam, that's what we called guys who were close, with an undertone of being even... closer. At the time, Gordon and I were best buds—but not that close. I was still chasing skirts and so was Gordon. Now there are guys who are asshole buddies, if you know what I mean." Brady's eyebrow arches. We all laugh.

Again I hear a reference to 'Nam. "So you also fought in 'Nam?" I inquire.

"Yeah. Our last mission was horrifying, to say the least." Brady recoils at the memory. Gordon gets a bit edgy.

"How so?" Craig chimes in.

"We were ambushed," Brady recounts. "Bullets were flying everywhere and our buddies were dropping like flies. We thought Gordon was dead, which is funny because he thought we were dead." Our rapt attention focuses on him as he continues. "I still have the scars where the bullets were dug out of me, just like Gordon. It's what bonds us, in addition to this gay thing. We fought for our country and they still won't let us marry in all 50 states."

"Why did each of you think the other was dead?" I ask as I try to work out the narrative. Gordon is visibly uncomfortable. He keeps fidgeting and gulping down his drink. That's number two in less than five minutes.

"Well..." Brady is just about to answer, when Gordon interjects.

"I don't think the guys want to hear about something that happened over 25 years ago, Brady."

"Of course we do," both Craig and I cry in unison.

"As I was saying before I was so rudely interrupted," Brady says, winking at Gordon, "we were separated. Gordon crawled to the river and disappeared. Our cavalry arrived just about that time and saved our sorry butts. The Vietnamese army we were working with had gone on patrol and expected us to sit tight. Well. We showed those chumps."

Craig and I turn to Gordon to see if he will fill in any missing pieces. We just stare at him as if he's dinner. The silence elongates and I swear a touch of blush colors his cheeks.

"There's nothing to really add," he finally says, trying hard to smile at us, the pack of wolves.

"Nothing?" an incredulous Brady says with an arched eyebrow. "At the reunion, you mentioned a female pulled you out of the river and you were nursed in some jungle village." He drops the info at our feet.

"You what?" I practically shout at Gordon.

"I was saved by some villagers. I don't remember most of it. I was bleeding to death, in shock. I can't recall many of the details."

"Oh my god. The village I am from nursed one of you Ghosts. My mother pulled the soldier from the river." It is getting harder and harder to breathe. I take another hard look at Gordon.

"You don't say?" Brady says under his breath. He sits up straight. "You don't think that you two also met in that village?" The whole table stares at Gordon and me, holding its collective breath.

"No," Gordon says, dismissing the very idea. "I think I'd remember Vy. There were two people taking care of me, a child and an old man."

"Old man? What did he look like?" I ask.

"It's all a blur. I've spent these years trying to forget it, to leave it all behind," Gordon says.

Craig looks at me and asks, "What did this... Ghost... look like?"

"Well, I can't say. Most of the time, he was bandaged and mumbling. I remember seeing his circumcised dick and thinking he had been mutilated," I laugh. "It was such a sight it burned itself into my memory. Vietnamese guys are not circumcised, as a matter of routine. To see it was shocking to a young Vietnamese kid like me. When the monk told me that American parents do that on purpose, I remember thinking how barbaric they must be."

"What are the odds that you two would have such similar stories?" John asks.

"What else do you guys remember?" Craig interjects, who flares with interest in our stories.

"Mother fished the Ghost out of the river and sent me to get the village monk," I recall. "I do remember bringing him food every now and then."

"Why do you keep calling the guy a Ghost?" Brady inquires.

"Yes. Why do you do that?" both Craig and John ask eagerly.

"It's what we call white people. You guys don't have this rich, natural tan we yellow people sport," I laugh. "We could spot you guys practically in the dark if we didn't smell you first. Guys who drink a lot of milk sweat it out. What a stench!" I exclaim. The whole table laughs.

"What else do you remember, Gordon?" I ask. I was getting excited about the prospect of him being the soldier my mother saved.

"I don't think it was your mother," Gordon counters. "A young girl found me by the river. There is no way she was old enough to have had children. The boy who fed me couldn't have been older than 10. The crazy old man who watched over me was just that. CRAZY. But he did speak some broken English."

I sigh, knowing in my heart that it would be too good to be true. We already had our miraculous coincidence, back in Birmingham. But this, it can't be.

The entire table sits quietly, as if in meditation. All are wondering whether Gordon and I did, in fact, first meet in that village in 'Nam all those years ago. Is fate pulling us together? I can tell that Gordon is getting agitated.

"Hey, guys. Let's leave the war in the past and move on," Gordon says in an exasperated tone. He looks right at me, his eyes probing, asking if I'm making this all up. A lot of guys were ambushed in and around villages during the war; it would be natural for

Gordon to believe the similarities in our stories are just coincidence.

"Yeah, I agree with Gordon," I say out loud, even though I want nothing more than to continue probing him. I honestly do think we might've met. I can't prove it, but I can tell Gordon is tired of talking about that terrible memory. I now see the patterns in my life, like my connection to Gordon in Birmingham, then D.C., and now here in Boone, where he lives. Is this the path for me? I've come more into my faith of late. Buddhism rewards me with wisdom and peace. I wonder if it is doing that now.

When I was involved with the Belly Fetish Man, I was the eighth person on the waitlist, which I interpret as a cosmic sign. Eight is a powerful number in Buddhism. I knew it was Karma's way of telling me of the consequences. I can learn the lessons in this life or the next.

"Okay," Brady surrenders, and the dynamics of the conversation shift. "What are we doing for tomorrow?" Brady looks at Gordon expectantly.

"I think we'll head down to the Blowing Rock Canyon in the morning and then have lunch in town," Gordon replies.

"That sounds like fun," John says. "We looked up this region before coming out. We also want to see Grandfather Mountain."

"Hey, Vy. You're joining us, right?" Brady asks, his voice full of hope.

"Sure," I reply and then remember all the trouble that my "Sure's" have gotten me into over the course of my life. Jerry's still a little mad that I forced him to go to Michael's pool party. After that whole scene, Michael and Gary had a terrible argument that almost derailed their relationship. Secrets and lies can do that; foundations must be made of sterner stuff. Of course, Jerry and I think that desperation is the glue sticking those misshaped pieces together.

The next morning I show up at Gordon's around nine in the morning. I know never to arrive when the roosters wake the land. When you hit dreamtime after witching hour, it's difficult to greet the sunrise. I once told Gordon that waking up before nine isn't a crime. His response was, "Yeah, if you're five years old."

"Hey Brady. Is anyone else up?" I ask as I enter Gordon's home. Brady's in sweatpants that show off a nice bulge, and a tight t-shirt outlining his pecs. He's still lean from his years in the army and he's obviously maintaining it. I find it amazing that he rock climbs with a bullet still in his shoulder.

"No, just me," Brady replies. "Even at home, I get up at six in the morning. I've been reading at the dining table for an hour. I've got coffee going. Interested?"

"No thanks. I'm not a coffee drinker. I'll fix myself some tea." I make my way to the cabinet where I find the tea and pull a cup from the dry rack next to the sink.

"You seem pretty comfortable around here," Brady observes.

"Hmm. I never thought about it," I say and look into Brady's green eyes. He's about the same height as Gordon. He and John are also about the same height, but John is a blond, blue-eyed surfer boy from California. "Funny. Once I moved here I thought I would come here more often," I say. "Unfortunately, that doesn't happen." I don't share the pointlessness of coming over, especially if Gordon and Craig are swinging together.

"How do you know Gordon?" Brady asks.

"I got to know him in D.C. I met him a few times at some mutual friends' parties. In our last encounter, I also met Craig, who owns a rental here with his partner, Tom." As I'm steeping the tea in the hot water, I add, "Oh, and in a very weird coincidence, I ran into Gordon in Birmingham, Alabama, while visiting on Spring Break."

"Wow, how did you put those pieces together?" Brady asks, bemused.

I tell him to wait a moment as I head into the living room and fetch the photograph. I bring it back into the kitchen and hand it to him. "Here. See if you notice anything odd?"

Brady studies it for a few minutes and then a bewildered look crosses his brow. He looks right at me and then back to the photograph. He does this a few times. "Oh my!" he exclaims. "Is that you behind Gordon and Maggie?" He points to me in the photo.

"Yes. And the guy..." I point "...is Tim, who I was seeing, and the reason for the trip." I stare right at him and then break the silence. "I didn't connect the dots until my first trip here, when I saw myself in the photo. I practically fell to the floor. When I pointed it out to Gordon, we both stared into it as if we were looking at some divine prophecy from the stars."

Brady just keeps looking at the photo, even after he replaces it. "You know, it's not that far-fetched that you guys met at that village," he whispers in a subversive tone.

"My gut feeling says so. But, I know that if I don't have inconvertible proof, then Gordon is going to dismiss it as coincidence," I whisper back. "He likes to be in control. That much I've learned in our short time as friends."

"Very true," Brady says, nodding. "Gordon's been like that since I fought alongside him in the jungle. If he couldn't control the outside world, by God, he was going to control what he could put his hands on."

"Hey guys," a voice sounds from the kitchen entrance. Brady and I turn to see a groggy Gordon enter the living room. We both give a start. It certainly feels like we got caught committing a crime.

"Just chatting your army buddy up," I say calmly. I can see that Gordon is very suspicious. His icy blue eyes scan the room, looking for evidence.

The house wakes up after Gordon's entrance. From the kitchen I can hear Craig and John moving about. As I drink the lukewarm tea, I think about our schedule for today. We'll see the gorge and Grandfather Mountain, and then we'll eat lunch in Blowing Rock. I think at that point I'll make my escape.

"Gorgeous vistas!" John exclaims as we take our seats around the table on the patio. "I see why people buy houses that are planted into the side of the gorge. I'm not sure if I could look out the back window and see no ground. It gives me the shivers," he continues.

"Watch out for that first step out the back door," Craig chimes. We all laugh.

Spending the day confirms how much I have missed Gordon and Craig. Our conversation flows naturally and effortlessly, and we banter back and forth. I try not to stare at Gordon. We do touch a few times. His skin feels electric as it slides over mine. Our old chemistry ignites...well, at least on my side. His wall is pretty thick and the drawbridge is up. There's no crossing the moat.

I can't help grinning when he grins. I hope I don't come across as a love-sick puppy. I admit that Gordon and Craig do look like a couple. I see how easy they bounce off of each other. I wistfully hope for that type of camaraderie and closeness with Gordon. I bear silent witness. I don't feel the need to drop a stone in that placid lake. I hope whatever relationship Gordon and

Craig have makes them happy. I'm feeling myself get emotional. Dammit, I've got to go.

When I refocus, I see that our food has arrived. I'm also coming in on a story that is producing a lot of laughs. "Sorry," I interrupt. "What's so funny? I kind of spaced out."

"We're laughing at Brady here," Gordon says. "When he first got to 'Nam, the heat was such a monster, it mauled him for weeks. He whined about it louder than the rest of us, so we got to calling him Baby Brady." Gordon can hardly control his laughter.

"You can get off that high horse, Mr. High Country Mountain boy. I do recall a few heat-related mishaps you experienced," Brady admonishes with a laugh. "You should have seen him. That fur coat of his was soaked every day by mid-morning. We always wondered who got the dog wet," he roars. "It got so bad he kept his hair shaved to stop the stink!"

Another round of laughter sweeps the table. Gordon takes a bow. He gives as good as he gets.

"You better watch yourself, asshole buddy," Gordon says to Brady. "You might never see it coming. And to think that now, you've become a real life asshole buddy." Gordon's laughter fills the table.

"Were you guys asshole buddies?" Craig asks.

"Hell no!" the men yell in unison.

"I think they doth protest too much," I howl back, winking at Craig.

The table erupts into another round of finger pointing, lip smacking, and riotous laughter. The rest of the
patrons on the patio turn to sneak a peek at all the
commotion. We raise our drinks to the crowd to
acknowledge the disruption we're making.

Once we pay the check, I stand up and announce
my departure. I use school work as my means of a
clean getaway.

"Do you really have to go, Vy?" Gordon asks.
"Your company has been great."

"School work never sleeps and I would like some. I
have a paper due Monday," I apologize. I give hugs to
everyone. When I'm hugging Gordon for a split second
I close my eyes and make a wish upon a star. When
my eyes open, I see a smirk on Brady's lips. I wonder if
I held the hug a bit too long.

Monday arrives as another weekend bids adieu. On
Sunday, Brady, John and I hiked through the back
country and climbed rocks at the river. John acci-
dentally slipped off one of the rocks and splashed into
the frigid water. The group suppressed their laughter,
but John was good-natured about it.

On Monday night, Brady and John decide to make
their leave.

"Gordon," Brady says, "John and I want to thank
you for a wonderful weekend, even if you did try to
drown John. You must come out to Portland and bring
Vy. He's a hoot!"

"We'll see. This weekend is the first real visit with Vy since he moved here. I'll have to make an effort," I say.

"You shouldn't let him slip away," John says with a wink.

"What do you mean?"

"Gordon!" Brady interjects. "Even a blind man can see that Vy is into you." Both Brady and John give me a sharp look. "You can't be that obtuse! I can understand if you're still in the closet, even if it does have a glass door. Maybe you haven't come out completely."

"Yeah. You must not be dating. That explains why you're so CLUELESS," John adds.

"Okay, guys." I hug them both to send them on their way and to cut this conversation off. "I'll visit at some point." I wave as they get into their rental and head off to the airport. What they said lingers in the air and floats around me. I take a whiff to see if the idea turns bad. Vy and I passionately kissed that one time in D.C., but I've put those feelings away. That moment is complete and I've not given any more thought of letting it out in the present. I decided that as long as I'm living in Boone, then I would keep my gay life under wraps where it is easier to control and won't have to worry about any consequences.

I go inside and close the door, marking another end to a glorious weekend. But something keeps nagging at me. As I look at the closed door, I can't help but wonder: why do I feel so trapped and out of control?

32

"The guys said that Vy has a crush on me," I announce to Craig over cereal. What a way to start a Tuesday morning.

"You don't say," Craig responds. He looks at me with that bemused air about him. "Sweet. Vy is handsome. He's a catch."

I try to read his expression, but he has put on a mask of apathy. "Are you saying I should pursue Vy?" I've known Craig for more than five years, ever since we met at a private gay party celebrating ski season. That's when I also met his partner, Tom. Things have become a bit weird ever since Tom found out about our indiscretion. Tom doesn't come to the mountains anymore.

"Let me count...oh that's right," Craig laughs. "Prospects, like none." He smiles up at me, probably wondering why I ask idiot questions.

"The way Vy is keeping his distance, I'm not so sure there's any interest," I counter. I wonder what it's like dating someone like Vy. I'm not sure if I'm ready. Commitment requires a passport and a visa. My map from the days of dating women is useless. I'm lost without signs, outposts, and guardrails. The paths lead nowhere.

"School could be taking a toll on him," Craig says. "It's not like he came right out of undergrad. It's been a long time since he was in school. Now, he's living in a strange place, knows few people, and he quit his job. It could be any reason. Maybe some we don't even know about."

"I'm going to call him right now and see what's up," I brashly say. I'm interested in knowing more.

"Hello, Vy?"

"Yes. Is this Gordon?"

"Yeah. What are you doing later this week? I think it would be fun to hang." I do my best smooth talking.

"Sounds like fun. I have a paper due Thursday, then I'm free. I need to go shopping for a few items. The apartment is missing a few things to make it feel like home."

"Kewl. I know this flea market down the mountain in Wilkesboro. You can find pretty much anything there," I say with a smile. I can feel Craig's eyes on me.

"Wonderful. Should I come by Saturday morning?" Vy asks.

"Why don't Craig and I pick you up around seven? The good deals are gone by nine," I counter.

"What, you're going to be up before nine? Stop the presses!" Vy laughs. "Now I've got to go, to be a part of history. So it's a big sure!"

"Ha. Ha," I respond with playful sarcasm. We say our good-byes and hang up.

So Craig will be joining us. He and Gordon seem more like a couple every day. I do need to find something to cover the wall I see when lying in bed. I find it too plain. Plus, I miss Gordon although it's not like he's promising me anything. It's time to get out of my head and back into the real world.

That Saturday, I find myself prospecting the closet for something to wear. Even if Gordon's not interested, I want him to see what he's missing. I pick a pair of slim-cut black shorts and a tight red t-shirt that weaves in orange highlights to create a fiery crimson pattern. That should catch some attention.

"What a gorgeous t-shirt, Vy," Craig says as I open the door to my apartment. "You always wear things I want. When you buy shirts, you've got to get two and make mine double large."

"This is the first time I've been here since you moved in, Vy," Gordon remarks as he enters. "I see your art is on the wall."

"I'm still unpacking, and it's been almost four months. I have boxes that won't see the light of day, even when I'm done with the degree," I laugh.

"What are you shopping for?" Gordon asks.

"Well, in the master, there's a blank wall that I look at when lying in bed. That empty space disturbs me. I'm not sure what it is about blank white walls. They sort of remind me of a sanitarium. I've got to get something up," I say as I lead the group upstairs to show them what I mean.

"Is this the wall?" Craig asks.

"Yes. See, the bed is up against the window. When the afternoon sun breaks in, it bleeds across the wall. As the light dies, the wall projects a look of decay bathed in yellow. Yuck. I prefer a mirror. I'd love to lie in bed and see the sun setting," I explain. I lie on the bed to demonstrate. Thankfully, I made the bed this morning.

"Comfy."

I hear a voice in my left ear while simultaneously feeling Gordon's weight on the bed next to me. I turn to my left and look right into those blue eyes. They are my absolute weakness. This must be how Superman feels every time he's around kryptonite. Here is Gordon, in my bed.

"Room for a third?" a smiling Craig announces as he lands on the other side of Gordon. Mood killer.

"It's time for everyone to get out of bed!" I shout nervously and roll off, leaving the couple dangling.

"Spoilsport," Gordon says with a hint of mischievousness.

We drive 30 miles down the mountain and into Wilkesboro. Gordon says the flea market includes vendors from all the surrounding communities. You'll never know what you'll find among the discards of rural townsfolk and displaced urbanites.

As we are coming down the mountain, I can't help but hear the song, "She'll Be Coming 'Round the Mountain," over and over in my head. The children's song is based on a black spiritual number. I learned it when living in the Virginia Mountains, and never understood its meaning. It was only later that I learned that it's sometimes thought of as an end of the world spiritual about the second coming of Christ. Being Buddhist, I never understood how the end of the world would be a wonderful thing. Now, it seems quite karmic, one stage of life ends and another begins.

"Here we are!" Gordon announces with a big grin. We hop out of the car and survey the bustling market. We arrived just after seven—peak time to get a good deal. "We'll head down the far left aisle and work our way around," Gordon says with a sweep of his right arm.

"Any idea what type of mirror you want?" Craig asks as he looks over the place. I watch Craig and Gordon move in sync. We follow Gordon to the far left aisle and snake our way around the countless tables piled high with stuff and more stuff. There's already a large crowd of people mingling about.

"Not sure. I figured it's like pornography; I'll know it when I see it," I smile and chuckle. The guys roll their eyes.

By ten, we've uncoiled four-fifths of the market. I still haven't seen anything that I'd hang on my walls to greet the day. We're deconstructing people in the crowd, making catty comments, and joshing each other on our dubious taste in clothes, furniture, and knick-knacks. You truly see the underbelly of American capitalism when you spend time at a flea market. It's astounding the type, amount, and quality of the stuff. One person's trash is another's treasure. That old saying rings loud and clear here.

"Hey Vy, over here!" Gordon shouts. He's standing at one of the aisle's end caps, where an old couple is de-cluttering their lives.

"What's up?" I say as I come alongside Gordon.

"What do you think?" he asks, pointing to a mirror. I follow his finger and gaze upon the object of my affection.

"It's gorgeous!" I exclaim. There, on a makeshift saw-horse stands an art-deco wall mirror, about five feet by four feet, with a single center pane of glass framed with beveled panels that are raised slightly inward. It gives the effect of a flower blossoming. In the upper corner of each raised panel is a design motif etched and frosted, an abstract geometric shape. I'm afraid to ask how much. Thankfully, Gordon asks first.

"How much for the mirror?"

The elderly woman smiles. "Where do you intend to hang it?" she asks.

That's a strange response. "There's a blank wall that I see when lying in bed that this mirror would fit perfectly," I respond, wondering if the price has just gone up.

"You're hanging this in your bedroom?" she confirms.

"Yes."

"Ah..." she breathes. "This mirror is a present from my true love, Henry, who is right over there. For many years, we too hung it in our bedroom. But, it's gotten too heavy for our bodies to keep moving it. Do you have a true love?"

I blush. "No. But maybe one day." I nervously smile as the response is filled with a mixture of regret, remorse, and revelation.

"It may bring you good fortune. It certainly has for us. We've been together for 50 years and if the Good Lord is willing, another 50 years." She smiles. She then locks into my eyes and says, "For you, $50."

"Yes," I quickly say in astonishment. You can't get a cheapy from China for that and certainly not real lead glass that has beveled panels.

"This mirror is fuckin' heavy," Craig curses as he and Gordon maneuver it up the stairs.

"It's kind of you guys to help," I respond with a big grin.

"I can see why the couple is letting it go," Gordon grunts as he and Craig carry it into my master. "It's damn heavy. Are you sure that those hooks will hold it?"

"As long as we find studs and use four of them," I say triumphantly.

"Studs here in Boone, who would've thought?" Craig deadpans.

After 30 minutes, the mirror hangs on the wall. I plop on the bed with the curtains open and from my angle, I can now see the right side of the bed and the sky beyond. The gorgeous sunsets will now feed directly into my line of sight. Also, twilight is my favorite time of day and I'll be able to enjoy it lying in bed. A smile of satisfaction escapes my lips.

I hug Craig goodbye with a peck on the lips. As I embrace Gordon, I can't help but hear the elderly woman's voice echoing in my ear. "My true love gave it to me..." The mirror was Gordon's find. I quickly peck his cheek and hug him with a little extra force. I say goodbye and disengage rapidly. Crazy old woman talk is messing with my brain. I keep chanting silently, "Stay in reality, stay in reality, stay in reality." I force a smile.

"When Vy was hugging me, I thought he wouldn't let go. That hug was harder than the one he gave upon our arrival," I muse to Craig.

Craig turns towards me. "It's clear that his mood went straight down all of a sudden. I wonder what that was all about."

"You know, Vy likes to ride bikes. I'm going to see about us going to the falls. It's a nice hour-long bike ride. We can hang on the rocks and then ride back. Just the two of us getting back to nature and spending some time together," I comment.

"Sounds good. You guys make a good-looking couple."

"You're getting ahead of yourself," I flatly state. I'm not sure if I'm ready to date anyone. "Are you ready to head back to D.C. tomorrow?"

"Yep. I got all the house work done. Thankfully, it's before the next rental. I'll be leaving right after lunch," Craig explains.

As I drop him off at his place, I yell, "Call me about lunch," from the car window. He's been working on his house quite regularly. You'd think he's living in it as opposed to keeping it as a rental. He hints he may retire here when city life finally loses its luster. I find that hard to believe, but then again, Vy's here.

"Did you talk to Vy?" Craig asks over lunch the next day.

"Sure did. We set up the bike trip for the first weekend after Labor Day. We're both busy over the next few weekends," I explain.

"That's not so far off," Craig replies. "It's about three weeks."

"True," I remark. "Funny thing. Vy seems a bit apprehensive about riding for an hour in the middle of nowhere. Since it's after Labor Day, the summer crowd will be done until the leaf season crowd returns for the first three weeks in October. We'll be all alone in the wilderness."

"What? He thinks you're going to dispose of him where nobody can find the body?" Craig hoots.

"Maybe so. I think Vy is more urban than he lets on. All this back woods adventuring is something I think he prefers to do under glass," I grin. "Or, he could just be afraid of being alone with me for an entire Saturday afternoon."

33

The sun pulls a gorgeous hat trick and splashes the mountains and towns with a cerulean hue. The yellow rays warm the blue skies as the earth cools the mountain shade. The lushness of the valleys is a hair past peak and still intoxicates a green paradise overflowing with wild flowers, brier patches, and old growth trees. The animals come out to taste the crisp apple of a day. The 70-degree climate is pitch perfect.

"We're going to be out there for an entire afternoon?" Vy asks in a tone broadly painted with horror.

"What else are you going to do on a Saturday afternoon?" I respond with a good-natured jab. "With the season over, hardly anything is open. No reservations are needed; you just need to make sure the restaurant is actually open," I continue in defense. "It's the best time to be out here. There're no crowds. We might not see anybody all afternoon." I see Vy getting nervous. His eyes dart left, then right, then front, then back, and then all over again. I'm practically getting motion sickness from watching it. "The trail is decent," I say. "There's one climb and then mostly flat terrain all the way to the falls. And coming back will be quick, since we'll be going downhill." I try to get Vy to make eye contact with me to stop the darting all around bit. I lock up the car and hop on the bike. Once we're in the saddle, off we go.

What the hell did Gordon mean by one climb? He's pulling away from me. I can barely keep up. This climb is practically killing me. We're going up the side of a small mountain, and he's so far ahead I can barely see him. I can't pedal anymore. I hop off the bike and start walking up the mountainside. My legs ache and my back feels like a rack is going to be needed to straighten it. Thankfully, I have water.

As I crest the hill, I see Gordon lying on his back, sunning himself. It took me a good 20 minutes to catch up to him.

"Well, my fitness level is crap," I say, panting. "You're certainly in better shape since you've had time to sun yourself." I'm working hard to catch my breath.

"At least I'm not like my friend, Ben, who would come back to taunt you with a whole basket full of names, like slug, weakling, poor baby."

"I'd tell him to go fuck himself," I say with a smile. Gordon laughs, gets back on his bike and takes off. I've barely gotten my breath and off he goes to catch the wind. All I'm left with is my loud rasping to keep me company.

Vy is so cute when he's exasperated. I know that he wants to at least make this look respectable. He looks good; he holds his own; he's in pretty good shape. He may not be explosive in his physicality but he keeps at it.

"By the way, on the way back," I say, "you'll want to control your descent. I had another friend who lost control going down that hill and wiped out. He broke his arm and collar bone in addition to skinning most of his legs bare. It was an ugly sight." I wink.

"Great. Thanks for telling me," Vy groans. "You could've waited until after we got back." I give Vy some slack, but make sure to stay in his line of sight. He's not built for this sort of endurance, nor is he used to the thinness of the air. I suddenly see the trail-head leading to the falls and my excitement gets the better of me. I hop off the pavement and quickly break for the dirt path.

"Are we there yet?" I hear Vy yell behind me, mocking a child's whine.

"Oh, stop!" I laugh. "Or I'll pull over and give you a thrashin'." We both laugh. It's amazing how in sync we sometimes get.

"Promises. Promises," I crack back. Gordon and I get on the same wavelength sometimes. It's scary. I still reminisce over our kiss. Is this how Ken got trapped? At the time, I'm sure a connection emerged, fully alive with electricity. The chemical reaction ignited. For a gossamer moment, I felt our spirits touch. Whatever defenses I ring around my heart disappear. Inside that exploding moment, I can watch myself wake next to Gordon every day. That place is what I think is called 'home.' But, alas, it seems only true for one of us.

'We're here!" Gordon shouts as he jumps off his bike. He walks it to a tree and wraps the lock around the trunk. He then motions me over and locks his bike with mine.

"I don't see any falls," I anxiously say.

"We're still about 25 minutes away on foot. The terrain is too rough for bikes."

"Great. First the bike ride of death and now a forced march into the middle of nowhere. I haven't seen any other human beings since the ones enclosed in their little metal coffins passing me as I walked up the mountain. You're trying to dispose of the body, aren't you, Mister?" I say as I poke Gordon in the ribs. He just flashes me his signature Cheshire Cat's grin and jogs ahead. He dares me to keep up.

The jogging gets us to the falls quicker than 25 minutes, and when I see the water, I suddenly forget all the pain it took to get here.

"It's beautiful, Gordon," I breathe. I enter the clearing and see a sheer cliff pouring white water over its edge into a pristine river.

"Be careful on the rocks and follow my lead," Gordon says. "We'll head over to that big center rock, where you'll be able to see downriver. It's a gorgeous sight."

Once we get to a perch in the rocks, I glance down the cliff face. "Wow, what an incredible sight," I exclaim. As I shift to follow Gordon's lead to sit down, I step on a slick patch and lose my balance. I desperately get low to reduce my center of gravity. No luck. I scream as I slip off the rock.

"Vy!" Gordon screams. He lunges his hand forward to grab me but only catches air. I'm fighting gravity and losing. Thankfully, we aren't that far up and the river is directly below. As I splash into the water, I see Gordon diving in after me. The water is icy cold.

I break the surface as the cold water needles my skin, screaming at the sudden chill. Gordon breaks the water and lunges toward me. I feel his strong arms hook around me and pull me to shore.

"Aw, Fuck!" I shout. "I'm a drowned cat." I shiver and cough.

"You okay, Vy?" I ask, fear stalking my every word. The fright that Vy gave me sliding into the water burns into my brain. It was like watching a slow-motion action stunt. I knew I had to get him out of the river before the current carried him away. Even pulling him out as quickly as I did, we still moved about 100 yards downstream.

"Vy, you're shivering looks bad," I say.

"I ha-hate the c-cold. That water might as well be i-ice. I'm thankful I didn't b-break anything. I'm bruised all o-over," he manages. "Tha—thank you for pulling me out."

"I know this is going to sound crazy, but you need to take off your clothes and let them dry in the sun. We'll rub together to stay warm." I say this to Vy dispassionately, to reassure him that I mean no harm. I'm not trying to get into his pants, not at this moment. Yet, I can see his eyebrow arch.

"Is this how y-you get your dates out of their cl-clothes?" he asks, trying to put on a grin through his violent shivers. "You know, a simple 'l-let's fuck' would suff-ice."

I'm horrified at the thought of being naked in the middle of nowhere with Gordon, the man of my dreams. It's one thing to be naked in a group, like at a hot tub, than one-on-one with no one around. This feels too intimate, too personal. What else can life torture me with in one afternoon? I silently cry. "Fine," I finally tremble. I strip. Before long we're both naked and our clothes hang in the trees under the sunlight. Gordon wraps his hairy body around mine. I wince as his cold fur hits my hairless torso.

"You okay?" he whispers as I wince.

"Your hair is c-cold. As you can s-see, I'm hairless." I look into those incredible blue eyes. I feel Gordon's powerful hands stroking my skin like rubbing sticks together to create fire.

"It'll be okay," Gordon whispers in my ear. "Once we dry out it's a short walk to the bikes and we'll be off."

My head spins. I feel Gordon's body press against mine. I know it's for warmth but I'm starting to get excited. The worst he can do is say no. With that thought, I press my lips against his and surrender. The surrender is accepted as I feel his tongue dart inside of my mouth. I also feel his hard-on pressing against me.

Amazing what an incredible kisser Vy is. I'm just as excited as he is. Why not? I stroke my hands over his cute ass, grab a handful of his left cheek, and pull him even closer. I plunge my tongue deeper into his mouth before he breaks contact. Whoa. I feel Vy's cool mouth envelop my cock. I nearly lose it right there. I think Vy could suck paint off a wall. After a few quick thrusts into the back of his throat, I pull out and bring him up close for a French kiss. Then I'm down on my knees.

Oh wow. Gordon's mouth is electrifying my cock. His tongue swirling over my head is sending shock-waves deep inside of me. Being uncut makes the head a hundred times more sensitive. I yank my cock out or else I'll unload. I see his shit-eating grin as I guess that he realizes what's about to happen. I pull him up to French kiss him. We lock lips and mash our bodies together. I swear we are trying to occupy the same space.

There's something I want. I spin Gordon around and push him into a bend. I spread his crack with my hands and plunge my tongue into his hole. I feel Gordon's body shake and a moan escape his lips. My right hand grabs his cock from behind and jerks. I feel it get incredibly hard. I know he's close.

"I'm going to shoot!" he shouts.

"Feed me," I demand as I spike his cock into my mouth. Instantly, I feel warm cum shooting into the back of my throat. I spit some out, swallow some, and lick some onto his shaft. I can see his whole body shiver as I milk out every last drop. I come up and French Gordon with his cum as lip gloss.

I taste myself on Vy's lips. I drop to my knees and plunge my mouth over his uncut cock. With a quick swirl of my tongue over his head and my right hand jacking him, Vy unloads into my mouth. I spit it back onto his shaft and then lick it back up. I stand and lock lips again. We taste each other over and over.

We collapse into each other's arms as we hold each other up. I can feel Vy's cum drying on my face and I can smell mine on his face. I pull us apart. "We'll have to go back to the river to wash off. Or, we could just let it crust," I say with a wink.

"Last one there is a rotten egg!" Vy yells and runs to the river. It's no contest: I'm there in a flash.

"Okay, Mr. Big Shot!" I call out. I make my way to the river and squat to splash water onto my face. As I do, I notice Vy has stopped in his tracks. He's staring at my arm intently. I cock an eyebrow as he traces the tattoo on my shoulder with his index finger.

"Hey, man. That's my tat you're playing with." I step back and look down at Vy. His eyes are wide as saucers. "Sorry. I get a little sensitive about it," I sheepishly say. I notice Vy isn't saying anything. He's still stunned. I watch as he slowly gets to his feet.

"I have the same tat as you do," Vy says as our eyes lock.

"What the hell do you mean?" I demand, maybe a bit too forcefully. Vy doesn't say anything. He turns so I can see his right shoulder. My jaw drops open. Lok was right all those years ago. My tattoo has a twin, and it's on Vy. We stare at each other in all our naked, cum-soaked glory.

"That crazy monk..." Vy says just loud enough for me to hear.

"What do you mean, crazy monk?" I demand.

"You're the Ghost that Mother fished out of the river. The monk ordered me to bring you food and to help clean you up when you made a mess. You lay in the temple for a couple of weeks. The whole village was scared to death that the Việt cộng would discover you. They destroyed whole villages to teach a lesson to any who dared harbor Ghosts. The monk basically ordered Mother to take you out of the village because you got a fever and it wasn't breaking. He feared you would become a real Ghost."

This story again? I shake my head. "That can't be right. A girl pulled me out of the river and a little boy fed me and cleaned me. I also remember an old guy who sometimes spoke broken English."

"How old do you think I look?" I demand.

In that instant I knew Vy was right. I always perceive Asians to be much younger than they really are and Vy is no exception. I thought he was in his thirties, not his forties. My god, we were in that village together. Vy's mother saved me that day, and took me on that dangerous journey.

"Our lives began to intertwine on that fateful day," Vy says solemnly.

"I don't believe in pre-destiny," I say harshly. "I make my own choices and do what I want. Nobody makes me do anything I don't want to do."

"The crazy monk tattooed me on the day we left," Vy explains. "He must have marked you earlier."

I grit my teeth. I can't believe what Vy's telling me.

Vy continues. "The monk said that one day the path would blossom for me; that the tat would be a beacon on my life's path; and that I would have to listen to what's in here." He points to his heart. "My inner truth, my inner mindfulness will guide me among and beyond the outside world's illusion."

"The hell with that!" I exclaim. "I don't believe in any of this manifest destiny crap," I'm not sure who or what I'm so angry at. All I do know is that it's time to go. Right now. I stalk off to get my clothes. I see Vy following me.

"If you feel that strongly about the tat, why haven't you removed it? You certainly can afford it," Vy shouts.

"Lok told me in Germany that a master artist did this..." I stop, turn, and grab my left shoulder. "That a twin existed. So I was intrigued. I know I got this in 'Nam but I have no memory of anyone inking me. It looks like a cat in silhouette and I thought maybe one day I'd track its origin. I never entertained the idea that it was stalking me."

"And what do you think I've been doing with my tat? The monk marked me, too. He was one of the most revered people in my village. Even when Mother discovered it, she held her tongue. I could see the conflagration in her eyes but knew she wouldn't act on it. The monk's wisdom is not for us to question, only to contemplate. For more than 25 years, I've meditated

on the meaning of this tat. I now have the other piece.
I don't have the luxury of not knowing where it comes
from. I was left with the knowledge of who did this
and the pain of waiting a lifetime to solve its mystery,"
Vy shouts.

"That's bullshit about letting someone tattoo you,"
I spit.

"You don't understand the culture. You were just
there to kill some commies. Vietnam is over 2,000
years old. What do you know of tradition? What do
you know about carrying the weight of your ancestors
and descendants? What do you know about me?" Vy
hurls as he fights back tears.

I stare at Vy and watch the tears that he is trying
so hard to suppress sneak down his cheeks. I don't
know what to think. I don't like the feeling of being
directed towards anyone. How does someone 12,000
miles away tattoo two people and expect they'll meet
again in life? How?

The last time I saw Gordon so worked up was when
he had returned from visiting his neighbor—the woman
with the brittle bone disease. He hated the idea of being an invalid. I wonder if the notion that we are
meant to be connected, regardless of Gordon's choices,
is making him feel spiritually invalid. Perhaps it makes
him feel as though he does not have full control over
his life.

Our bike ride to the car is in silence. I make it down the mountain in a controlled fashion while Gordon flies down like a bat out of hell. It's as if banshees are chasing him as he pushes himself to get back to the car. I do my best to keep up.

I can't believe Vy's the boy who cared for me in Vietnam. I could barely sit up, eat, wash, or go to the bathroom. Vy took care of me when I was helpless. I need time to process this miraculous story. I'm taking this mountain descent too recklessly. I've got to slow down or Vy may have to help me again. With that thought I start applying the brakes to control my descent, even though I feel I've already lost that. It's not Vy's fault. Hell. His family saved my life because I couldn't save my own.

When we arrive at the car, I load up the bikes. Vy climbs into the car and we take off. I can't seem to make eye contact with him.

For me, it is wonderful news that my faith has rewarded me for listening to my inner spirit, for being mindful and purposeful, and for following the karmic wheel no matter where it brings me. I don't know much about this concept of Western destiny, but we Vietnamese believe that our choices in our past and present lives pre-dispose us to a probable future. We continue on our lessons until we free ourselves from the cycle of death and re-birth. Coming to Boone represents a death of one stage of my life and the re-birth of another. I'm filled with an inner peace with this knowledge, but Gordon can barely contain his fury. I silently meditate on the ride home and wish for a quick end to his turmoil. I want to reach out and comfort Gordon but I know that he would see it as charity, as me helping, as my way of saying that he can't help himself. So I close myself like a lotus blossom.

I get my bike off the rack and move towards the driver side window. "I got the bike. Thanks for taking me out to the falls," I gingerly say. Gordon diverts his eyes.

"Sure thing," I sputter and drive off. I gaze into the rearview mirror and watch as Vy shrinks in the distance. I need to be alone, especially away from Vy. I still can't believe all the coincidences. It's absurd to think that Vy and I were meant for each other, that destiny keeps throwing us back into each other's lives. And the tattoo! Have I been following some damn script?

As I glance back, I can no longer see Vy. A sense of dread weighs heavy on my heart. Damn, I can still smell him on my fingers.

I linger on the side of the road as Gordon drives off. He could barely say goodbye. I watch his car grow small yet I still smell Gordon on my fingers. I roll my bike up the front porch and over the threshold. As I park the bike against the wall of the front foyer, I turn to shut the door. With that act, the summer shimmers away and we plunge into the season of the dying. I can't help but wonder if I will ever see Gordon again. If our passion on the bank of the river was just another fleeting moment like our first kiss back in D.C., what will that mean for me? For my future? Karma must be punishing me for a past life transgression. I can feel tears channeling down my cheeks. My ears perk up as I hear a lonesome wolf howl in the distance, signaling the possibility of a future of walking the path alone.

Once the door clicks shut, I let the tears fall freely down my face.

34

"Why the funk? You've been stinky these last few weeks. It's been quite unbearable," Jeff rants.

"Yeah, Gordon. What's up?" Sara adds. "The Halloween party is coming and we're talking about going as the Marx Brothers. You seem distracted." She crosses her arms and waits for my response.

I know they mean well. Jeff's a friend from high school and Sara from college. They're my closest friends. I don't know if I want to open this can of worms.

"Does this have something to do with the bike ride with Vy?" Jeff goes for the jugular.

"Whaddya mean by that?" I icily respond.

"Ever since that bike ride, you've been distant and distracted." Sometimes Jeff can be overbearing. He stands at 6'2" and uses that height to intimidate others. He likes to lock his green eyes onto you and dare you to look away.

"You know, Jeff, you may be onto something," Sara chimes. "When Gordon and I ate lunch..." She traps me in her line of sight. "...you were totally out of it. I didn't think much about it until now..." She trails off and twirls her blue scarf between her fingers. Sara is a plus-sized Madonna with a heart of gold.

"Fine." I pause and reel in their full attention. I cast deep into the whites of their eyes. "I discovered Vy's mother is the one who pulled me out of the river in 'Nam." I can see their mouths drop open.

"Are you sure?" both of them ask simultaneously, with that oh-my-god look etched into their faces.

"Positive!" I exclaim. "Vy showed me proof. No matter how much I want to deny it, it stared me in the face."

"What proof?" they again simultaneously demand.

I reel them in closer. "We have the same tattoo; but his is on the other shoulder. Vy also told me who gave us our tattoos. The old man I remember through my haze was actually the head monk of the village monastery. It's his village that kept my death at bay," I softly say.

"Amazing," Jeff breathes.

"Well. It certainly explains the mystery of the tattoo," I state.

"But you don't know why," Sara interjects, slicing to the heart of the matter.

Before I can answer, Jeff drops a bombshell of a question.

"How did you see Vy's tattoo? If he's like you, he doesn't flash it around."

"We were naked." I let it out like a slow leak of a bike's tire. Again, with their mouths dropping, I quickly add, "Vy fell into the river and I went in after him. Once we got back to shore, we took our clothes off to dry." I hope that ends this line of questioning. I can feel Jeff's suspicions stalking me, sniffing around for any crumbs left behind. I pray silently for Sara to save me.

"That's so cosmic," Sara drops. We both turn to her. "Don't you see, Vy's mother pulled you out of the river and then you did the same thing for Vy. That's so like a wheel, very karmic."

Again, I'm hearing about a greater force exerting itself into my life. I prefer to make my own choices. I stare at my friends, lost in thought, my mind trying to deny it.

"Well, how's Vy doing?" Jeff again goes for the jugular. I jab my eyes into his and stare him down.

"I don't know," I simply say.

"What?" they both howl simultaneously...again.

"I freaked out. I couldn't get away from Vy fast enough. I dropped him off at his place and took off. We haven't spoken since." I feel the intensity of their stares spiking my nerves.

"You learn one of the biggest secrets of your life, the identity of who saved your miserable, rotten life, and all you do is freak." Sara hurls the javelin through me. "As long as I've known you, you've pined for the answer. It must've been a shock to Vy. Or are you only thinking about yourself?"

"I agree with Sara, Gordon," Jeff says. "You've obsessed over who saved your life ever since you got back from 'Nam. How many times have you said that you wanted to find that person to thank them?" Jeff shifts his tone into disappointment territory. "Now that you know, you run scared?"

I have no answer. Sara eyes me suspiciously and asks, "What else aren't you telling us?"

'Nothing," I firmly announce. I'm hit with their disbelief; I don't give a shit. I'm not telling how Vy and I passionately sucked each other off.

"Well, if you're not interested in Vy, I am. I've always found him attractive, but thought his heart belonged to someone else." I don't believe it. Jeff keeps going for the jugular.

"Fine. Whatever," I say to end the conversation.

"I want to say, as a final comment..." Sara makes sure she cements my attention before continuing. "...as shocking as this news is for you, imagine what it's like for Vy?" She lowers the boom. She's right. There're two people involved. I'm so wrapped inside my head I never thought of how Vy would be processing this revelation.

Weeks go by. I'm feverishly trying to make Gordon an afterthought. The fact that the crazy monk marked the both of us is incomprehensible. I shout, "Why!" over and over like a stuck record. Why did the crazy monk do this? When did he mark Gordon? Why does Gordon hate me? All I've got are questions with no answers.

The monk said that one day I'd understand. Well, I don't. The tattoos are some sort of lesson, just like the one when he and I walked down to the river. That took a long time to understand. I don't think I have enough life left in me for this answer's auspicious debut.

Gordon's kisses exponentially infect my DNA when we share our bodies. Two moments now merged into a larger whole that can't simply be divided into halves. I remember how he smells, feels, and tastes. We're inside a heartbeat where my ending is his beginning, where separation fades, and where the karmic wheel balances. My Buddhist faith rewards me. This must be what Evangelicals mean when they bear witness to faith.

A piece of me died when Gordon pulled away from me. This chance on love has swept me excruciatingly under the tidal wave. The rawness has flayed open my reason for being here in Boone. Maybe by telling my-self I am here to get my degree has polluted my cour-age to take a chance on love? I certainly didn't have the courage to come all this way only for Gordon.

Deep down, I need the reason for coming here to be about me. I watched Mother do something similar, when she shifted her motivation from moving for Dad to moving for the children. What about me? Does that weigh down my intentions like cement shoes? I came to Boone to test the waters, as if it were a laboratory ex-periment. I've waited for the experiment to start, for Gordon to enter dating mode, and then to test the hy-pothesis: "Am I his type?" I've been trying to test that ever since the pool party when we first met. Life is bio-logical, not chemical. That's my fatal flaw. It's ex-traordinary that Gordon and I have been crossing paths since I was 14.

I've got to stop obsessing over this. I've got mid-terms. No way can I let Jerry's worst case scenario come true. I can't leave Boone without my degree. I grab my Master's thesis materials and hike down to the library, descending the hill onto Grand Boulevard under the shadow of nightfall. To think Main Street is also called King Street. I'm a pauper this evening. I'm going to have to accept that Gordon isn't on my path.

"Hey Gordon," Mitch greets when I open the door.

"What a surprise? I didn't know you were coming back," I say as nonchalantly as I can manage.

"It's a last minute trip. My client wants a few more assurances about how the donation is to be used and I thought, why not handle the details personally?" Mitch grins as he enters the room. "How about a gin and tonic?"

"Okay," I say unevenly, as I lead him to the kitchen. I fix Mitch the drink and make a double for myself. Some surprises should be left outside, I think.

"You know, that last time was hot," Mitch says, downing his glass. "Maybe you're up for another go?"

I suddenly feel his lips press against mine and his hands squeeze my ass. Before I can react, I feel his tongue licking my neck. "Whoa!" I break contact by stepping back.

"No worries. I brought condoms and lube," Mitch says and again attacks.

His left hand grabs my crotch and his body presses me into the kitchen bar. My zipper goes down.

"Back off," I hiss. With my forearms, I push him off. I gain a couple of steps and smooth out the disheveled mess of my clothes.

"What's the matter?" Mitch whines. "Last time you fucked me a new asshole."

"Last time I was smashed. That shouldn't have happened," I counter. My muscles grow tense because I'm not letting him bear hug me again.

"Hey." Mitch shifts to a more soothing tone. "It's Mitch, your college buddy. Just want to relieve some stress. You help me out, I help you out. It's just like the good old days." He spreads his words thickly, like honey on toast.

"You're not in college anymore," I declare. "You're married with kids."

"Gordon. Be reasonable. I can't just pick up any guy," Mitch declares, as if I'm both judge and jury.

"Mitch," I say and make sure I have his full attention. "It's time to go."

"You're kicking me out?"

I don't say a word. I basically muscle Mitch out the door and slam it. I don't care where he gets his rocks off, but it ain't ever gonna be with me again.

I look out the window and watch Mitch's frustration boil over. He paces outside for a few minutes, clearly looking for a plan B. Suddenly, he stops in his tracks. He looks at me through the window, smiles, and heads off towards town.

As I am studying in the library, I look up from my desk and see this attractive man in a suit sitting across from me. We're on the basement level, in a secluded spot behind the shelves of books. It's quiet and very few people are about. Most stay on the upper floors, away from the mustiness. I spy the massive hard-on pole tenting this man's pants, and can even see the ring of its head outlined in his trousers. He smiles. I think about it for a split second and then I smile.

"Hey. Looking for a study break?" the man oozes. He closes the distance between us with a few strides.

I'm sitting at crotch level and definitely see the pole as he approaches me. I slowly lift my eyes and get stuck in the spark of his deep brown eyes.

"I could be," I purr.

"You have a place we can go?" he grins.

"There's a typing room just behind us on the left," I say. I'm not about to bring a total stranger over to my place. Those days are long gone. But, somehow, having anonymous sex with a total stranger in a semi-public space seems okay. The absurdity hits me like a meteor.

"You're so hot," he claims as he envelops me in the cramped typing room. It's basically a closet with a desk and chair. It's for those who want to use their typewriter without disturbing others. I'm sure the designer had no idea that it would also be used for this. Doesn't matter if you are gay or straight, these rooms are perfect places for quick sex, like hitting the keys on a Selectric.

Our tongues fight for space inside our mouths. I feel his hands stroking my cock through my pants. I do the same to him. He's pretty big. With each stroke I hear him moan, and he dives his tongue deeper into my mouth. I slowly zip down his pants. I want the one-eyed monster freed. Just as it flops out, the smell hits me. I immediately jerk back and reality comes sharply into focus. This man before me is basically undressed. His blue-gray suit jacket is on the chair; his white shirt is open, exposing his v-neck t-shirt and chest hair; his fly is open with his hard-on at attention; and, finally, his wedding band is sparkling under the office light.

"What's the matter?" he asks with a bewildered look on his face.

"I've got to go!" I pull myself together as quickly as I can. I abruptly get up and push him out of the way and I'm through the door. I catch a glimpse of his surprised, contorted face with that what-the-fuck-just-happened expression squeezing it.

I grab my things and flee the library. I run all the way home as if pursued by Cerberus. The chill in the air smacks my face, cracks my lips, and stings my lungs. I can't stop until I'm home behind locked doors. I pour into my home and slam the door. I fumble with the lock until I hear it click and drop on all fours, panting like a dog on a hot summer day. As I get my bearings, I slowly bring my breathing under control. The realization shatters my soul. The smell of Gordon suffocates me.

35

"Hello?" Mother says into the phone. Her tones are all over the map. Mother's English sings in a happenstance rhythm. She applies all five tones from Vietnamese onto unsuspecting syllables when she speaks English. They stretch and bend at the most obscure and obtuse angles possible. Strawberries become stomberries, for example. Also, when she is angry, her application of tones betrays her intent. Sometimes I find myself playing the same musical chairs with my English.

"Hi, Mother," I respond and wait like the dutiful son that I am. When Mother gets excited or stressed it sometimes takes her a few minutes to translate. Some of the most outrageous phrases fall from her lips.

They're typically unintended and yet when she wants to be serious and intentional, her tones drape her words in friendly, humorous flavors.

"You no talk in a while. Only one Mother you have. When she's gone, she's gone. I no live forever," she opines. I sift through her tones to figure how upset she is about me not keeping in touch.

"Mother, please. School takes up a lot of my time. I've been really busy with mid-terms and I'm getting ready for end-of-semester exams," I whine. I'm trying to match the right level of guilt across generations and culture. It's exhausting.

"Study good. Still, you no forget Mother. No good thing to do," she pushes.

"Okay," I warmly say to move the conversation away from being the bad son. "How are you, Mother?"

"Father drive me crazy," Mother says, and I know she's being metaphorical.

"What's he done this time?" I ask, and wonder how long the story will take. Ever since we moved to America, Mother and Dad have been at war with each other. Dad's biggest strategic error was leaving us behind in Pulaski. The marriage never truly recovered after that. They both tried to win the culture war with their children caught between the ever shifting lines of enemies and friends.

"We go north to see his family. One minute he goes, the next no. Him drive me crazy. I no care if we go."

"If you come up, will you visit?" I ask, wonder and apprehension in my voice.

"Yes. We visit. On way home, be good. Spend night with you," Mother states with excitement coloring her words. "Will see no good son, who forgets Mother." She lobs the guilt bomb back across the line.

I remind myself to let it go. No reason to fight like we did when I was younger. I take her on because I push past my pain of being a son lost in America. I forget she's a wife lost in America. "I would love to see you, Mother. When are you planning to come?" I ask.

"Father, him drive me crazy. We be there when we be there," Mother explains.

"That will be fine. Please call so I am here when you are."

"Why you no be home? You study or run around?" Mother asks. I can picture her looking into the distance for salvation. Better metaphor—looking inwardly for the peace of mindfulness to counter the chaos of American life. She doesn't like it when I mix Christianity into her Buddhism. She says Christians are on their own path to salvation, like me being on my own path to Enlightenment. I just smile.

"No, Mother. I do study in the library," I offer in an attempt to assure her that her oldest son is not partying his life away. He may be throwing it away on unavailable men, though. My mother's love has overcome her sadness that her oldest son might not have children. But that's another story.

"Good to hear," Mother says and I can hear a smile in her tone.

"Mother..." I start, pause, and make sure I've captured her attention. "The Ghost you fished out of the river lives here in Boone. I know him." I wait for her to translate and ponder. The minutes tick by. "Did you hear me, Mother?" I repeat with concern in my voice.

"No funny," Mother hisses back.

"No, Mother. I'm serious," I respond with an edge. I want her to hear the plainness in my tone; that way she knows I'm not making a macabre joke.

"How you know?" Mother demands.

"We have the same tattoo but on different shoulders," I share. "Crazy Monk marked Gordon like he marked me." I communicate how upset I am by tightening my vocal cords for tautness instead of loudness.

"Gordon is Ghost?" Mother clarifies.

"Yes. He is the one. I told him what I know. It's very little. I still do not know why Crazy Monk did that to him, or why or when."

"I no like you calling Monk Thanh 'Crazy Monk.' You very disrespectful, you no good son," Mother chastens me. "You bad in America," she continues. "He take care of us when first father go way. He look after us. Shame you."

"Fine," I quickly say to appease Mother. She no doubt picks up on my irreverent tone. Depending on her mood, she may continue the fight.

"What he mean to you?" Mother inquires out of the blue.

"Not sure what you mean, Mother," I hesitantly respond. My defenses go to Def-Con 1. After Mother accepted my sexual orientation, she decided that she wanted to discuss my relationships in fine detail, as if she were buying produce and meats for her restaurant. The scrutiny embarrasses me. I long for a mother who would follow the 'don't ask, don't tell' policy. I'm not that fortunate.

"I hear tone in voice when name mention. You care for him," Mother points out. Her perceptions are uncanny. She always knows when I'm not speaking the truth. She may not know exactly what I'm saying but she can hear it in the tones.

"It doesn't matter anymore what I feel." Suddenly I deeply want this line of conversation to end.

"He mean?" Mother asks.

"No. I don't think he's dating anybody, either. I just don't think he's interested," I explain. This short interplay wears me down.

"Invite him to dinner," Mother suggests.

"What?" I practically shout back in surprise.

"Me want to meet Ghost again."

"I don't want to," I counter with a bit of disgust.

"Not for you, for me. For mother who son forgets," Mother triumphantly remarks. She wins the verbal duel and knows it. I'm too focused on the battle and she's won the war.

"Fine," I reluctantly agree. "I can't guarantee that he'll show, though. You must give me a date. I can't tell Ghost it'll be at some vague time in the future." I make it clear that nondescript dates and times don't work when inviting people outside of family.

Once Mother calls back with a better date than, "Father drive me crazy," I leave a message for Gordon that my parents are coming for dinner on the Friday before Christmas. They change their plans to see me before heading to the Virginia Mountains so when they're ready to leave, it's a straight shot outta there and back to Florida. Father loves the warmth now.

"You're going, right?" Sara asks me. "Here's your chance to thank the woman who saved your life."

"I haven't seen or spoken to Vy since our bike ride," I reply. "What would I have to say?" I look at Sara for an answer.

"Why don't you start with 'thank you'? Why are you so against this? The almighty Gordon is playing chicken shit. Puleaze." Sara mocks me hard.

"You wouldn't understand." The stink of that ill-prepared phrasing derails me. It's an amateur move that a Master like Sara can handle blindfolded, with her hands tied behind her back.

"What's there to understand? You've told me that you'd give your right leg to find out who saved you. Now you know and it didn't cost you a right leg. Seems incredibly simple." Sara closes in. "Really, Gordon. What are you afraid of?"

"Nothing," I say and realize at that moment that I will be going to Vy's dinner to meet his parents. Deep down, I do want to thank the woman who saved my life. The one I've always wanted to meet. "Do you want to go with me?" I beckon Sara to throw me a lifeline.

"If you want."

Friday comes much too quickly. Thankfully, exams finished a little more than a week ago. It's not enough time to prepare for wilderness survival when the guy you have a crush on is meeting your mother again for the first time in 20 years. The sun burns bright, yet it was not warm all week. The temperatures fall below normal and the winds howl down the mountain slopes. Chemical peels aren't necessary when Mother Nature provides her own cool blast for your face.

"He late," Mother states flatly. I look at her midsection and realize that the bacon cheeseburgers have taken their toll. I've told her that small Asian women get rounder when they eat too much. I challenge her why she does not keep to the Buddhist diet, vegetarian. She tells me to mind my own business. So I counter by telling her that her black outfits can only hide so many diet sins. I get another scolding for mixing Christianity with her Buddhism.

"I told you I couldn't make him come," I retort, as I look around the restaurant. I'm a bit upset that I had to do this in the first place. Until the phone message, I haven't spoken to Gordon since the bike trip, even though I did smell his odor on that guy in the library. That freaked me out badly for days.

"I'm hungry. I want to order," Dad announces. He's reading the menu with his back to the door. Dad has aged less gracefully than Mother. His diabetes and gout ravish his body as it ticks down. He's stable for now, but is getting slower each time I see him. He's become round like Mother.

"Okay, let's give him a few more minutes," I say. Maybe he won't show. He never actually said yes or no. But I don't tell Mother that.

As I look toward the entrance for the tenth time, I finally spot Gordon walking in, along with his friend, Sara, whom I met once before. Sara makes eye contact first and then pushes Gordon along. He seems nervous.

"Hi Sara," I warmly say as I stand to hug her. I see Gordon is a bit surprised that I'm so familiar with her. "Hey, Gordon." I move in for a hug, but he quickly sticks his hand out. I shake it but I'm disappointed that we aren't hugging. It's not like I haven't touched everything. I then turn to Mother and Dad to introduce everybody.

Gordon sits next to Mother, Sara sits next to me, and my father sits at the head of the table. I can tell that Gordon is studying my mother's face, looking for a hint of recognition.

"You heal good," Mother announces with a smile.

"Thank you, Mame," Gordon responds.

I watch and listen to Gordon's interaction with Mother a bit too intently. Thankfully, we order immediately and the food comes quickly. I'm uncomfortable and want this to end as soon as possible. The whole time, Mother is surveying everyone. Dad just wants to eat and I can see he doesn't care what happens. Sara is bubbly in her slate-blue mock sweater and skirt while Gordon reinforces his defenses. He's handsome in his gray pullover with the red seal over his right chest and blue jeans. Crazy Monk is where I lay the blame for this current scene.

"Son tells me that you Ghost I pull from river," Mother remarks. The whole table except for Dad freezes. We hold our collective breaths.

"Yes, Mame." I can barely hear Gordon's response.

"He says you have same tattoo."

"Yes, Mame." Again, he can barely muster a response.

"Monk great artist before we leave behind. He paint. One day heart broke, he give all up," Mother says to a hushed table. I never heard this before. Mother had known the Monk before we ever arrived in the village. By the time we moved in, they were already on friendly terms. "He become Monk to learn Enlightenment. Leave world of not real. Travel inside," Mother continues. "He risk everything for you."

"He did?" Gordon asks, clearly seeking more clarification. He's wearing a perplexed look on his face.

"Việt cộng no good. If you found, whole village punished. He knew. He do so anyway. You fever no break. He grow concern." Mother enters a remembrance trance. We are all so enraptured with her story that we stop eating, except for Dad. He's content to eat and amuse himself with his own thoughts. "Day to day the fever no break. He say must go. So we go," Mother trails off.

"I remember you guys arguing," I say to help clarify.

Mother looks at me. "Yes, we argue but over leaving childs behind. He wants me leave childs with him in monastery be safe. No mother leave childs behind. I fear no see anymore. Family stay together; live together; die together. Whatever the path bring, bring," Mother exalts. "He thought me foolish. I thought him stewpeed. I no leave childs behind. I prefer die than do that."

"That's so courageous," Sara sniffles, holding tightly to her tears.

"We trade all for water buffalo and cart. No need except clothes we have. You heavy and stinky. Smell like bad milk." Mother shakes her head with the recollection.

"Why did you risk taking me away from the village?" Gordon asks. I can tell that Mother doesn't quite understand the question.

"Aiee. Very dangerous. If caught, bad things happen," she confirms. "Việt cộng or Americans, good or bad, no way to know."

I look over to Gordon, and see that his eyes are glistening. His mouth is trembling as he searches for the right words. When none come, he silently reaches his hand over the table and embraces hers. Mother beams.

"You grow big, strong. You do good. Good choice to save you, do you agree?" Mother asks.

"Oh, yes," Gordon concurs through the wetness in his eyes.

I'm astonished at how Mother has disarmed Gordon's defenses. She skillfully maneuvered through his facades like a master weaver. She now holds his hand and squeezes it. She seems genuinely happy. I would say that she likes the consequences. She saved a man's life, saved her family from poverty and an uncertain future, and saved her heart for a new love that drives her crazy.

"I want to thank you..." Gordon says. He's about to continue but she waves her hand at him.

"No. no. No thanks due. Choice I make. Glad it work out," Mother protests. "See you today is thanks enough." Mother smiles and bows her head.

I knew my mother was an amazing woman, but this display tops it all. She's really only wanted to see that Gordon was doing okay today. I watch as Gordon stands up and gives her a warm, wet hug.

I look over at Sara, who is now trying hard to suppress her tears. I can feel the rawness of the emotions seeping around us, filling the air like a London fog, coating us in a fine mist. Dad seems immune, though. I can see he's ready to go. "Let me get the check," I say to the group.

"Our treat. Dad pay." Mother stops me. Dad pulls out his wallet from his back pocket.

"No, please. Let me," Gordon says as he disengages from the hug. Mother looks at Gordon with a withering glance and he stops in his tracks.

"Our treat," Mother repeats herself and we all get it.

On the drive back to the apartment, the night holds the sky's diamonds in perfect position. With no clouds, the air grows colder, ringing the moon that casts a sliver light over the Boone valley. The snow on the trees climbing the mountain sides glisten in the moon's soft glow.

"Did you like meeting Gordon?" I ask Mother as we sit in the dark of the car cabin heading to the apartment.

"Good man. Be together one day," Mother says nonchalantly.

"What? Be together one day?" I respond with a heap of skepticism. "He wants nothing to do with me. I'd be lucky if he wants to be friends."

"He know not where he go. Path unseen for him. Him stop in place. I see you like him. I also see he like you. He not know he likes." Mother smiles after her broken English sings a song, although off key.

"Mother," I say, exhausted from fighting her.

"Mother not give false hope to son. You see," Mother interjects and closes the conversation. I'm reminded of the Crazy Monk and his sayings about the Path and that we blossom on it like the lotus blossoms on the water. The flower does not think but does as is. That is the Tao. I'm awake, I think. My Path is nowhere to be seen.

"What an amazing woman!" Sara exclaims as we drive back to my place in town. "How can you not admire her determination and courage to help a complete stranger who could've cost her everything?" she marvels.

"How very true," I respond. "She wants no thanks from me because what she did was expected. While she held my hand, I think she was reading my mind. When she squeezed it, I nearly jerked it back." I see Sara rolling her eyes. "I know. I'm reading things into the ordinary."

"Is there a reason why you and Vy aren't friends?" Sara gently asks.

"What do you mean?" I respond, my voice full of incredulity.

"What happened on the bike trip?"

"Nothing," I answer a bit too quickly.

"Gordon, I know you. Don't insult me," Sara demands. "We've been friends for far too long. You can confide in me."

I allow a pause to build between us before I respond. It shelters the confession that's coming. "Before we discovered our tats, we were having sex." I spy Sara rolling her eyes. "It's true, dammit. He fell into the water and I went in after him. When we got to the shore, we took off our clothes for them to dry. Vy was shivering badly so I hugged him to keep him warm. He then kissed me and I kissed him back." I let it all out. Sara becomes my priest.

"I knew it! Over that dinner, we knew you weren't sharing everything. Suspicion flowed like a 500-year flood. Even Jeff knew something was up when you first mentioned the tattoo," Sara admits.

I go on the defense. "I freaked. It was Vy who spotted the tattoos' similarities. When he showed me his tattoo, my self-denial crumbled around me. I was forced to admit that I had been in that village, and that Vy's mother had rescued me."

"Gordon, you can't control everything that comes your way. Vy also received a revelation that day. You guys never talked about it," Sara points out with force. "Without that talk, your emotional tinsel hangs and will get in the way. It's gone from decorative to hideous in one fell swoop."

"After I freaked I was embarrassed. It's easier to let it lie than to pick it up and examine it."

"Well, just to let you know—and don't kill the messenger—Jeff's going to ask Vy out." A bomb has been dropped. Right on my foot.

"What?" I'm smacked.

"Hey. You snooze you lose," Sara mocks without any remorse. "You can't put your life on hold so that you can control the consequences of dating someone."

I shake my head. I just met Vy's amazing mother and recognized where Vy got his bearings from. I've been a jerk about the whole tat thing. Sara's right. I've been cat napping and Jeff's making his move. I'm not sure if I have anything to offer Vy. I'm not really dating and I work all the time. I wonder if it's best that I walk away from this.

I pull into the carport and walk Sara to her car in the basement garage.

"You know, it doesn't mean Jeff's going to be successful," Sara elaborates. "It takes two to be a couple. Vy's the wildcard in all this." Sara grins and gets into her car.

As I watch her back out, I marvel at the women in my life. They can see all the truths that I keep buried from myself. They kick me in the head when I need sense. And they push me to strut forward when I want

to be stuck. I realize that it's about damn time I dug
myself out of the mud.

36

"Hey, Vy. It's Jeff," the recording says. "Call me sometime. Maybe we can do dinner?" He sounds positively upbeat.

The holidays are nearly over and school re-starts next week. There aren't many prospects for companionship unless I want to go mining through the student vein. Most arrive with no intention of staying, which is the direction I'm heading. Jeff could be a nice diversion, someone to know while finishing up the degree. I don't see any other prospects on the horizon. I need to burn the mining map and return to the prospecting office. Time is ripe to leave behind the gear.

We decide to meet at a pizza place near campus. I want a low-key affair with good food, and the Mellow Mushroom fits the bill.

"Hey Jeff, it's great to see you," I smile as I approach the table. I study Jeff as he rises to hug me. His striped blue shirt brings out the blue in his eyes, which the harsh mountains have etched handsome lines around. His smile radiates across the terrain and gently heats the surface for a crinkly snapshot.

"Glad you could make it. How's school?" Jeff asks warmly and then returns to his seat. The restaurant is a nondescript, heavily wooded square room. The country-style dining table and chairs give it a rustic feel. It's all about the pizza.

"The first semester kicked my ass," I respond. "By the end, I wrote ten 10-page papers and the introduction for my Master's thesis. I'm told if I ever want to pursue a PhD, then having a Master's thesis is the way to go. At this point, I'm crawling across the finish line." I breathe a sigh of relief. I bathe in Jeff's smile.

"Does it get any easier?" Jeff winks in response.

"I've heard from my professors that the first semester strips the chafe from the stalk. I feel first-hand how taxing and draining all that stripping is," I say. "Now they say the concentration for me is to finish the Master's thesis. Since I survived, my reward is no longer proving I belong. That's a good thing. If I had another semester like the first one, I'd seriously be homicidal."

I grin to let Jeff know I'm not being serious. I enjoy academics.

"Have you thought about life after school? Are you going to stay?" Jeff asks. I can see that he is hanging on for my response.

"I haven't really thought about it. Boone is a small university town. I'd need to find employment if I have any hope of staying," I respond. "It seems to me that the main categories the people here fall into are old-timers, students, faculty, and retirees. I don't find many over-40, single gay men ready for nesting, empire building, and relationship hunting."

"I know what you mean. Unless you've got money, it's hard to live here. Of course if your family has been here since the beginning of time, then you've got some advantages. You know people. People know you. People make it happen," Jeff laughs.

"Sounds like the mafia," I squeal. We both laugh and sink into an easy rhythm of conversation.

"What do you do, Jeff?" I inquire as we finish our meal.

"I run a lunch-only restaurant in Downtown Boone. It feeds the students and university personnel during the weekdays. It offers another choice besides the cafeteria. In the evenings, I wait tables at my friend's restaurants."

"Ingenious," I exclaim. I pull my focus off Jeff and casually scan the restaurant. "I think this place wants to close," I remark.

"What gave it away? The chairs on the tables?"

"Smart ass." I poke him. Since we paid an hour ago, we get up and head towards the door.

"Thank you, Jeff. I enjoyed our dinner," I smile. I'm content with how the evening went, and am ready to walk away when he stops me.

"Let me see you home. I did drive and there's no need to walk."

"Kind of you to take me home. I seem to rely on the kindness of strangers these days," I say as he pulls into the driveway. The idea of inviting him in snakes around me as the car halts. I'm not ready for that. I lean in to give him a thank you kiss before pulling the escape hatch and ejecting from the confines of the cabin. That way he won't need to get out of the car. I'm working to save us from any awkward moments. Of course that would be too easy for me.

Jeff grabs the opportunity, literally, with both hands as my face squeezes small and my lips pucker. He passionately returns the offer. I can feel his breath pump into my mouth as if I were a balloon. He tries to insert his tongue but I outmaneuver his attempt by meeting him half-way.

"You're very handsome," Jeff whispers as we disengage. "I wanted to do that all evening. I fought the urge to feed you pizza. I kept myself in check as a good boy."

"I'm flattered," I manage. I don't want to string him along; I'm enjoying the companionship. "I don't want to ruin our friendship or get ahead of ourselves."

"Ok." I hear the disappointment like a fog horn in the dark alerting the ships from the rocky shores. There is a pregnant pause. "Gay Ski Weekend at the lodge is coming up," he says. "It's the second weekend in February. You want to go?" I can tell that Jeff is not going to give up so easily.

I see the expectation light up his blue eyes. As I focus, I can't help remember the other blue eyes that had me searching open skies. I lose my way between them with nothing to guide me across the vast space. I can't seem to find my place. "Sure," I hear my voice say and I wonder why I give it away.

As the days tick by, I kick myself for saying "Sure." There's a part of me that wishes the word "no" would enter my vocabulary. I often wonder why I can't form that one-syllable word. That one word has some real power. That one word allows me to claim choices for myself; it comes from the I-place. I'm the type if I say I will do it, I will move heaven and earth to do so. That gets me into so much trouble, especially charity fucks.

Jeff wants to come by and pick me up as if this were prom night. I dread going under that charade. I'm not much for winter sports so I beg off anything outdoors. Saturday night is the big dance. One of the few times there is anything resembling a gay festive outing around here. If you want that, then you have to drive to Greensboro or Charlotte, and that's at least a couple of hours. I put Jeff off for as long as possible, and a stroke of luck hits me like a bolt from the sky. A very good friend of Jeff's who is catering the food needs help when one of his workers gets sick with the flu.

"Got bad news, Vy," I hear a humbling Jeff on the other end.

"What do you mean?" I ask in hushed tones.

"I'm going to have to help set up and maybe work a little during the dance," Jeff moans.

"I'm sorry to hear that," I respond in soothing tones. I'm glad for my good fortune. "That's the bad news?" I hope that my tones do not carry relief, joy, or excitement.

"Yeah. Its impact is the bad news," Jeff remarks. "I won't be able to pick you up and spend the night dancing away under the wall of windows." He's clearly bummed.

Whew. This may be bad news for you but it's a major relief for me. I won't have to work through a plausible reason for meeting at the dance instead of doing a pick up. This will severely limit any extracurricular activities between us. And there won't be any friends-with-benefits shenanigans happening either. "Bummer. I'll see you there then," I say.

I arrive at the dance wearing a tight black t-shirt, jeans with holes in all the right places, and squared-off, black leather ankle boots. When I was in D.C., the look I went for was called "high fag attitude." It was a look I barely pulled off with as much aplomb as before, due to how my fat settles around my mid-section. I may still have a 32-inch waist, but it now has handles for carrying purposes, the bane of a single gay man, regardless of age. For this evening, I want to catch just a glimpse of my former youth in the vanity mirror.

"Hey Jeff!" I call out as I round the corner into one of the rooms off the main reception area. The room doubles as the dance floor and overlooks the backyard and mountains. Every time I'm here I marvel at the wall of windows. I've discovered that all the dance events have the same basic set up. I find Jeff in the other room, behind the bar.

"Vy! You look hot," Jeff grins.

"Kind of you to say," I bounce back with a hint of attitude. The outfit's desirable effect heats the air around me. I'm basking in being an attention whore. "Are you working all evening or just until the party gets going?" I ask.

"Most of the evening. I'm sorry," Jeff says with puppy dog eyes. "I may be able to break away every now and then since I'm doing this as a favor."

"Okay," I note with a hint of disappointment. I may not want to lead Jeff on but I would like a dancing partner who can lead.

I work my way around to the dance room and slide down the right side. When I get to the wall of windows, I set my drink on the window ledge and see both the dance floor to my left and meadow to my right. It looks to be about 30 guys here in all sorts of arrangements: singles, couples with sparks, couples without sparks, groupings, and a few mixed groups. Unless you ask, you're never sure how each individual relates to another individual. It gets quite political, comical, and farcical. You never want to say the wrong thing because it becomes your calling card.

As I sway to the music, I exhale and allow the rhythms to roll over my body. I un-focus from the gyrating, pulsating bodies and see them as a sea of grass swaying in stormy winds. I step into the sea and take my place. Soon, I'm whirling, twirling, and swirling through the sonic landscape. I catch the eyes of some of the other dancers and make imaginary connections. I create stories of how we ended here together. I silently laugh at some of the absurdities I concoct.

"You should go and dance with Vy. He's scorching tonight," Sara announces as we both see Vy dancing by himself.

"He seems completely into himself. I've not really been a friend of late. There's no telling how he'll react," I counter.

"Who cares? Go. Or I'll do it," Sara persists.

I watch Vy's body gyrate masterfully to the music. He seems like he's having a great adventure by himself.

Sara's right; I should slide next to him and see what happens.

I turn and instantly see Gordon matching my movements. I smile and lean in. "So nice of you to join me," I coo. I'm too much into my element to care about the water under the bridge. I still have a weakness for Gordon. I pretend this night that Gordon is mine.

"I couldn't let these other guys think you're alone," he flirts.

"You say the kindest things," I smirk and pivot away from him. I see Gordon step forward to close the distance. Soon, our bodies are matching movements and I can feel his breath on my nape. I relax my back into him. For a moment we are moving in sync. I feel through my back the solidness of his chest. Some of his hairs poke me. I giggle slightly at the tickle.

I feel Vy's body against mine and grind closer. I catch his scent off his nape and bury my nose into his flesh. I pull him tight so I can feel the beat through his body hitting mine. I grip his hips and dock him into my crotch. We do a little dirty dancing, and I feel myself getting excited. I've got to be careful; Vy always seems to get past my defenses.

I think Gordon might be getting a bit excited. I feel a poke as we grind together. I laugh it off, letting my guard down around him. It feels too comfortable. I can listen to his stories all night. I want to watch him sleep; I want to make plans for two; I want him to be the beginning and the ending of my days. I must pull it together. I'm slipping back into fantasyland.

With that thought, Gordon pulls me over to Sara. I wouldn't be surprised if she's the one who pushed Gordon my way.

"Hey, Sara. Great to see you, Ms. Beautiful," I beam and give her a smooch on the cheek. I watch Gordon out of the corner of my eye picking up his drink on the window sill. "Is that your usual gin and tonic?" I smile.

"Got me dead to rights," he exclaims. "Best concoction ever."

I just smirk. I wonder what number he's on. "I'm happy I ran into you. I thought I would be dancing with myself, a la Billy Idol," I remark.

"Certainly can't have THAT," Sara deadpans and then looks right at Gordon. I see that I'm right about who pushed who towards dancing.

"Vy, it was great meeting your mother. I should have said something earlier. She's an amazing woman," Gordon says.

I blush at the compliment. "Thank you, Gordon," I simply say. I did wonder how the meeting had gone for him.

"Yes Vy, I agree with Gordon. She's so courageous," Sara interjects.

"What a love fest you two have got going!" I grin. Frankly, I'm getting embarrassed. At the time, we saved Gordon because it simply was necessary. We didn't expect anything in return. Mother always does what she thinks is her duty. Back to the present, I'm touched that they feel this way.

I smile at Vy. He seems a bit embarrassed. I can see the blush spreading across his cheeks. That's sooo cute. "How about dinner next week?" I blurt. Sara and Vy snap their necks toward me, like I'm a mouse to starving barn owls.

"I can't," Sara quickly answers. "But you guys definitely go." She pushes hard as if her life depended on it.

"What do you say, Vy?" I follow up with a hint of expectation and hope mixed into my voice. "For old time's sake..." I add as a gentle nudge.

"Sure," I say, using my old faithful. I'm not quite sure what to do. I do like Gordon and I'm not sure where he's at. If he's in dating mode, I could get clues to where he's likely to make landfall. It's the same reasoning behind hurricanes. When they're stationary, they can go anywhere and their paths are obscure. Only when they're moving can you hope to get an idea of where they are going. If I'm not careful, he'll strike somewhere unexpected and I'll be left with the emotional disaster. There's no FEMA for that.

Our conversation is interrupted by a familiar voice. "Hey, guys!" We all turn to Jeff as he ambles up.

I try to look relaxed and content. This is supposed to be our date. It's every guy's nightmare. You show up to an event with the boy of choice and he goes home with someone else.

"Jeff," I acknowledge.

"What's up?" Jeff continues.

"We've been dancing and drinking," Gordon says. He winks at me and raises his glass.

"Sounds great," Jeff comments. "I've got to get back to work. But Vy, let's have dinner. It's my treat to make up for a bust this night's turning out to be." I smile politely, and Jeff heads off.

I can see Gordon and Sara looking at me, cornering me for an explanation. "Jeff asked me to the dance but then ended up working it. He's filling in for someone who's sick," I elaborate.

"I see," Sara smirks. She then turns to Gordon and passes him a look. I wonder what that's supposed to mean.

"Jeff's a nice man. He wants more than I can give. I don't have any solutions there." I feel the need to defend myself. "I see us becoming friends, but nothing more," I state.

Vy is certainly making a spirited defense. I can't blame him if he wants to go out on a date with Jeff. I haven't actually shown any strong interest. It's not like

we're dating or anything. It's fun to watch him squirm,
though. I should throw him a lifeline. "How about you
come by 7:30 next Saturday?"

"That'll be great." I grab the line and reel myself to
shore. I best go before I overstay my welcome. I do feel
strange, like I'm cheating on Jeff even though there's
no dating relationship between us. It's that whole who-
you-come-with and who-you-leave-with thing ricochet-
ing in my brain. "It's getting late. I see that it's already past two. I better leave."

"Or what? You'll turn into a pumpkin?" Gordon
laughs.

"Age cripples me; youth forgets me," I plea. "Anyhow, I don't like driving in the snow and ice. It'll take
me 10 times as long to get home," I comment.

"Gordon, you should take Vy home," Sara offers.
We both turn to look at her. She has become Medusa,
having turned our stares into stone. "I'm actually going to stay the night here."

"You are?" Gordon asks with a mixture of disbelief
and incredulity.

"Yes, Gordon. You know I always take a room just
in case. We always seem to stay too late and get
smashed. Now go." Sara pushes us away.

I turn to look at Gordon. "It's okay. I'll be fine. I'll
make it."

"For heaven's sake." Sara throws her arms to the sky. "Just go!" She commands and pulls us along in her wake.

As we leave together, I catch a perplexed look on Jeff's face as he watches the two of us exit the lodge. The last thing I see is Sara moving towards Jeff.

"You want me to drive?" Gordon asks.

"Sure. I'm not that good in this type of weather." Ah, Gordon: my knight in shining armor.

The road home is mostly quiet. I sit back in the passenger seat and marvel at how the evening has turned out. I come with one person and leave with another. I realize the man I left behind must be traumatized.

"What are you thinking, Vy?" I ask. I look over and study his pensive expression.

"Oh, nothing. I'm just marveling at how white everything is. It's been a while since I've seen this much snow and ice. It's quite beautiful." When he says this, his eyes lock onto mine.

As I pull into his parking space, I wonder exactly what I'm doing. Unless he's driving me home now, I will have to become his houseguest. So I just go with the flow. It's not like we haven't already done it or seen each other naked.

"I can sleep on the sofa," I offer.

"Or... you could share the mattress?" he throws back.

I don't want to lead Vy on, but I'd like to spend the night with him.

"Look. We don't have to do anything. We can just wake up next to each other," he says, throwing me a lifeline.

"Ok, Vy," I say and hope the awkwardness passes.

As we climb into bed, I turn to my side and close my eyes. I lay there, hoping Gordon will touch me. I don't want to look directly at him for fear that it'll be too intimate. I want to feel his touch. That would be enough. Just as I begin to fade away, I feel Gordon snuggling up against me and his nose burrowing into my neck. I sleep in paradise, at least for one night before I'm cast out of the garden.

37

"I'm ecstatic that you're doing Spring Break with me," Jerry announces. "I know how much you hate the cold, and I'm sure you'd rather be visiting the parental units in Florida."

I look around my favorite restaurant and see a kaleidoscope of patrons. "Yes. You must be my best friend," I deadpan. "I don't want to spend the money this year."

"Money issues?" Jerry asks, his concern wrapping around me.

"Unfortunately, yes. I'm finding that full-time school is eating through my savings quite rapidly. I'm stuffed with debt. It's a vacation home payment without the good times," I remark with a hint of desperation. I stare at Jerry and decide to drop the bomb. "I've decided to sell the condo."

"What?" Jerry explodes. His alarm at the prospect contorts his face.

"Yeah. I think it's time to move on. Plus, it'll solve my current cash flow crisis," I explain.

"Are you planning to stay in Boone? What's happening between you and Gordon?" Jerry panics. The concerned tide rises up like a tidal wave about to smash the coastline.

"There's nothing going on between Gordon and me. For a split second, I let myself believe that there was, especially after he stayed the night." The tidal wave curls higher above me.

"What?"

I smile because his total attention is on me like a spotlight. "Remember the gay ski weekend a month ago? It was late and the weather was awful. So I was scared to drive home. After Jeff showed up and announced a make-up date, I felt that it was time to go. Well, Sara practically commanded Gordon to take me home on account of my fear of driving. I don't really mind the snow; it's the ice that petrifies me. So he did." Jerry's anticipation pours from his skin like beads of sweat.

"But how did you guys end up together?"

"Well, he drove me home, and I wasn't about to take him back to his place in that awful weather," I explain. "At first, he said he'd sleep on the sofa, but I told him we could share the mattress." I pause to check Jerry's trip status. Don't want to lose any passengers. "Once we climbed into bed, he spooned me from behind. Man, it felt great. That must be what heaven is all about, having a man's man holding onto me. Even though we both were wearing t-shirts and boxers, I could feel everything from the curve of his body, to the poking of his fur, and to the rise and fall of his breathing. I could have died happy at that moment."

"And?" Jerry opines as he tugs on the fishing line for that elusive catch.

"And?" I mimic. "And nothing. The next morning he was up and dressed and waiting for me downstairs. I made a joke about him doing the walk of shame, wearing the same thing he wore the night before. He responded with a blank look. He might've thought it was shame."

"I'm sorry, Vy," Jerry says, trying to console me.

"Oh, it gets better," I interject. "At the dance, he asked me out for dinner the following Saturday. After our evening together, he called that Saturday to see if it was a problem to meet at the restaurant. What was I going to say?"

"No he didn't," Jerry mocks as he waves his index finger around in his most put upon southern black woman persona.

"Oh yes he do," I fire back. "He even brought someone." I wait for a moment. "We all had a pleasant dinner and then it was time to go. As I left, I couldn't help wondering what parallel universe I was living in. For every step forward I think I take with Gordon, he ends up three back and one to the side."

"It's not you, Vy," Jerry affirms. "I think Gordon doesn't know what he wants. And where is Craig in all this? Do you think they're still carrying on? And who is this person he brought?"

"Actually, he brought Craig to our supposed date," I respond.

"What?" Jerry exclaims. This time his jaw drops and his eyes explode.

"I hadn't seen Craig for a while until that night. He's usually working on his rental when he's in town. Or drinking with Gordon. Who knows?"

"That's fucked up," Jerry says.

"Well. I did enjoy myself that night. I like both of them. We laughed and talked most of the night away. Tom's still not coming to the mountains, and as far as I know, he and Craig are still together. At the end of the night, Gordon and Craig left together."

"I still say there's something going on there. I'm sorry," Jerry says.

"It's okay. I should never get my hopes up. I know better. Besides, I'm thinking of moving west, like to Seattle or Portland, once I get the degree."

"That's so far away," Jerry remarks. "What am I to do with my best friend across the country?"

"Visit," I say. "D.C. isn't home anymore. I think that's why I'm so restless. I'm in search of a place to hang my hat. Living in an army family gave me a new set of friends every few years. Families rotated in and out of the military housing we lived in. I watched our block change over completely almost every two years."

Days roll by, and soon it's time for me to leave D.C. Since I'm selling, my place is already empty of furniture. I brought along my sleeping bag for the night, since I'm coordinating the resurrection of my abode. Renters suck the life out of the place like building vampires. Some colors will do the place good.

Walking home from the restaurant, I'm lost in thought. Without noticing, I brush past a solitary figure under the street lamp at 17th and P Street. "Hello, stranger," I hear from out of the cone of darkness. Startled, I turn to the source of the sound and watch the solitary figure take shape, depth, and color.

"Hey. Is that you, Tom?" I project towards the shadowy figure. He's edging into the cone of light.

"It is. You're looking good, Vy. The mountains seem to agree with you," Tom grins. He's lost weight. I'd say about 15 pounds. His fighting shape pushes against his clothes, ready for a rumble.

"You're too kind," I blush back. "Where have you been? I've seen Craig every now and then."

"I don't go up to the mountains anymore. I find it an ordeal on many levels," Tom states in a matter-of-fact tone.

"Really? I'm thinking of moving west once I get the degree. There's not much in Boone to keep me."

"But what about Gordon? He isn't enough?" Tom asks. I immediately perk up.

"Why would you say that?" I quickly strike. He must know something that might be coming from Craig.

"Craig mentioned that there might be some energy there," Tom explains.

"I don't really think so. I fell for Gordon during a window of opportunity but the window slammed on my fingers. I've been smarting ever since."

"He's a great catch. You might want to stay with it," Tom affirms.

Tom's thunderbolt smashes me with surprise and sucks all my oxygen away. I expected a neutron bomb as opposed to a humanitarian shipment. Why the endorsement? I ponder. I can't help myself after that comment. "Tom. I know this ain't my business, but I heard Gordon and Craig are in a down-low relationship. Every time I ignore that, I walk away with emotional wounds that no ER can heal. I constantly wake from traversing a parallel universe, where I think Gordon is interested until his actions scrub those intentions away."

Tom laughs. Is a psychotic break coming? I'm unsure what to make of this display. I wait for something, anything, to make the water less murky so I can view the bottom. My patience pays off.

"I don't think so. I think I'd know if a romantic relationship existed between the two," Tom states. He asks for clarification. "What have you heard?"

The street lamp becomes the interrogator's weapon of choice. "I hear Gordon and Craig are involved but keeping it on the down low. My source is third-party, though. Anyhow, I'm sorry for bringing it up," I backpedal and admonish my curiosity that kills the cat.

"You're fine. I expected you'd hear about it sooner or later. Boone isn't that big, as you may have noticed," Tom laughs. "One night Gordon and Craig were caught having sex in Gordon's hot tub. What they never knew is who told me. The irony is that no one did. I went to Boone as a surprise and stumbled upon them. I watched for a few minutes to make sure of what I was seeing and then left." Tom pauses and collects himself. I wait patiently. "After a few weeks, I confronted Craig. He swore it was a mistake and that there was no premeditation. He said there wouldn't be any ongoing friends with benefits. I've been with Craig long enough, over 20 years, to know when he's lying. I didn't think he was when he told me that, but I know he's not telling me everything. I wouldn't be surprised if they had been messing around for some time."

"I'm sorry to hear that," I reply. "I know you guys are having difficulties."

"I know. It's obvious. I'm not sure why I've been using it as a hammer these last few years. I've made peace with what I saw. What makes me mad is that somehow our relationship reached a point where our love was taken for granted. How can you just happen to cheat? Well, you can if the relationship is painted in a for-granted color. We've been together a long time. It's time to stop making excuses; it's time to bite the bullet; and it's time to hire the lawyers to unwind us." Tom gazes at his feet. "We aren't living. It's like zombie land. It looks like Abby and I are on our own."

I hug Tom for sharing and head home. I'm confused by this new information. If Gordon's free, then why is he stepping back three and over one for every one step forward? I can't figure this puzzle out and it paralyzes me.

With Spring Break in effect, the grocery stores are less chaotic here in Boone. This eye-of-the-storm moment—just after the students have left and before the tourists arrive—gives us residents a respite from the crazies, except for the home-grown variety. I can actually run in and grab items without having to pack rations in little green cans for extended patrols.

"Hello, Gordon." A familiar voice stops me dead in my tracks as I'm about to round the aisle's corner. I turn towards the trapper.

"Hey Jeff! It's been a while. How are you?" I start the small talk and hope it's quick.

"I'm doing the best I can. What have you been up to lately?"

"Nothing but the family business. It keeps me busy," I respond.

"Hanging out with Vy then?" Jeff throws the gauntlet down. Jugular attacks are his specialty. Even with the wide grocery aisles, the collateral damage is sometimes high. His eyes narrow with anticipation.

"No. I saw Vy a week after the ski dance. Craig and I joined him for a Saturday dinner. I haven't seen him since," I say.

"Well that explains a couple of things," Jeff sighs. His tone wraps into a smug blanket.

"What do you mean?" I fall for the trap.

"Mid-week I had dinner with Vy. His demeanor had changed. He told me that it wasn't fair for him to lead me on and that he hoped we could be friends. He said he'd understand if I couldn't accept that." Jeff lowers the boom in his voice but still hangs back.

"I'm sorry to hear that. You guys would've made a cute couple." I work to soften his disappointment.

"You don't say," Jeff icily responds. The blizzard blows through the aisle after it scrapes across the graveyard. "You guys have a one-night stand after the dance?" Jeff lobs it in.

"No. Did Vy say we did?" I get annoyed at this potential falsehood.

"No. He didn't. I asked him what happened. He said you guys shared a mattress and nothing more." Jeff puts me at ease with his reply.

"You see, just friends," I triumphantly remark.

"You damn fool!" Jeff explodes.

The eruption of such strong emotions involuntarily pushes me back a step. Jeff pounces on the confusion pouring from my face and stinking up my body.

"Helen Keller can feel how much Vy wants you; a blind man can see how much Vy longs for you; a deaf man can hear Vy running after you. Hell. I noticed you guys leaving together from the dance. And Sara! Her attempts to smooth over whatever she thought I was going to do with Vy was the icing on the cake. She shouldn't bother, not in Vy's case, because his intentions are a lighthouse for woebegone ships," Jeff hisses under his breath. He wants to scream and make a scene but he's doing his best to keep it in.

"Jeff—"

"Don't 'Jeff' me," Jeff spits out. "I've known you since high school. I don't know what your problem is. How many shooting stars do you think you get to capture here in Boone? How many Vy's come walking through here? Dammit, Gordon! We could be in our 60s before someone like him comes through here again," Jeff bellows.

"Take it down a notch, man. I don't know what's getting you so worked up. Yeah, I think Vy's a handsome guy—"

"Oh for the love of God, stop!" Jeff interjects. "Open your damn eyes and live a little. After the idiot stunts you've been pulling, I heard that Vy is leaving town once he gets his degree in December." He cuts the jugular clean. The spray coats us.

"He is? I'm sorry to see him go." I subtly shift away from Jeff's emotional display, hiding my reaction.

"For the love, you're so THICK." Jeff tightens his vocal cords into a fishing line capable of slicing heads off. I'm puzzled and it must show. "Don't give me that stupid act. You can't be that thick!" Jeff throws his hands up and marches off in a huff.

I'm totally turned around as to why I'm in the center of this maelstrom. I stalk after Jeff. "Dammit. Stop, Jeff," I whisper harshly. I don't want this scene to get too out of control. You never know who's watching in this small town. I grab Jeff's shoulder and he turns, revealing the rage contorting his face. "What the hell are you talking about?"

"Really?" Jeff says with the thickest sarcasm he can spread. When he sees that I'm not taking the bait, he continues. "Do you think Vy is intelligent?" Jeff exasperatedly asks.

"Yes," I note, confused.

"Vy could have gone anywhere to get his Master's. So why did he choose Appalachian State University?"

I shrug, roll my eyes, and put my hands up, palms out. I display a simple, mentally challenged look.

"I'm tired of this game. You truly can't be that thick," a defeated Jeff moans and walks away.

I stand, rooted in place. I don't believe Vy is in Boone because of me. Why would he do that? I don't think I've led him on for him to do something like that. My head won't wrap around what Jeff's pushing.

38

Fantastic! My favorite table is open. It has a great view and a power outlet for my laptop. I get all set up and lose myself in the thesis. The writing is tough, but fun. I've never written anything longer than 20 pages and here I am, planning at least 50 pages. My index cards are filled with stats, quotations, and references. I put them in an order that should drive the structure of the paper. The hypothesis is right up front to remind me what it is I'm working to prove.

Occasionally, my mind drifts, and when it does it's time for a break. The coffee shop's food is decent. I go for the turkey sandwich and chips. It's during one of these breaks that a path appears and the object of my affection rolls in.

"Hello, Vy," Gordon projects when I spot him entering the diner.

"Hey Gordon," I respond as I set down the turkey sandwich. What are the odds that he'd come in? It's in the freakin' middle of the day on a Wednesday afternoon. There's at most five people here; well, six, counting Gordon. "How are you?" I try civility.

"I'm fine. Mind if I join you for a few minutes after I grab a coffee?" he asks.

"Sure," I say. What harm can come of this? I've pretty much given up. Nothing's ever going to happen between the two of us.

When he returns he takes a seat and asks, "What are you working on?"

"I'm starting the writing process for my thesis. It takes about six months, start to finish. That doesn't even count the defense," I say.

"Impressive. And how are your classes?"

"After this semester, I'll be done with nine classes out of 12. I'll take two over the summer, leaving me one for the fall with thesis hours. Then, I'm finished." I smile. I look into those incredible blue eyes and, dammit, I can still see the flicker. Electricity fires on my side of the table. I instinctively search for a ground to sever the current. I hear the echo of Tom's words like siren calls toward the rocks. Sailors beware!

"I see," I remark. Well, this isn't going anywhere fast. Vy seems distracted or disinterested. Our conversation remains all business. I'm getting the news but not hearing the heart of the matter. I can't blame him for keeping his distance.

"What have you been up to?" he asks. It sounds like he wants me out of here. Damn. He looks good today.

"Just work. Managing the rentals means never a dull moment," I respond. I like Vy in black. The turtle neck makes him seem even more studious and artsy. He does stick out at a right angle here in Boone.

"Okay. Well I should get back to writing," he says, signaling the end of the conversation.

"Sure thing," I confirm and get up. I turn towards the door with my coffee when I stop, turn back, and blurt out, "We never took that bike ride down on the abandoned rail line. It's pretty flat and quite scenic." I can see Vy's wariness slice through me. I wait to see if he'll take the offer.

"Remind me about the rail line again?" I inquire with a great deal of suspicion. I'm caught off guard. I don't understand why Gordon wants to do anything with me. He starts down a path and then he aborts. We may have the same tattoo and some of the same idiosyncrasies, like drinking water with no ice. That doesn't seem enough to keep us in orbit of one another.

"The trail head is actually close to where you live," he explains. "It's an old freight line the town turned into a scenic bike path. Even though the calendar says

April, you'll want to layer. No telling what the weather will be like this Saturday."

"How long is this adventure?" I ask. The last time we went into the wilderness, a huge skeleton fell out of our closets after we had sex. It was like a slasher flick of bad consequences.

"It'll be an afternoon. It's a good two to three hours."

"Okay, Gordon. Sure. At least I'll get some use out of my bike. What time should I expect you on Saturday?" I smile. I'm amused by the whole conversation. The hidden agenda stalks behind the line of sight. I feel its eyes on me.

"How about I come by two o'clock?" he grins. I just know he's trying to ease back into hanging out with me again. He doesn't want this to be an all-day event. Not yet.

"Sure," I say for the third or fourth time now, and watch him disappear through the door. It's not a lunch date but a play date. I'm intrigued about all this effort. I must remind myself to stay firmly planted in reality. That's my mantra for anytime I spend with Gordon. I must remain in reality.

Saturday sneaks up on me as I lose myself to the thesis writing. There are a couple of times I almost called to cancel. It's hard not to hang out if it's available. I let myself flow.

"You're right on time," I announce as I open the door to a smiling Gordon. He's holding his bike, and wearing a white T-shirt and blue shorts. It is 68 degrees outside, which is warm by Boone standards. Of course I'm in sweats, a thermal shirt, and a jacket for good measure.

"Vy, it's not that cold out," he grins.

"I'll bring my backpack in case I need to shed a few layers," I fire back. I hate being cold and Gordon remembers that.

"Did you want to take my car?" I ask since he's holding his bike.

"Not necessary. The trail head is about two miles from here. We'll just ride out. That way we won't have to deal with the bike rack and parking."

"Ok. Here's my visitor's parking pass for your dashboard." I give Gordon the permit.

Off we go. We weave through the traffic until we get to the trail head. I follow close behind Gordon. He's still a much stronger biker. We plunge onto the path together. It's practically flat and easy to keep up. Gordon says there's a spectacular lookout point where the valley vista spreads outward to the mountains as a backdrop.

It takes a little more than an hour before we burst upon the scenic spot. We break out of the forest canopy into a meadow of flowing grass, wild flowers, and tufts of stone and stumps. It's a rugged landscape and spring is pushing itself through the frozen tundra. Complementing the explosion of color through the brown carpet are the mountains that ring this valley. We stop and dismount our bikes, then prop them against a huge fir. The scene is breathtaking.

I hear a "swish" and turn to my left to see Gordon hurling apples into the clearing. After a couple of throws, he stops. He motions for me to stay still. I stand next to him and focus on where the apples land. I close my eyes and reach deep for a meditative state. I call upon my faith to quiet my mind and stay in the moment. I open my eyes and see deer converging on the apples.

I witness Vy's startled looks as I hurl the apples. I don't tell him that they're for the deer. After I throw a few, I place my index finger to my lips and motion for him to stand next to me. I see he's meditating. Vy's breathing slows. A moment actualizes between us as he opens his eyes and deer approach.

In that early spring meadow with the mountains watching and the deer eating, I feel connected to the land and to Gordon. I see the flecks sparkle in those deep blue eyes. The contagious grin warms me every time I see it. I want to fall into his arms and I want to hear his voice until the end of my days. But these things are just out of my reach. I ache with longing.

I see Vy swaying in the wind, watching the deer eating. He's tucked in tightly. He's most likely reveling in his cold weather gear. He's cute trying to stay warm. I remember feeling the softness of his skin. I catch his scent every now and then and find myself aroused. I imagine looking into those brown eyes every day.

The moment expands and Gordon and I are engulfed. The meadow, the mountains, the deer, and we are all suspended across wires that invisibly connect all living things. Time takes a breather and lays down its charge. We return to the moment between our heartbeats. The flow we encounter erases the distance.

I lean forward and my lips touch Gordon's. That act, like eating an apple, expands awareness and sends the soul shards racing through us. Whatever keeps us in balance ripples outward with a quiet force. It's a force with no sound. We plunge into each other and the ground breaks our fall. We laugh and roll, all the while kissing and tasting each other. When we come to a rest, I find my head resting on Gordon's strong chest and my right hand clasping his left hand. We look up and see the cumulus clouds float by. We watch odd shapes form and dissolve. We lay there, perfectly in sync. I listen to Gordon's heartbeats and match his breathing. I'm at home.

Soon the angle of the sun tells us that late afternoon is turning over its chores to its sister, night, like an unwanted houseguest who's overstayed its welcome. We help each other up. I kiss Gordon again and hang on for a few more moments. I pick up the rest of the apples and throw a couple. Gordon throws the others. We walk hand in hand to the bikes. I'm scared to let go. I'm afraid the space will become solid and keep us apart. I dread the out of sight, out of mind condition.

It feels good having Vy's head on my chest, and walking together hand-in-hand for the bikes. I wonder why I'm holding back, why I have my life on hold. He's a great catch and I fear that I'll have to throw him back. Is Boone a place that can offer Vy enough? Would I be able to offer him enough? He's keeping up as we ride back to his place. I smile. Whatever happens, I'm glad for the moment. That'll sustain me in an uncertain future.

"Thanks for the afternoon, Gordon," Vy smiles as we arrive at the car. I place my bike into the rack.

"You're very welcome. It's good to get out and explore," I respond and finish tightening the straps. That should keep the bike from slipping off.

"Next week, if you're free, you want to come over for dinner?" Vy asks, his voice trembling with anxiety.

"I'd like that," I respond. I then hug Vy and get into the car. I roll down the window and look right into those deep brown eyes. "When would you like me to come over?"

"How about Wednesday, around seven?" he asks, relief washing over his words.

"I'll see you then," I say and wave good-bye. As I look into the rearview mirror, I realize how much I like spending time with Vy. I feel at peace. It doesn't matter what happened to us in Vietnam. A connection has sparked to life this day. One that will last.

"That smells wonderful! What is it?" Gordon asks as I place our dishes on the table.

"Vietnamese Ginger Chicken," I proudly announce. It's my signature dish and one of the few that I can make.

I take my seat and we begin eating. We have a casual conversation, and Gordon can't get enough of the chicken. He absolutely loves the dish.

I pour us some after-dinner drinks, and we take our seats on the sofa. As we talk, my mind flashes to the meadow and I inwardly smile. The comfort of that moment fills the living room, dancing off of Gordon's voice. Time flies by, and suddenly its past midnight. I wonder if Gordon will stay. I hesitate to close the conversation without knowing for sure.

"As I've said before, I'd love to learn more about Asian cultures," Gordon proclaims. "There's so much history we don't learn in school here."

"You should return to Vietnam as a traveler. The country is very different than when we were there. I've been back twice now. It's amazing how it's changed and grown." With that, I kiss Gordon, pressing my advantage. We make out on the sofa and then...

"I best get going." I disengage abruptly from Vy and stand up.

"You can stay," I quietly counter.

"I'm not ready for that," I reply. I realize that was a bit too harsh. I quickly retread my words. "I had an excellent time tonight, Vy. The chicken was amazing. We should hang out more."

The "hang out more" phrase hangs in the air, in that cushion that continues to hold us a part. It doesn't matter that my heart breaks when it can't find traction and momentum. I'm living through the nightmare of 1001 first dates. "Sure." I realize that my "Sure" is really a defense mechanism to keep my real feelings inside. What harmony am I protecting when I'm the one suffering for keeping my mouth shut?

Throughout the summer, we do precisely what Gordon suggests: we hang out. Sometimes it's just us; sometimes it's with his friends; or sometimes it's with Craig. I eventually stop kissing Gordon. I want him to pick up the ball, to meet me half-way, to let me know he's as interested. He'd kiss back after I'd start, but then I begin to feel like an unwanted sexual harasser. We slip into an easy pattern, an easy flow, an easy state. The more the summer wears on, the more my decision to leave once I get my degree feels more right. I keep planting a field of potential but it keeps coming up fallow.

Our special moment in the meadow grows harder and harder to keep alive. The connection we created ripened, but fell to the ground. A sinking feeling lodges in the pit of my stomach that the moment might not be perennial. It becomes a nightmare for romantically challenged fools who get left behind when the laughter ends. I keep reminding myself that Gordon hasn't promised me anything. No matter how many times we hang out, that's all we're doing. Creating a home is more than that and we aren't doing that.

I enjoy how comfortable I am when spending time with Vy. I wonder why he's stopped kissing me. I wonder if I've upset him somehow. Jeff still maintains that Vy cares for me deeply, that I'm the sole reason he came to Boone in the first place. He informs me that it's so bright a blind man can see it. But Vy doesn't surface anything and it makes it hard to know where we stand.

As the warmth of the August dog days come to an end, I find myself walking with Vy outside of Skip's shop. We decided to meet up in Blowing Rock today to hang out. As we are walking to the car, I quickly turn to Vy and drop the question at his feet.

"You didn't come to Boone for me, did you?"

I walk in silence for a couple of more steps. The chill eats through my clothes and seeps deep into my marrow. I'm unsure of what to say. I finally blurt it out. "Yes and no, Gordon."

"What do you mean?" I stop in the middle of the block. This was not the response I was hoping for.

"I took a chance. I hoped that if you entered into dating mode while I was near, maybe I'd find out if our kiss in D.C. meant anything," I remark. "I know that sounds crazy, but it's the truth."

"You came all this way to determine if our kiss in D.C. meant anything?" Jeff and Brady were right. How could I have been so clueless? First the story in Vietnam, then our shared tattoos, and then his coming here. Were all those actions driving some master plan? If so, for what purpose? My back braces against an imaginary wall, spiking my spine, paralyzing me to the spot.

"No! I didn't just come for that. I decided to get my degree, which I had wanted before I knew you," I counter. My anger builds inside of me because we're about to step back three and over one again. How many times must I be put through this? Buddhism condemns me to repeat and repeat until I learn the right answers. I'd like for once to know the right questions, too.

"But still. You came to Boone because of me," Gordon exclaims.

"Partly," I redirect. "I'm not the type of psycho to stalk a guy until he surrenders."

"No. You came to Boone because of me," he demands.

"Fine. I came to Boone because of you AND because of school. I couldn't come here only for you. I also came here for myself. It doesn't matter since I get the distinct impression that you had decided to shut down the gay part of yourself. I don't think you'll ever go into dating mode as long as you live here." What is Gordon angrier about, that he's not good enough to be my sole reason for coming to Boone or his losing control of the situation?

"I never asked you to do that; just like I never asked that monk to mutilate me," Gordon callously spills.

"What the fuck are you talking about?" I yell. "I knew damn well if you thought I had come here because of you, you'd shut me out from day one. And what the hell does the monk have to do with any of this?" I grab my right shoulder. "I didn't ask him to do this. I didn't know he did it to you until after we sucked each other off."

"Fuck you," Gordon shoots back. "I didn't ask you to come here. I'm not responsible for that choice."

"I never said you were. Where do you get off telling me about my choices? I decided to come here. I own that decision." My voice tenses to the point of a loud screech. Rage builds inside from all the might-haves, what-ifs, and forward-jump-back actions that only serve to rip my spirit into slivers. It takes everything not to get hysterical.

"You have no right to push me into anything! I control my destiny, not you, not your monk, not your faith!" he screams.

"Fuck you. I didn't push you into anything. It's your own blind desire to control that leaves you cold. I hope it sucks you off at night," I cry out. "Damn you, Gordon. You've nothing to worry about. At the end of December I'm gone!" I scream and stomp off.

Thankfully, we drove separately. I slam the car door and cry. What the fuck just happened? I left Gordon stewing on the sidewalk. Every part of my body heaves and shudders. I need to relax. Minutes crawl by as I plunge into a deep meditation, to calm the fibers of my muscles, to slow my breathing and stop the escalation to hyperventilation. The fight leaves me raw. I'm confused, damaged, and stifled. I can't keep doing this to myself. When summer travels down the mountains of Boone, I've got to do the same thing, too. I finally put the car into motion, even though I feel stuck.

Dammit. How could I lose control like that? Why am I so upset? Vy practically ran to get away from me. All I can hear him say is that he is here for me. Why? I never asked him to do that.

I get into the car and drive home. I'm too agitated to calm down. Once I stomp through my front door, I change into running clothes and shoes. I can't sit still, so I take off down the street. I run and run and run. I finally return home after 10 miles and yet I'm still wired. I fix myself a gin and tonic. I sit. Even though I'm looking out the window, I still feel like I'm running.

39

October roars in, heralding a bitter winter. I find myself constantly in foul weather gear. The skies turn concrete gray; the wind bites as it crawls on the ground; and most of the leaves have sung their swan song. I don't have natural fur for insulation. Even though this is my second October in Boone, this time it feels like more of a promise of death than a chance at something new.

I chant to myself that the Master's thesis comes first. I'm not going to let anyone ruin my favorite holiday of the year. I missed it last year and I'll be damned if I do that again.

"Hello, Jeff?" I say over the phone.

"Hi. Is that you, Vy?" Jeff answers back.

"Yeah. I'm calling to see if you're going to the Halloween party. I'm wondering if you want to go together," I ask with a hint of hope coloring my words. It's tomorrow night. I waited until the last minute since I'm playing the yes-I-will no-I-won't routine obsessively.

"We can do that. But I thought you'd go with Gordon," Jeff says.

I wonder if I should explain. "Gordon and I fell out, again. We just see things differently." I hope to get past this topic relatively easily.

"You don't say. What happened?" Jeff directly points the gun.

"A couple of months ago, Gordon asked me if I came to Boone for him. Then he got righteous angry when I mentioned he was one of the reasons I came out here. That seemed to unhinge him," I sadly admit. "We got in a dragged out shouting match in Blowing Rock. You should have heard it. It was like two alley cats howling on the sidewalk." I sigh.

"I'm so sorry, Vy," Jeff's consoling voice answers. "Gordon likes to be in control. If he thinks he's not, he goes ape shit. I bet he freaked because he didn't control your decision yet it involves him on some level. I've known him since high school and sadly that part of him hasn't changed. I sometimes think that he's keeping his life on hold for some reason," Jeff continues.

"Thanks for understanding," I say.

"Come by at nine tomorrow and we'll head over to the lodge," Jeff says. "We'll rock the town together."

"Also, may I ask a favor?"

"Ok," Jeff answers with suspense in his voice.

"Would you help me with my costume?" I practically beg.

"Of course!" Jeff shouts. "Come over in the afternoon instead."

"Thank you so much," I respond and I'm grateful that Jeff still likes me. I'm glad we are not in-law friends, in which the person who introduces us is the connection and once gone, the friendship goes with it.

The many days after the big fight with Vy still ambush me every now and then. I hate losing control. I'm agitated when I meet Sara for dinner the night before the Halloween party. She wants to talk about what to wear this year since we went as the Marx Brothers last year. I go, even though I'm in a lousy mood.

"Hey, Gordy. Why the blue face?" Sara inquires.

"Nothing," I flatly say.

"Puleaze. I can tell something's eating you," Sara pushes. "You've been distracted all through dinner and I bet you've only heard ten percent of what I've said."

"Look. I'm just out of it. Vy and I got into a huge cat fight on the sidewalk in Blowing Rock a couple of months back. I haven't spoken to him since," I admit.

"Really? What over?" Sara asks, her eyes wide.

"Vy told me that I was one of the reasons he moved here. I freaked," I share. "I'm so angry that he would do that."

"Not surprising," Sara remarks in a matter-of-fact tone that's painted in a shade of ho-hum.

"What?" I exclaim. Her comment catches me by surprise. I can't believe I'm thrown off balance.

"Dear," Sara says, shaking her head, "you and I had a dragged out cat fight in New York City because I wanted to eat at Dean and Deluca and you didn't. It's all about control with you." Sara lights the fuse.

I do remember that. That time I was the one who stomped off. I just sit and stare at Sara for what seem like years. Sara waits for me to respond, or more likely to agree with her. "Okay. I agree," I breathe.

"All right. Let's say you are the main reason for Vy moving to Boone. So what? Why are you so bent?" Sara interrogates.

"He shouldn't be here because of me. I didn't want that responsibility."

"Did he ask you? Did he hold a gun to your head? Why do you feel that you're responsible?" Sara probes.

"It's like the damn tats. I didn't ask for it and Vy didn't ask for it; yet we both got one. Some monk, who didn't ask permission, just did it. I've never felt so out of control," I explain.

"So Vy being here somehow represents this loss of control? Would that be a bad thing? Are you afraid you won't be able to control the consequences of dating someone? Are you afraid your closet with the glass door is finally tumbling down? I think you both possess great chemistry together. You make a very handsome couple—when you aren't trying to control it," Sara muses.

I ponder what Sara says and wonder where that leaves me. In this restaurant, at this precise moment, I think I'm still running and still hiding. I ought to be flattered that Vy would come here for me; yet, I drove him away so that I could stay in control and hide in plain sight. What a lousy outcome.

"I'll come by at nine and take you to the party," I offer.

"That'll be great," Sara smiles.

The day is spent getting into our costumes. The weather holds out. It'll be cold with no snow or rain. The air is teeming with electricity, especially due to the dryness. The veil between what might be and what is thins through the collective attire of masks and costumes. This is the best time of year for wishfully thinking yourself into a larger-than-life persona. You can be anybody, real or imagined, magical or mundane.

Sara and I walk into the Venetian Carnival-inspired theme. The kaleidoscope of colors, painted bodies, and thumping music assaults our senses. I don't have much peripheral vision with this mask on but that's okay. Sara is dressed as Little Bo Peep. I look ahead and wonder if Vy is here.

"Jeff. Thank you so much for altering my costume. It's gorgeous. I'm already getting compliments on it," I purr. We've been at the party for an hour and guests keep pouring in. I'll be ready to go soon since I'm here to be seen, not to overstay my welcome. I'm sure Gordon is here somewhere. I'll only recognize him depending on what he's wearing. My best indicator is Sara. She's a difficult woman to hide.

"I'm glad," Jeff replies. He's wearing a gallant Robin Hood costume. "Let's have a great time and dance the night away."

"Well. Look at what the cat dragged in," Wonder Woman chimes in.

I turn to see who dares. "Oh my god. Is that you, Jerry?" I scream.

"A girl never tells her secret identity." Wonder Woman bats her eyes.

"What a great surprise. Jeff, this is my best friend, Jerry, from D.C.!" I exclaim and hug her to death. "She won the costume party at least year's D.C. Drag Halloween Bash in THAT outfit."

"Pleasure is all mine," Wonder Woman extols. She extends her hand that's covered in a cheap imitation gold bracelet, now glistening with disco ball lights. It certainly wouldn't stop any bullets.

"So who's your Steve Trevor?" I ask Wonder Woman, eyeing her partner. He's wearing an old military uniform. Before she can answer, the man steps up.

"I'm Phil," Steve Trevor says as he extends his hand.

"How did you know that was Vy?" Robin Hood asks Wonder Woman with a puzzled look on his face.

"I talked to Vy this morning. He didn't know we checked in earlier than planned. We are staying in Blowing Rock. He told me what you were doing with his costume," Wonder Woman confirms. "Plus, I stood next to you until I heard Vy's voice, just to make sure." She smiles. "It's gorgeous! What a sexy outfit!"

"So who's Phil?" I ask Wonder Woman in a low voice.

"Great guy I met in the office. He was thinking of transferring either to D.C. or Philadelphia. We hit it off immediately as our chemistry ignited. I'd like to think his decision to move to D.C. was in part influenced by our meeting. Also, he wanted to see me in this once he saw the pictures." Wonder Woman twirls. "I couldn't keep this from my adoring public." She clangs her bracelets together. Imaginary bullets stand no chance.

We all laugh as we head to the dance floor. We decide to dance for a bit and then head back to Jeff's for a night cap to catch up. Jeff already prepared some late night nosh for us.

"Look at Wonder Woman!" Sara shouts as she points.

"That's kewl," I agree. I scan the crowd, searching but not finding. I wonder if Vy came. I don't blame him, if he decided not to.

"Gordon. Let's dance." Sara grabs me by the arm and leads me to the dance floor.

I twirl and pounce and laugh at everyone. I feel such joy with Jeff dancing at my side. I'm lit up like a Christmas tree; I'm the star leading the Wise Men; I'm a gift that everyone wants to open. I then focus on the woman in the Little Bo Peep outfit as she brushes past me with Batman in tow. As I gather all of her into my field of vision, I recognize her. Wow. It's Sara. Oh my god, that must be Gordon in the costume. I'm lost to the beat to think clearly. I twirl and twirl, gyrating to the funky jungle rhythm.

I get an impulsive power surge. I lean into Gordon and plant the most passionate kiss I can channel. As we separate I whisper into his ear and quickly breakaway with the group heading to Jeff's, "You know, Catwoman stole Batman's heart."

What?! I'm caught off guard as this Catwoman plants a kiss on my lips. There's something oddly familiar about this kiss. WAIT. I know who this is. The bolt of recognition fries my nerves. A tear trickles down my cheek and a grin spreads across my lips as she races off with my heart.

40

November streaks by. I finish the thesis, defend it, and hand in my final project for my last class. I still revel in Jerry's surprise visit and the great time at the Halloween party. They're blown away with the kiss I gave Batman. I do tell them it was Gordon after a lot of teasing and wrong guesses.

The semester is fading away and my time grows short here in Boone. In these next few weeks, I have much to do in order to wrap up this life and plan a new one, a metaphorical death and rebirth cycle in full bloom.

"Thanks for coming over to help me pack," I say as I hug Jeff, Sara, and Skip.

"So what's next?" Sara asks as we get ready to pack up the living room and kitchen.

"Not sure. I'm putting this stuff into storage while I head to Portland. Once I get settled, then I'll send for my stuff. Thankfully I purged before moving here." I look around. "Well, I know it doesn't seem that way," I sheepishly add.

The afternoon of packing, labeling, and hauling boxes exhausts us. We make a pile in the living room for the movers. The rooms are now bare as if my life is dissolving away. Soon, only hints of my passing tingles the memories of those who still have warm thoughts of me. I'm becoming a Ghost.

"What do you want to do with the mirror in the bedroom?" Skip asks as I enter the master to see what's left to do.

"I think I'm going to leave it with the bedroom furniture. Ironically, Gordon found the mirror at the Wilkesboro Flea Market. It took both Craig and Gordon to help me move it here and mount it," I reminisce. "It's too big and heavy to move cross-country. Besides, it belongs here in Boone and the mountains."

Even with their help, it takes all day to finish packing up. The sun moves across the sky but provides no warmth. The days get colder and grayer. Occasionally, the ground whitens but thankfully no more than a couple of inches.

I share my love and gratitude over a pizza dinner. "Without your help, even by the end of the week this task would be unfinished," I grin. I've certainly come to love this group, and in many ways, depend on them.

"Are you staying with Jeff through the week?" Skip asks.

"Yep," Jeff interjects.

"I still need to tie up a few more things for the university. I have to make sure I get the degree after living here for a year and half," I laugh. "Also there's the cleaning once the movers clear out my stuff on Monday. The plan is to turn over the key by 1 pm next Saturday."

"Then straight to Portland?" Sara asks.

"No. First, I'm off to Florida. I'd like to visit my folks before I go. I'll spend the holidays with them. Mother thinks I'm going too far away." I sigh and look over the group. A cry is coming on. I stifle it and then I see a tear in Jeff's eyes. I lose it. We all cry and do a group hug. I'll miss them deeply. Jerry and Phil will also fly down to Florida to spend New Year's Eve with me.

The week launches into high gear as a beehive of activities scrubs the landscape. There's a burst of students wrapping things up and faculty winding things down. Boone is shutting down for the winter.

"How was the packing event?" I ask Sara over lunch on Tuesday.

"Sad. I'm going to miss Vy," Sara laments.

"When does he leave?" I inquire.

"His plan is to turn over the key on Saturday and then drive to Florida on Sunday. Are you going to say good-bye?" she continues.

"I'm not sure if that's wise," I offer. I still remember the kiss he gave me at the party, of me frozen in the moment, of him racing off with my heart. I wanted to surge forward and wrap my arms around him and lose control.

"You're plain stubborn," Sara quips.

I give her a puzzled look as I bore my eyes into her.

"Well, you are!" she exclaims. "You're letting Vy go even though you know one of the reasons he's here is because of you." She pounds her point. "He may not have moved here strictly for you but you can give him a reason to stay. You stand at the edge of something wonderful. Why not fall into it? Love can change your perspective."

I sit and stare.

"Ultimately, who cares why the two of you have been crisscrossing each other's lives for more than 25 years? I think the universe is saying somethin'. Control is a lonely option."

"I don't know," I breathe with a tattered sigh. With that I leave to return to work. I have a string of rentals to get ready for next semester. I'm moving people out in order for others to move in. It's a never-ending cycle. I'll be doing this till the next generation takes over. Most likely, it will be my brother's kids. I keep hearing Sara's words echo inside my brain.

I turn over the last two years of adventures with Vy. The good times far exceeded the bad times. I laugh; I cry; I wonder. Life's giving me a window of opportunity, which I can take now, or hope that it comes back around. There're no guarantees and no safety nets. Letting go of control is spinning my insides inside out.

My hectic week finally comes to an end. I race to finish the last few chores and get my 'i's' dotted and my 't's' crossed. Sometimes the university's bureaucracy hammers me into the wall. Once I get clearance that I earned my Master's, I go out and celebrate with Jeff and Skip. Sara's work interferes with her participation, but a warm call from Jerry and Phil cheers me up. With this phase ending, I'm left tying up loose ends.

I finally finish cleaning the bathroom, stripping the grime from the white wall tiles and the black and white checkered floor tiles. The whiteness of the room reminds me of a sanitarium. Whew. This Friday is shot. Thankfully, it's the last major room to clean and now it's done. Hooray! I shout as I enter the master. I catch the dying sun splayed across the picturesque window like a crucifixion of something heavenly brought low.

The room feels desolate now that it's been boxed up and emptied, except for the bedroom set and the flea market mirror. I enjoyed lying in bed with the window as my headboard and the mirror reflecting back what's behind me. I laugh. I told myself to be careful with Gordon. Yet he never closed the distance, either too short or too long.

What am I going to do with a mirror that is five feet long and four feet high? It takes two people to carry it. I'll talk to the landlord and see if she wants it. Maybe I'll give it to Craig for his shop. Maybe someone will want to buy it without the baggage of my true-love-gave-it-to-me. What a sight it was to watch Gordon and Craig struggle to bring it up the stairs and balance it on the hooks. We held our breath when we let go. When it stayed, we exhaled. The mirror transformed the wall into a looking glass into another world. When the dying sunlight struck the mirror, the reflection deepened the shadows that hinted of places at the edge of my peripheral vision, much like my relationship with Gordon. I would be in direct line of sight, yet the action would occur at vision's edge. The mirror belongs in Boone. It's sturdy like the mountains—it's been around a long time, and has passed through many generations. It fits here. It'd be out of place anywhere else.

"Hi, Vy." The familiar voice rolls up the back of my neck, handed off by the hairs standing on end. I jump.

Once my heart starts beating again, I twist around slowly to name the voice.

"What are you doing here, Gordon?" I ask with little enthusiasm. "I didn't think we were friends anymore. Are you here to say goodbye or are you here to make sure I follow through?"

"I'm sorry for acting like an asshole," I simply state. "Whatever your reasons for coming here were, they were your reasons. I overreacted." I watch Vy's face for the emotional gallery, his endearing habit of showcasing his inner world to the public. Portraits of confusion, pain, arousal, joy, and sadness appear under the spotlight and then fade for the next and then the next. Vy is mostly hurt from taking a chance and losing. As I scan downward from his facial portraits, I notice the beautiful striped shirt that sums up his mood. The long vertical stripes in various widths streak against a white background that incorporates random knots of exotic bamboo. The green brings out the lush cream in the wall and the violet dances with the dying sunlight. It's gorgeous. He's a blossom about to close, taking with him his ephemeral tones and hues.

Gordon stares; I stare back. I project amazement that he's only wearing a navy blue pullover with white cuffs and a three-button, front-over pair of jeans that shape his legs and ass in the right proportions. The cold must be afraid of him. I'm more sad than angry at this crossroad of our paths. "Hey, I'm sorry, too. The Blowing Rock fight wasn't one of my shining moments either," I offer. "The hostility blindsided me as it wrestled a straight-jacket on me. And white's a hard color for me to pull off. I thought you would have been flattered to know that you were a reason for me being here. I didn't think my secret would hurt you. And just for the record, you weren't the only reason." I ramble to get it out. I wish he had been the only reason, but I couldn't have done that to myself. I needed a plan B, even if I never activated it.

I must speak before I lose my nerve. "I don't know what I want," I tell Vy. I practically say it under my breath. "I've always been in control." I hang back and a pause erupts. "I should say I want to be in control. Over the last couple of years, I laughed and cried with you. I tried hard to be the tour guide, showing you the charm, the magic, the reasons why Boone is home. Maybe you coming here without those reasons made you too independent for me." I struggle to get my words out. My college education fails me when I need it most to gift wrap my emotions.

I watch Gordon and listen to what isn't said, like the fear of living life out loud for all to see. Sometimes our eyes connect and the electricity arcs through our bridged heartbeats. The chemistry ignites a shared chain reaction, causing a loss of control in the both of us. When he takes his three steps back and one over, I wish we had never met. As I struggle to behave differently around him, I lose the war. I win a battle only to stand alone amongst the debris. His speaking, his laughing, his take-no-prisoner attitude towards life intoxicates me. He's a man's man, the 007 whose license is to sweep me off my feet. I'm so alive and wonder why he doesn't stay. I also sense he wants to clamp down on his life so as not to be too alive. I don't seem able to solve the riddle of why men leave. Yet, I hear in between the spaces of his words a calling, an answer, a reason. The brain teaser is twisting my thoughts into, around, and through the solution.

Without window treatments, the rays of Earth's fallen star cast a deep shadow over Gordon's face as he stands at the foot of the bed. He's ancient and eternal through the channels etched in his face and crowned with a white Caesar crest on his head. I'm off to one side thinking of how many crimes against nature we've committed, by the river, the abandoned rail line, the dinners across town, the conversations with his friends. I stop listening to the outside. In a pure meditative moment, I know what it is. My answer strikes with the force of a shooting star and I'm part of the oneness of my faith. I blink and a tear escapes.

I catch a blank look and a tear. "Hey, Vy. I'm not here to listen to myself talk. I'm not here to make you cry." Dammit. Already, I'm losing control.

"No, that's not it," I reply, shaking my head. "I thought about the river, the meadow, the town, your friends, to all the places you've taken me. My emotions, both physical and spiritual, tell me what I've been searching for is a reason to belong, to stay. Like Mother, like Son." This is starting down a well-worn path with a twist. I must stay focused on this moment right in front of me. If I blink, I'll miss it.

"Every one of those experiences was exciting for so many reasons," I concur, yet think I miss the point.

"You were right, Gordon. I did come to Boone for a chance with you but I wasn't courageous enough for that to be the only reason. My Master's was secondary to the mix—my plan B. I can fly only with a safety net. I require an anchor. Look around here. You're from here. You have generations of roots that dig deep into these mountains. If I go back to Vietnam, I might stand on the ground that 17 generations before me stood on, but I wouldn't feel connected. Hell. I barely speak the language anymore. No more sing-song for me." My voice trembles at the admission.

"I'm thinking how unfair that is to me," I share. "I want so much to force you to accept that I didn't ask you to come here; that I didn't ask you to leave behind your big city lights for these provincial street lamps; that I didn't ask you to actually come." I make eye contact with Vy as I offer up my own fears of what it would be like to have someone want to change their life for you. And then another truth surfaces. I was also afraid that Vy's presence here would force me to date openly as a gay man. I couldn't even begin to control the consequences of that momentous event.

Wisdom creates itself through a sheer force of thought of its own accord. "I know that," I state as if I'm already gone from this life. "I know my time here created situations neither one of us wanted to deal with. I connected with you and cannot understand why. If you got a whiff that I was coming here for you, your macho, I-don't-need-any-fucking-body, attacks," I remark. I feel so raw and worked over that I instinctively hug myself and realize I'm at peace with the answer. "Normally, Gordon, in this situation, I'd say it doesn't matter anymore. As you can see, my stuff is gone. I even finished the cleaning." I sweep my hands across the room for dramatic effect. "I didn't listen as the Great Thầy taught me. I derided and disrespected him by calling him Crazy Monk. I can't move here on a chance for love and you can't tell me to move here as if to exert control. You show me by example why Boone is home and why its life pulsates so hard you can't hide it." More tears flood my face. It's not about getting men to stay; it's about getting me to stay, the one person I can influence. Mother showed me that instinctively all those years ago in Pulaski; it was why she stayed when her marriage faltered. She stayed for her children. Instinctively, Gordon did that as well.

What is Vy saying? I hear the tick and tock of my heart and it sounds like a countdown to my last chance. I showed him what life was like in Boone; I was his personal tour guide. That's all. I couldn't control Vy so I showed him all the wonderful things that beat in Boone's heart and how it beats in my heart. It would be absurd to hide the life of Boone just as it's absurd for me to hide my own life. I may not know exactly why I'm here but I do know I want Vy to be on the same path. Together, we laugh and enjoy each other's company. I must thank Sara for casting me off in Vy's direction.

I edge closer. I'm within arm's reach of my true love. Damn the consequences. I reach out and grasp Vy's face with my hands and pull him into me. It's my first time initiating intimacy with Vy and it frees me of the gilded cage I've wrapped around me. My lips explore his and our tongues lock onto each other.

I let go into Gordon. My body, spirit, and mind flow without edges. Tears of relief find their way into the world as children must to become adults. Gordon gently kisses them away. I'm enthralled looking into his clear blue eyes. I see the flecks dance and know its lightning. The electricity hums between us. The very ends of my hair stand up to meet the goose bumps.

"You know, once this reaction starts it can't be stopped," I warn. My feelings tear through me like a hurricane as my hands claw into Gordon's clothes.

"I've been an idiot, Vy. Every time you got past my defenses, I erected them higher and deeper. I want you in Boone because of Boone, not me. The crazy logic nearly caused me to lose you." I sigh and squeeze Vy closer. I go for broke to match Vy's release, and we dance to the rhythm of our yin-yang.

I follow the opening of Vy's shirt and undo his buttons. I tear open the gorgeous green-violet striped shirt, another one of his beautiful shirts. I lift his white t-shirt over his head and nuzzle my mouth over his right nipple. I brace against him, reach around and squeeze his ass.

The peace arising from my realization swamps my inhibitions. I want to occupy the same space as Gordon. His tongue feels so good sliding over my nipples. I love the way he playfully bites them, like some overgrown kitten learning to chew. I shake and know that I'm hard as a rock. Whoa. I land on top of the naked mattress. I feel my pants slide right off and then his hands clawing off my socks. I can see the mirror staring back at me.

Vy's hard-on is poking through his boxers. As I shimmy out of my clothes, I climb on top of him to make sure he doesn't squirm away. I feel his soft skin against my hairy body. I wonder how that must feel for him. Vy says he loves hair. Well. I've got plenty, except on top of my head. "You feel so good, Vy," I exclaim.

"I love the feel of you; I love the way your body caresses mine; I love how you make me crazy looking at me." I smile up at Gordon. He laughs back and a twinkle sparkles in his eye. I get lost looking into those icy blue eyes, but his voice and steady hands anchor me.

I feel my boxers slide off and then a warm, moist mouth push my foreskin back. My eyes roll backwards. The pressure created by his lips sucking up and down my shaft sends ripples through every nerve in my body. Then a finger kneads the folds around my ring. Yes. I'd give it up right now. Right at this moment, I want to feel Gordon deep inside of me, connected through me, so deeply that we're connected forever. Of course there's no condom or lube. You packed it away, the evil thought laughs. Whoa. I feel the edge of his tongue circling and penetrating my ring. My heels are acting as if they can walk on ceilings. My ring expands and it seems his tongue is weapon enough to make me pre-cum. My eyes explode open when I realize that something bigger is pushing inside of me.

I slide on the condom that I pulled out of my wallet. I see surprise on Vy's face—another adorable portrait. I love catching him by surprise. I want to make love to him. I slowly sink and feel him bearing down on my shaft. The warmth of his insides startles me. I thrust slowly and then rhythmically pick up the pace. I can hear moans escaping Vy's lips. Wow. He's squeezing so hard on my shaft, I'm about to explode inside of him.

With every thrust, I feel Gordon going deeper than I've ever experienced before. I'm so stimulated. I feel a tremor rising from my balls up through my cock. "I'm going to explode," I gasp. With that, Gordon slides out of me and swallows my cock. I release. He takes my seed deep inside of him. I feel the coarseness of his tongue licking all that threatens to escape.

The sensation of Vy's cum sliding down my throat rocks me harder. I feel him traveling down inside of me. I want every last drop of him. I lick down the shaft and back over the crack of his ass. He squirms. That's my confirmation that this is driving him crazy. He likes the way I make his ring sing. I feel the tension let go and that's my cue that admittance is allowed. Our connection bridges us to the next level. I've been cradling my shaft in my right hand and can feel how stiff it's gotten. I'm about to explode. Then I hear Vy's urgent plea. I enjoy this.

"Feed me," he implores.

I reach down with my left hand and cradle Vy's head. His mouth opens and I slide my cock down his throat. I actually don't make it that far when I feel his mouth closing and sucking my shaft. I explode 10 years' worth of seed. He's ready for it. No gagging; just the happy sounds of slurping. He pulls out every last drop.

I swallow as quickly as I can. I know it's coming from the hardness of his cock; I'm surprised there's so much. Where has Gordon been keeping it? I see, hear, and feel his enjoyment feeding me. I reach up and pull him down next to me. "Oh baby. The things I do when I'm around you."

"Well, you're always a willing partner in crime," I smile at Vy.

"Don't be so smug. I should be mad at you," I mock. We cradle each other and the moments flow like an unbridled river. The last of the sun reflects in the mirror, and the beveled, raised panels pull an image together. "Oh my God, Gordon, look at that!" I exclaim as I sit straight up. I prance towards the mirror in my birthday glory.

"What?! What is it?" I shout in surprise. Vy's standing at the mirror playing peek-a-boo with his tattoo. He's got cute dimples above his ass cheeks.
"Come here, come here," he exclaims frenetically.
"Okay. What am I looking at?" I stand in matching birthday suit, laughing at Vy's kinetic motions.

I move Gordon so that his left shoulder is lined up with my right shoulder. The image of the tattoos fits together perfectly. Individually, depending on the lighting, the images coalesce either into a single cat profile or an abstract figure with an eye. "Look at our tattoos in the mirror," I gently command.

Gordon's expression says it all. "Vy, it forms the face of a tiger."

"Great Thầy told me that one day I'd understand. We all travel many paths, sometimes alone, and that's fine; sometimes together, and that's fine. Yet, when traveling together, we can be so much more." I study Gordon and can tell that he understands exactly what I mean. "You know, thích, as a noun, is an honorific Buddhist title, and as a verb it means 'to tattoo'." The many layers and nuances of the Vietnamese language would take a lifetime of meditation to uncover minuscule fractions of meaning or beauty.

"Our pieces come together and a face of a tiger looks back," Gordon muses with a big grin.

"Tiger is a potent symbol in Vietnamese culture. It represents power, cunning, control."

"It will take me a lifetime of study to learn your culture, Vy," Gordon remarks.

I grow serious as we stand in the mirror with our tiger watching over us.

"Is it too late for us?" I turn and face Gordon. "I'm all packed up and ready to move away," I calmly remind him.

"From here you are," I reply with a grin. "I'd say your next stop is Elm Street."

"WHAT? You're asking me to move in?" Vy asks, dumfounded.

I do enjoy catching Vy by surprise. "Look. We don't really know what the future holds. But who am I to go against the Great Thầy?"

"You're mocking me now," he replies with a smile.

Gordon and I gently rock in each other's arms, holding ourselves upright in the paling glow of the sun's twilight. Gordon's right. The future lies ahead of us and our path remains untraveled. We need to recognize what's in front of us while living in the moment. I realize the question that I'm trying to answer: "Would I move for love?" is wrong. The better question is, "Would I stay for love?" Gordon gives me reasons to stay whether he had planned it or not. The decision is ultimately mine, though, which is his gift of letting go and accepting the consequences of whatever happens.

As our pieces fall into place, I have a strong feeling that we will meet life with a new sturdiness, one with the face of a tiger.

ABOUT THE AUTHOR

WE Coble is a war baby with East-West parentage. He writes stories with gay themes, supernatural tones, and strong, women-centric points of view. He often travels among Philadelphia, Washington, Raleigh, Saint Petersburg, and Omaha, which is his current home, to stay connected with his family of friends. He was once asked by his late grandmother, "Why do I get older and you don't? Did you make a deal with the Devil?" He replied, "Grandmother, I'm Buddhist."